NOT OF THIS FOLD

WITHDRAWN

Also by Mette Ivie Harrison

The Bishop's Wife

His Right Hand

For Time and All Eternities

NOT
OF THIS
FOLD

Mette Ivie Harrison

Copyright © 2018 by Mette Ivie Harrison

All rights reserved.

Published by Soho Press, Inc.
227 W 17th Street
New York, NY 10011

Library of Congress Cataloging-in-Publication Data

Harrison, Mette Ivie
Not of this fold / Mette Ivie Harrison.
Series: The Linda Wallheim mysteries ; 4
I. Title
PS3608.A783578 N68 2018 813'.6—dc23 2018027716

ISBN 978-1-64129-093-7
eISBN 978-1-61695-943-2

Interior design by Janine Agro, Soho Press, Inc.

Printed in the United States of America

10 9 8 7 6 5 4 3 2 1

To MWEG (Mormon Women for Ethical Government)

Helpline. But, it had mostly been dogmagnetic games of truck, or t_____ attacks.

It was already, I knew, I wanted to ____'d left a message and ____ _____ to point to a _____ I got scared, but I didn't really want him to know I was leaving to hide for twelve. I'd promised Kurt he no longer on that hotline, I'm not myself, anymore investigating murder cases, but this was different. How could I be in any danger? but I knew he'd still be angry if he found out.

After that, I waited at the front door staring outside for five minutes, until Gwen arrived. I thanked myself — the moment she pulled up, Gwen's customary dark was unlocked, so I got in. I was less worried about Gwen as that, excited my anxiety ____ the way I knew this was a bad idea sneaking around, getting in trouble. I guess I had, broken laws, out of my custom as _____ ____, I'd been up busy following all the rules like a good Mormon girl, for my best year of my twenties.

I didn't cast that but Gwen's car around me.

Gwen smiled and scratched his forehead, then circled the rest of the ____-de-sac and turned her down the main street that would lead down ____ downtown. From the occasional light of street lamps, I saw her face was still stripped of makeup and under the w___ ____, her eyes looked puffy by my mind, She wasn't in a talkative mood. She slid her brights on, which was fine since there was no cars for a couple miles in each direction. All the good Mormons were home, asleep.

She drove down to the Fire-Seven gas station I'd seen in the news clips. It looked empty, it was still cordoned off, but there were still flashing lights, but I could see a couple of police cars.

Gwen had swallowed her attention to me, but only at the gas station, my adrenaline returned, and I wondered if Gwen

CHAPTER 1

Every year on the Friday night before Halloween, we put on a ward Trunk or Treat in the gym for the whole neighborhood, Mormon and not. It was organized by the Primary Presidency, but the bishopric always manned the activity booths in costume. This year, Kurt and I were dressed up as Frankenstein's monster and the Bride of Frankenstein, costumes we constantly had to explain to children who were more accustomed to comic-book heroes and Disney characters. We also enforced a rule that the children only received candy if they could compose a limerick, which we demonstrated first.

The first counselor and his wife, Tom and Verity deRyke, wrapped in long strips of cloth as mummies, were running a variation on musical chairs, and I could tell they were enjoying it. The Primary children loved Verity and Tom, the honorary grandparents in the ward to families whose eldest generation had passed away or weren't able to be with them.

The second counselor, Brad Ferris, was sporting vampire fangs, black capes, and drips of blood down the sides of his chin, and had set up a booth where kids could make a witch or a ghost out of candy pieces. Brad had become second counselor just over a year ago. At the time, his wife, Gwen, had been emotionally fragile, struggling terribly with her infertility diagnosis and the tragic history behind it. I'd hoped that she had come out of her shell lately. She'd been exercising and had put muscle on her petite frame, but the fact that she wasn't here and hadn't been to church in a couple of months made me worry that something had gone wrong. Was it that there were too many children around, reminding her that she and Brad couldn't have a "forever family?"

Then I saw her, with three small children and a generously figured Hispanic woman trailing after them. The children were adorable, the youngest apparently having just learned to walk. The oldest, a girl, was dressed as Wonder Woman, the younger boy as Captain America, and the baby in Gwen's arms as a peapod. Gwen seemed comfortable with them, leaning over to whisper to them something about what to do next, then laughing with their mother. It surprised and pleased me.

"And what are your names?" I asked when they came over to us.

The oldest girl informed me that she was Lucia, her brother was Manuel, and their baby sister, with the biggest, darkest eyes I'd ever seen, was Amanda.

I helped them through inventing a limerick about superheroes, and then passed out the candy. I hesitated when it came to giving anything to the baby, but Gwen picked out a pack of Sixlets and opened it to pop one into her open mouth.

She nodded to the mother of the children. "This is Gabriela Suarez," she explained. "From the Spanish ward I've been attending."

So that was why she hadn't been at our meetings. I wondered how I hadn't realized.

"I didn't know you spoke Spanish," I said.

"I learned in high school and took classes in college, but I'm not fluent. That's why I've been going." She turned to Gabriela and then introduced me to her. "Hermana Linda," she said, dispensing with my last name.

"Nice to meet you," I said, smiling.

"I hope you don't mind us coming to your party. Gwen said that we would be welcome," Gabriela said in slightly accented English.

"Of course not. I should have thought to invite the full Spanish ward." It had only recently been organized in our stake. I hadn't been aware we'd had so many Spanish speakers before now, and it hadn't occurred to me that they'd have children who wanted to celebrate this very commercial American holiday. I felt terrible about that now.

"It's pretty new," Gwen said. "We can think about doing some joint activities in the coming year. We're still trying to figure out how this works." This made me feel a little better, but not much.

She moved onto the next station, once again introducing Gabriela and the children. I could see that Gwen and Gabriela were close. Gabriela kept reminding the older two to say "Thank you" to everyone who gave them a prize, and she tried to keep Gwen from giving the baby too much candy. When Gwen put little Amanda down and she began running across the slick hardwood floor, Gabriela chased after her and caught her before she fell.

I stole a glance or two at Brad, who was looking on at the children's antics rather stiffly. I wished I knew what was going on behind the scenes in his and Gwen's home.

Unfortunately, I was probably not the best person to come to for marriage advice. Kurt and I had just gotten over an intense months-long argument about the Mormon Church's new policy of excommunicating married same-sex couples. Even now, we didn't talk as much as we used to.

I knew Brad to be a steady, compassionate man, but children were so important to completing a Mormon family that some men might have considered divorce so that they could have biological children who were "born in the covenant." Others might have demanded adoption. But so far, Brad had accepted the fact that children had not come their way. And Gwen had clearly found other ways to fill her own need to nurture, though she and Brad had kept her infertility a secret from everyone in the ward but me and Kurt.

I went to the bathroom and found Gabriela there alone, talking on the phone. I couldn't understand much of the Spanish, but I heard her mention "*obispo* hope," which was a strange combination of Spanish and English. She seemed agitated, and she kept glancing up. After a moment, she saw me and rushed out.

I didn't follow her, as I assumed she'd gone outside for privacy, despite the cold. I wished I could've comforted her somehow, but I didn't want to pry by asking what was wrong. I looked up the word "*obispo*" on my phone and found out it meant "bishop." Curious, I then checked the list of bishops in our stake and saw that the one for the Spanish ward was "Bishop Hope." I wondered if she'd been speaking to him directly, or simply about him?

The eleventh ward in the Draper stake, only a few months old, was created to attract the Hispanic members who were streaming into the area for work, since it was a more familiar space both linguistically and culturally. There were similar wards and smaller branches throughout Utah and most of the Southwestern United States, usually under the authority of a Hispanic member or someone who spoke fluently, often a former missionary who had become a bishop or branch president. There were also other language-specific wards, depending on the needs of the population, whether Tongan, Korean, Portuguese, or even Swahili. It had been the same in the early days of the church, when swathes of immigrants from northern Europe had necessitated Norwegian, Danish, Finnish, and Swedish wards.

I went back to the booth with Kurt, smiling at children as the bishop's wife and trying not to look for Gabriela and her children. I noticed that she was with them again when, an hour into the activity, Shannon Carpenter, the newly called Primary President, announced that it was time for donuts and cider.

These were my responsibility, so I hurried to the kitchen to oversee the seventy-odd children, aged three to eleven, lining up to pass through the door to the outside. Each received one glazed Krispy Kreme donut and one cup of freshly pressed apple cider from Farnsworth Farms to take outside.

I smiled at the Suarez children when they came through and said, "*Buenos días*," which was the extent of my Spanish. Gwen laughed at me and then whispered to the children to say "*Gracias*." As for Gabriela, her eyes were shadowed, and she still seemed unsettled.

Once the donuts were distributed, Kurt came to help me clean up. Then we headed out to say goodbye. It was still light out since we were on Daylight Savings, so children could walk home, but parents usually preferred to pick up their smaller children for safety reasons. I could see Gwen helping to bundle up the three

Suarez children and waving goodbye to them as they drove away in a tannish twenty-year-old Honda.

I watched Shannon Carpenter's husband, Glenn, usher their three sprites—three, five, and seven years old—into the back seat of his SUV. Then I headed back to the multipurpose room and I found Gwen and Shannon in the midst of a loud argument that Kurt and the other male bishopric members were attempting to ignore.

Not quite five feet tall, Shannon was even smaller than Gwen. She sometimes seemed like one of the Primary children, not the President. I didn't know where she shopped, but her tight-fitting knit dresses and tunics accentuated her petite frame. I was always impressed with her ability to manage a room of children, given her sweet disposition and the fact that any three senior Primary children could run her down if they put their heads together.

"I'm concerned about our children," Shannon was saying, her voice a high squeak. "They need to feel safe at church activities. I don't feel it's appropriate for you to invite random strangers to participate without getting any clearance from those in charge of the activities."

"Random strangers? Gabriela and her children are members of our church. They're in our stake. Why would I need to get approval for them to attend an activity?" Gwen asked, her face red.

As Shannon Carpenter considered an answer, I noticed Tom and Verity deRyke stepping out quietly, heading toward the parking lot with a couple of boxes.

"We should always remember the line of authority that God Himself has put in place for the good of all concerned. I have special charge over the children of this ward, and that means that I will be accountable before God for all that happens to them," Shannon said.

Gwen's face reddened. "If I'd brought some neighborhood kids who weren't Mormons, you'd have been fine with that as a missionary effort. But since they're Hispanic, it's all about protecting the children of this ward. Do you realize you're being racist?"

Kurt made a cautious humming sound next to me, but he didn't intervene.

Shannon looked past Gwen instead of directly at her when she said, "I don't appreciate you throwing words like that around when there might be children to overhear them."

As if the word had been a curse, instead of an everyday part of the English language.

Gwen glanced around the room, now clearly empty of children. "Well, maybe if you're so concerned about the children of our ward, you might consider teaching them to look beyond their own comfortable lives and see those in need. You could have done reverse trick-or-treating at one of the apartment buildings where most of the Spanish ward members live. Show our children how to act when we have so much and those who live next door to us don't. To aspire to be more like in the Book of Mormon, when everyone lived in complete equality instead of being rich or poor."

Shannon gave a dismissive wave of her hand, a gesture with no casualness to it. "We do plenty of other service projects. This activity was for fun. I think our overstressed children deserve that much one day a year."

I cringed at her condescending tone, and Kurt put a steadying arm on Brad's shoulder as he stared at the two women.

"Overstressed?" Gwen balked. "These are the most privileged kids on the planet. They have everything handed to them!"

"They need to know they matter to God, to learn to listen to the Spirit and become leaders. And they need to have good memories of church activities in their childhood, or we're going to lose them in those difficult teen years," Shannon said with an undertone of urgency. "More than a third of the millennial generation are leaving the church, and that's even among the most active families."

Frankly, I was surprised she knew these dismal statistics. Most Mormons didn't know about the Pew research group's statistics on millennials and decline in church activity. They thought it could happen to other religions, but not to "the one true church."

"So we're going to teach them to keep taking and taking? Because we're afraid they'll start looking for another organization that will give them more than we do? That will bolster their overweening egos even more?" Gwen said. Her hands were clenched, and her voice was hard and angry.

Kurt cleared his throat and was about to say something, but Shannon got there first. "You may think they're privileged, but there are so many moral dangers out there that they can't see because they're too young. That's why we have to keep them sheltered from the world. But you wouldn't understand that, because you don't have any children."

This was a dangerous button for Shannon to push. It was too much for Gwen. She let out a sob of embarrassment and frustration and ran out.

CHAPTER 2

I glanced around and saw Brad, who looked completely absorbed in picking up trash and folding up tables. It made me furious. His wife needed him, and he was ignoring her. What in the world was going on between them? Why had she decided to attend the Spanish ward, when her husband didn't attend and she wasn't a fluent speaker? Was she just trying to avoid the members of our own ward?

I didn't have time to figure it out now. I grabbed my coat and chased Gwen down the hall, out the door, and into the nearly empty parking lot.

"Gwen. Are you all right?" I called out.

She slowed, then turned around. Her face shimmered with tears. "What a mess I am," she said, shaking her head.

A mess? Then she was the kind of mess that made sense to me. I'd missed her over the last couple of months, but had assumed she needed space and that I shouldn't pester her. I wished now that I'd gone over to talk to her. I loved that Gwen wore her heart on her sleeve, and how fierce she could be, how sharply she felt injustice toward others.

"Gwen, I really admire that you stand by your principles. I hope you know that," I told her.

Gwen let out a long breath and wiped her face. "Linda, I just can't keep just going through the motions here while other Mormons stick their heads in the sand. We say we care about the poor and needy, but we're not doing enough to actually change their lives. All that money we pay in tithing, where does it go? We never see a real accounting. How much goes to build temples? To help with disaster relief? The church gets billions every year, and only gives out a pittance."

My eyes widened at this. I really didn't know how much was donated worldwide each year from tithing. I knew the church was proud of being fiscally responsible and always running a positive balance, after spending so many years in its early days in the red, thanks to Joseph Smith's poor financial handling of his bank. Tithing had become a major push under Heber J. Grant, after the church had gone into debt in the wake of the Great Depression. The church had prospered since then, but it was true that the building of an expensive mall in downtown Salt Lake City had caused progressive Mormons to question the priorities for the church's now multibillion-dollar assets.

"I'm sure the church does what it can," I said weakly.

Gwen shook her head. "You don't see it like I do. These immigrants are being told that security for their families only comes if they pay full tithing. They're living on the edge already, in fear of the government, of the gangs if they're sent home, and the church pushes them to pay tithing when they can barely feed themselves. It's unconscionable, Linda."

"But there are blessings for obedience," I said, aware that my words sounded flimsy and unsympathetic. I'd really believed this, at least until last year. Now I wasn't sure how to be obedient to a church I disagreed with on so many fundamental issues.

"And then there's the racism within the church."

There was that ugly word again.

"Don't make that face. It's everywhere, even decades after the revelation giving black members access to priesthood blessings. That was in 1978, Linda! But it doesn't even matter, because of the idea in the Book of Mormon that righteous people have white skin and unrighteous people are cursed by God with dark skin. It permeates everything in Mormon theology, this idea that being white is being of God."

"That's not how it's meant," I argued back at her. "It's not literal white skin. It's a glow of goodness." I was aware, though, that the Book of Mormon had certain passages changed recently in order to make it clearer that literal whiteness didn't equate with moral purity.

"People say that in the church, but look at our leaders. They're all white. Those are the people who are deemed righteous enough to be the mouthpieces of God. And it's even the same in the Spanish ward. Bishop Hope tells everyone they should give up their own culture for gospel culture, which is just white Mormonism."

I cringed at this. "It's a worldwide church. We're still learning." But I knew that wasn't enough for Gwen.

She said, "I can't stand it anymore. I have to do more. I've quit my job at Zions."

"I don't understand. Why?" Zions Bank, one of the biggest corporations in Utah, was a well-respected place to work. Gwen had been a manager there for nearly a decade, and they paid her well. How would quitting her job help her do more for the poor? And what would this do to her marriage?

"I've decided to apply to the Police Academy at UVU, down in

Orem. The more I see marginalized people being taken advantage of, the angrier I get. They need someone on their side. Someone inside the system who can change things." Her tear-streaked face was bright with determination.

But it was hard for me to imagine Gwen as a police officer. It was a physically demanding job, and she'd been so slight—until recently. I guessed this was why she'd been working out more and putting on muscle.

To be honest, I had briefly considered the police academy myself a few years ago, but had decided it wasn't for me. I was too old and too set in my ways, and my methods of information-gathering weren't always legal. I hoped Gwen had better instincts.

"Aren't there other jobs that would make just as much impact? You could go to law school or become a social worker." Both would be less dangerous.

"I'm not taking the easy way out. I want to be there on the front lines, not just sit it out in a comfortable office," she said.

Gwen herself had been abused when she was too young to know how to ask for help, and maybe she wanted to be the savior she wished she'd had. Was that what she was doing for Gabriela Suarez and her children? I thought about no one mentioning Gabriela's husband and briefly wondered what was going on there. Maybe he was abusive? Was that part of her conversation with the "Obispo"? The church didn't have a great history of hearing its women when it came to abuse. Many were told to go back to violent husbands to save their eternal family—and their husbands' church careers.

"I guess I understand why you prefer the Spanish ward, then," I said.

Gwen smiled and lowered her defenses a little. "Tomorrow morning, I'm running a road to citizenship workshop for the ward. The church supports it because it's trying to make sure families can stay together legally. But the way people talk up here, it seems they think their families are more 'forever' than others." She waved back at the church building and Shannon Carpenter.

Despite the conservative political climate of Utah, the Mormon church had made multiple pro-immigrant statements over the years, including support for the Utah Compact, which was meant to help immigrants find paths to citizenship. In addition, Mormon bishops were instructed not to ask about immigration status when giving out callings, and there was to be no prejudice on that topic among ward members, in a Spanish ward or anywhere else. Some argued that this was just the church trying to keep up its membership numbers, not to mention tithing. But it was one of the few areas in which the Mormon church as an institution was more liberal than many of its members.

"Do you want some help tomorrow?" I asked. "I don't speak Spanish, but I'm sure I could make myself useful." With an empty nest, my Saturdays were usually free, unless I was babysitting one of my grandchildren or hosting a family get-together.

Gwen immediately brightened. "Really? You want to come?"

"Of course. What time do you need me?" I said.

"It starts at ten and goes until one," Gwen said.

I nodded again. "I can do that. Where is it? Our local stake building?"

"No, the Spanish ward meets at another building." She rattled off an address and I typed it slowly into my phone, repeating it back to her when she'd finished. "It's close to the freeway, so it's easy to get to whether you're coming from the north or south."

"All right. I'll see you tomorrow, then," I said.

"Thank you, Linda. Thank you so much," Gwen said tearfully. She gave me a quick hug, then began her walk home alone. I still worried about the state of her marriage. Quitting her job was a huge step to take without consulting her husband, and even if Brad didn't mind the loss of income, it spoke volumes about Gwen's state of mind. She was thinking like a single woman, not a married one.

I went back inside and saw that Brad had gone already. Had Kurt told him to meet Gwen at home? I knew it wasn't my business, but it was hard not to stick my nose in.

For the next hour, I helped with the rest of the cleanup, stacking and putting away tables and chairs and loading our decorations into the back of Kurt's truck. In the front of the truck, I kept a couple of extra bags of candy piled on the floor at my feet.

"Dinner?" I said with a laugh. We hadn't had a chance to eat before we came.

"I certainly wouldn't mind," Kurt said as he pulled out a Snickers bar, his favorite.

I slapped his hand. "Don't ruin your appetite," I said with a grin, already planning dinner on my own terms.

Once we were home, Kurt unloaded the truck as I set the bar counter with plates and cups. The "entrée" tonight was candy bars. I plucked out a few personal favorites for my plate, including Mounds and Almond Joy, then gave Kurt the ones with peanuts.

"Do we have to use silverware?" Kurt asked, coming up from behind to kiss the back of my neck.

"We're civilized," I said and pulled away to unwrap the bars, then cut them into pieces using a steak knife. I stepped back and looked at the plates, then went to grab a bag of baby carrots from the fridge. I added a cup of cold milk for each of us. "There," I said with satisfaction. "Four food groups."

"Four?" Kurt said. "I see two food groups and candy."

"The nuts count as protein," I reminded him.

"That's still only three," Kurt said.

"You mean chocolate isn't a food group?" I teased.

"I won't argue," Kurt said with the grin that had won my heart over thirty years ago.

We ate our "dinner" with the same pleasure as we would have a meal I'd spent hours slaving over. Why didn't we do this more often?

I remembered why when the sugar headache hit after my fourth candy bar. Oh, well. There was always Excedrin Migraine, my main source of Mormon-approved caffeine.

"I'm worried about Gwen," Kurt said as we put our plates in the dishwasher. "Brad told me that she's been angry a lot lately, and that her anger is often directed at him and the church."

I was angry at the church a lot myself these days. But I could see how Kurt would feel like it was unfair to direct it at a husband. He didn't see sometimes how the men were part of the church system. They had the power, and sometimes it felt like the only choices for women were knuckling under or leaving. I still struggled with this and wasn't sure I was prepared to have a conversation about it now.

"You saw how she acted tonight," Kurt said. He seemed to assume that I'd agree it was her actions that were the most egregious. I didn't.

"I saw her leaving the building in tears and Brad not going after her," I said.

"He was just afraid she'd yell at him."

This was the only source of power women seemed to have within Mormonism: the power to make men feel bad. "Well, maybe he needs to work on listening to her more," I said.

Kurt's eyebrows rose. "I was hoping you'd offer to go talk to Gwen," he said.

What did he mean? I had already spoken to her. "About what?" I asked.

"About bringing politics into the church building and picking fights with other women in the ward who are just trying to do good," he said.

Complaints about bringing politics into the church seemed to come almost entirely from the conservative end of the spectrum when the liberal segment called them out on Christian principles of love, compassion, and helping the poor and needy.

My stomach tightened as I stared at Kurt. "I support everything Gwen said." My tone made it very clear that I wasn't in a mood to be cajoled.

"Well then, maybe you can ask her if there's anything we can do to help in the Spanish ward," he finished lamely.

I explained that I'd already volunteered to help her the next day with her citizenship workshop.

"Thank you, Linda," he said, and I believed he was actually grateful.

"I'll see what I can do," I told Kurt. That was the most I could promise for now.

CHAPTER 3

Early Saturday morning, Gwen texted to offer to pick me up. I thanked her and accepted, since it would be easier not to have to worry about finding an unfamiliar address.

Kurt was already up and eating breakfast in the kitchen when I came downstairs, dressed and showered earlier than I wanted to be.

"Why aren't you sleeping in?" I asked.

"There's a scout campout today, and I wanted to visit them and go on their hike this morning," he said.

At least he hadn't felt obliged to risk his back on a night's sleep on rocks.

"Good luck," I said and kissed him just as Gwen knocked at the front door. She was looking better than she had last night, more energetic and less frazzled.

"Are you nervous about applying to the Police Academy?" I asked Gwen after I got into her car.

"Oh, definitely," Gwen said with a little laugh. "Petrified."

But she was doing it anyway—was that bravery or stubbornness? "How long do you think it will take to finish once you've gotten in?"

"Well, it's about a year of classwork before certification, and then you have to find a position in a local department and get on-the-job training," she said.

"I've heard people complain about the pay," I said, noting that she hadn't mentioned the rigorous physical tests she'd have to pass.

Gwen shrugged, then started down the big hill toward the freeway. "Yeah, but Brad has never really depended on my income. Isn't he supposed to be the provider, anyway?" There was acid in her tone, and I decided not to press her about her marital issues.

It was hard for me to imagine life as a Mormon woman who wasn't a mother. We were told so often that raising children was the most important thing we could do with our lives; that mothering was an eternal role, and even when we were resurrected and living in the celestial kingdom, we'd be silently serving our spirit children somehow, as our rarely spoken-of Heavenly Mother did.

"How's Samuel?" Gwen asked me, glancing over when we were stopped at a light.

Samuel was my youngest son, openly gay and now in Boston on a mission for the Mormon church.

"I think he's doing well," I said, grateful she'd asked. Sometimes it felt like everyone in the ward danced around the topic of Samuel's homosexuality. They'd ask about my other four boys, but not him.

Gwen sighed. "I really admire him, Linda. He has a difficult row to hoe."

"He's incredible," I said. It wasn't an exaggeration; he'd known about the prejudice he'd be exposed to as an openly gay missionary, and he'd signed up anyway, never once complaining

about his own church's views on the evils of "practicing" homosexuality and on the inherent divinity of heterosexuality.

Somehow, I'd never been bothered by those views much before.
They seemed like someone else's problems. Until Samuel announced
he was gay at a family dinner at the end of his senior year of high
school with Kurt and all of our other sons there, as well: Joseph,
Adam, Zachary, and Kenneth. I would always feel mom-guilt about
never seeing the signs before that. How could I have missed something so major in the son I'd always felt closest to?

"I wish I'd known someone like him when I was his age,"
Gwen added. "It would have meant so much to see someone
show that kind of courage."

Her teen years had been spent with a father who'd sexually
abused her and her sisters—her infertility was a result of that
abuse. She'd been so innocent, and yet she'd faced such incredible consequences for someone else's actions—someone who'd
remained in a position of authority in the Mormon church for
decades. It was heartbreaking.

Gwen Ferris's life was one of the things I'd set on my "shelf,"
the place church leaders suggested we place our doubts about
various problems in the church. Her fate would be the first thing
I asked God about in the afterlife. I wanted some explanation—
why did some people get miracles, but not Gwen? Why did some
people suffer such enormous sins against them and never see
justice? The fact that she'd survived that to become a functional
adult was as a testament of her own strength, in my opinion, not
God's intervention.

"You're plenty courageous, Gwen," I told her.

"Thank you, Linda," she said, staring straight ahead through
the windshield.

I knew she felt that the other women in the ward judged her for not having children, even if they didn't know the circumstances. Shannon Carpenter wasn't the only one who made assumptions. Gwen could have set them straight, but it was almost as if she was proud to serve as a reminder that not all women had to fit in the stay-at-home mother box to be part of Mormonism.

I reached over and patted her leg. "Don't ever doubt that you matter, Gwen. We need faithful women like you in our ward."

She let out a breath and shook her head. "Do I still have faith? I don't know anymore."

Eventually, we pulled into the parking lot of a faceless industrial building on the other side of the freeway. It was cement on the front, and there were several businesses listed near the entrance inside. One of the offices bore a plaque with THE CHURCH OF JESUS CHRIST OF LATTER-DAY SAINTS engraved into it and beneath that, the same in Spanish: LA IGLESIA DE JESUCRISTO DE LOS SANTOS DE LOS ÚLTIMOS DÍAS.

I followed Gwen to the front door, which she opened with a key. The interior was chilly. There was a thermostat, which I turned up, hoping that would warm the room. It looked like they couldn't fit more than a hundred people in here, and there were no padded seats like in our building on the hill. I felt guilt at the contrast. I noticed the banged-up piano in the front for services— pretty bare-bones for a Mormon chapel.

"I've got to set up," Gwen said. "I have some signs in the car. Can you put them up so any non-Mormons who show up know where to go?"

I went back to the car, retrieved the signs, and posted them on the grass and in front of the building.

"Do you have anyone else coming from the ward to help?" I asked when I came back inside.

Gwen shifted uncomfortably. "I didn't really ask official permission," she said.

I knew there was more to it than that. "Do you think the bishop wouldn't want you hosting this?" I asked, confused. How had she gotten the keys to open the building if she hadn't gone through the proper channels?

"Bishop Hope didn't seem thrilled when I brought it up. That was the last time I went to talk to him about what I could do to help." It didn't seem like she was too pleased with him, and I recalled Gabriela mentioning his name during her unhappy phone call at our chapel.

"So you're doing this behind his back?"

She shrugged. "Not quite. He told me I could do it if I was willing to man it by myself."

"Do you think anyone will come?" I asked. In our ward, if the bishop didn't advertise and encourage members to come, an activity was dead in the water.

"I hope they trust me more than him," Gwen said.

It seemed like her relationship with the bishop was pretty adversarial. If he didn't like her, did he have the power to get her calling changed and kick her out, since she wasn't naturally part of the Spanish ward herself? It seemed like a bad omen for Gwen's last attempt to stay connected to Mormonism.

For the next hour we sat there, waiting quietly. Gwen kept standing up to check the door to see if anyone was coming. She clearly cared a lot about this workshop and the people in the Spanish ward, and I understood the point she'd made to Shannon Carpenter, that we Mormons could often be all too happy to remain where it was comfortable, to choose service that was easy.

"Maybe we don't always live up to the ideal in the Book of Mormon of no poor and needy," I admitted, thinking of the period after Christ had visited the Americas, when generation after generation lived in perfect gospel unity. They'd had everything "in common," the scriptures said. Times had clearly changed.

"The Book of Mormon," Gwen muttered. "Do you have any idea what it means for the people in this ward to be told they're Lamanites?"

"No. Is that such a bad thing?" Of course, the Lamanites were the descendants of the two "bad" brothers, cursed with dark skin for their unrighteousness, but they'd also been the ones who believed in Christ in the end. They'd been the ones saved when the destruction of the Land of Zarahemla happened at Christ's death in Jerusalem. By the end of the book, the Nephites had all fallen away and the Lamanites were the ones God wanted to reclaim.

Gwen rolled her eyes. "Look, I'm not interested in arguing about whether or not the Book of Mormon is a historical record of a real group of people or not, but Linda, surely you of all people can see the problems with telling Latinos that they're descendants of Israelites."

I felt a niggling worry. I hadn't meant to get into such a deep discussion about the history of Mormonism and race. In the early days of the church, Joseph Smith had sent missionaries to the native tribes near where the church was located—never with much success. But the message in those days was that the descendants of the Lamanites had to accept the gospel before the Second Coming of Christ. Then Joseph Smith had been martyred in 1844.

A few years later, when Mormons had come west to Utah, the new Mormon prophet Brigham Young had alternately made pacts with the American Indians against the United States government, blamed them for things the Mormons themselves had done, and used them as he wished. But after that, there hadn't been much discussion of Lamanites as real people until the 1970s, when Spencer W. Kimball had sent Navajo children into the homes of white Mormons as foster children and had claimed that their skin was getting whiter. The program had been so disastrous that the church was still facing lawsuits over it, for ignoring abusive situations in particular.

"What do you mean?" I asked.

"This idea that Latinos are the descendants of the Lamanites and that we as Mormons have a duty to bring the gospel to them, there's an inherent superiority and colonialist attitude about it. I see it in the way that Greg Hope interacts with people every Sunday at church. He's the white guy with the truth. They have to defer to him."

I didn't see Mormonism that way, but I couldn't deny I'd seen others who did. "He's white?" I asked, though it seemed obvious from the name.

"Yes. He drives me crazy, the way he refuses to listen to them. He pretends, for about two sentences, then goes back to telling them what to do. Just be more like him, pretend to be white. Or be subservient. Accept your place in the world." She spat out each word.

I held up my hands. "I'm sorry," I said. "Maybe he has other qualities that make him a good leader. Or maybe he's just the kind of person who needs to be called into leadership so he can be shown to be the selfish person he really is." That was my best

attempt at explaining the situation. I didn't know the man personally, but I'd seen other cases where the men who'd been
called to serve were exposed as evil, and that was the only reason
I could think of that God might have sanctioned their callings.

"We have to give up the Book of Mormon, if you ask me. It's
untenable. The history claims, the DNA evidence, the mistakes."
She shook her head. "It doesn't work as any kind of record, and
it reeks of nineteenth-century racism."

I had mixed feelings about the arguments about the histo-
ricity of the Book of Mormon. Just because we hadn't yet found
archeological evidence or DNA that supported it, didn't mean it
had to be invented.

"Gwen, I find some of its stories so inspirational. The one of
Alma the Younger's vision and return to the church, the story
of Samuel the Lamanite testifying of the coming of Christ, the
anti-Nephi-Lehites choosing death by the sword rather than
killing again, and Captain Moroni raising the "title of liberty"
to fight against the enemies of peace. Not to mention the whole
idea that wealth makes people too proud, and always leads to
a downfall."

Her expression was sour. "I find *The Lord of the Rings* inspirational, too, but no one calls Tolkien a prophet. Or says that a
church should be founded on its teachings in the most literal
way possible."

"What would we be without the Book of Mormon?" I asked.
No different than any other Christian church, it seemed to me. I
wasn't ready to give up Mormonism's unique points. Not yet.

But Gwen shook her head again. "A better church. Better able
to serve those who need us."

I could see why Brad was struggling to get along with Gwen

right now. I wasn't married to her, and felt like our discussion had somehow turned into a debate. She must push his buttons every minute.

But I loved her, despite all. "I try to trust in God that the church is moving in the right direction," I said.

Gwen let out a huff of breath. "After the new policy, you can still say that, Linda?" she asked.

Her question stung. The POX had been very difficult for me, and I still didn't know what to make of it. It was a major stumbling block to me believing that the current leaders of the church had special access to God's voice. I hadn't seen racism in the Book of Mormon and the existing church structure in the same way, but I should have. Of course there were other problems besides LGBTQ issues that our leadership wasn't addressing. I tried to remember that I needed to let Gwen vent to me, like I vented to others.

"I'm sorry," I said. "You're right."

We didn't talk again for a few minutes, and then Gabriela entered with her children. I hadn't known she would be coming. I waved at her, then at the baby, getting a smile and a wiggle in return.

Gwen stood up and embraced her. "Gabriela, so good to see you," Gwen said, and then greeted the woman in Spanish.

"Linda," Gabriela said, and gave me an embrace as well.

"*Buenos días*," I said in what even I could tell was a bad accent.

"I'm so glad you could make it," Gwen said, turning back to Gabriela.

"Of course. I'm sorry I'm so late. I had to get the children ready, and you know how children can be . . ." Gabriela trailed off and flushed. Gwen didn't know how that was, since she didn't have small children of her own. "They were very grouchy this morning," she finished.

"Well, let's get to work," Gwen said.

"Let me help with the little ones," I said, holding out my arm for Amanda.

Gabriela relinquished the baby, and I held out a hand to Manuel. Lucia followed after us to the other side of the meeting room, where we could play duck-duck-goose and Who's Got the Button?, both of which I had to explain to them.

Little Amanda kept escaping from my arms and crawling speedily toward the open door. I'd chase after her and bring her back, and then the process would start all over again.

After an hour of child-wrangling, I needed a nap. I'd babysat my granddaughter Carla plenty of times, but she wasn't as much work as these three. Maybe because she wasn't mobile yet.

I remembered that I had some candy in my purse, a couple of packs of leftover Sixlets and a few mini candy bars I'd stuck in my purse in case I needed to keep my strength up when I was out shopping. But I was willing to sacrifice them for a good cause. I let the children have a few pieces each, using the Sixlets as a lure to keep Amanda close by.

Finally, Gabriela and Gwen were finished talking about the possibility of applying for DACA—Deferred Action for Childhood Arrivals. Gwen gave her some numbers to call for further assistance and some paperwork to begin the process.

"Thank you so much," said Gabriela as she gathered Amanda into her arms.

"Your children are wonderful," I said. "I'm glad to have been able to help."

The children waved goodbye to me as Gabriela clucked for them to follow her.

I didn't tell Gwen about the phone call I'd overheard at the Trunk or Treat, but I did ask, "What about her husband?" since this was the second time I'd met her and neither she nor the children had mentioned him.

Gwen explained, "Luis was deported early last year. He first came to the country as an adult from Mexico on a temporary visa and overstayed it for several years. When ICE found him, they deported him immediately, and she was terrified they'd do the same to her, so she had to move and give up her job."

"How awful," I said. Deportations had become all too common lately, in hospitals, courtrooms, and parking lots. It made me wonder what our country had come to.

"They were married in the Salt Lake temple, but that doesn't make them legal citizens," Gwen added.

"At least they're sealed eternally, then," I said, but Gwen gave me a look that made me wish I hadn't said anything. What use was it for a couple to know they'd be together with their children after they died if they had no time together in the here and now?

"Gabriela's parents brought her to Utah from Mexico when she was fourteen. She was only supposed to stay as a visitor, but her parents kept her here in high school long past her visa permit. She's been getting removal orders ever since, but her parents didn't tell her anything about it. They've both passed away now, though, and it was only after they died that she realized there was a problem with her residency. By then, she felt the United States was her home."

"If she gets the paperwork filled out, she should be fine," I said.

"If they don't change the laws again," Gwen said.

It was true. The recent rise in anti-immigration sentiment around the country had made it dangerous for all immigrants.

Gwen and I talked about the tendency for Mormons to vote Republican, even when it seemed anti-family, because of specific social issues like abortion and same-sex marriage.

"You must worry about reversals on protections for LGBTQ people after the last election," Gwen said, making the transition to Samuel again.

"I am. Every day," I said.

It was nice to finally talk to someone who was at least as liberal, or perhaps a bit more so than I was politically. Anna Torstensen, my best friend in the ward, certainly wasn't. I'd learned not to talk to her about politics, but I felt it had made us less close than we had been. Maybe that was part of the reason I was talking so earnestly with Gwen.

Toward the afternoon, two more women and one man came in. Gwen talked them through the process, gave them some numbers to call, and loaded them up with paperwork. Then we packed up and headed home.

CHAPTER 4

As Gwen pulled up in front of our house, I spotted Kurt's car in the garage. So he'd made it back from the scout camp alive. I hoped he'd showered and put a load of laundry in. Since Samuel had gone on his mission, we'd divided some of the household chores. I still did all the cooking and dishes, while Kurt handled bathroom cleaning and laundry.

Gwen parked in our driveway and turned off the car, meaning she wanted to talk. "I just don't know how to reconcile the racism I see with what I think the church should be."

"The church is filled with flawed people," I said. "It can't be anything other than flawed. Our leaders speak to God some-times, but I'm not sure they can ever fully translate His perfection into our language—or into our institutions." That was my best way of explaining the gap between the ideal church and the real one for me.

"It's one thing to say that there's a gap. But how can you say that the prophets were listening to God and that they refused to let black people be full participants in the church? How could they have gotten it so wrong?"

I'd heard Mormons argue that God was behind the priesthood ban, but I couldn't see it. "I'm not trying to justify it," I said. "It's problematic, but I have to say that I don't see any other church that offers me more of the Christ I love. Mormonism is so good at community, so good at reaching out to the lost sheep, and at teaching us to be less selfish."

"I'm not sure that's my experience lately," Gwen said darkly. It was probably why she'd decided to become a police officer, because she felt like she could do more there than in the Mormon church to help other people.

"I'm sorry, Gwen," I said. "We all have spiritual crises, I think, as we realize that the old God we once believed in is no longer sufficient to our current needs." Maybe it was the wrong thing for me say to try to convince her about what her experience should be. I often thought people just needed to listen more, and I would try to model that.

"What? No calls for me to pray and read my scriptures more? Fast every week? Go to the temple?" Her sarcasm was biting.

I wondered how often Brad had made these suggestions to her. It had clearly been a bad idea. "I know you're a good person, Gwen. I don't need to preach to you."

"Well, Shannon Carpenter certainly feels like she does," she sniffed.

"I know," I said. "But that doesn't mean you're off base. It's not an easy equation sometimes. Humans aren't mathematical, and there's no right or wrong here. We have to try to give each other the benefit of the doubt, and look for the good people are doing even if it's not what we think is best." I could tell I was sounding preachy, even after I'd told myself I would listen.

She sighed. "It sounds like you're telling me to stay in the boat."

That was a phrase used in a recent biennial General

Conference pep talk, where the prophets and apostles speak to the members of the church about modern-day issues and their words are considered even more important than older talks or the scriptures. I shook my head, frustrated. "That's not what I mean at all." This wasn't going the way I'd hoped. I needed to be a little more vulnerable, offer her some real truth about my personal history.

"Then what do you mean?"

I knew Kurt would be furious if I encouraged Gwen to leave the Mormon church, but sometimes that was exactly what needed to happen. "Well, I don't know if you know this, but I left Mormonism for a while, many years ago. Before I had children."

Gwen looked surprised at this. "You, Linda?"

I wasn't sure if I should be offended or not. I smiled. I guessed this wasn't what people imagined when they saw me next to Kurt at church on Sunday. "Yes. I was going through severe depression, and I blamed God for some terrible things that had happened in my life." I wasn't going to get into the details now. "Time away was useful for me. I realized I missed that spiritual high, and even the frustration from interacting with people who didn't see the world as I did. I needed the community, I guess. I needed that challenge to look beyond myself."

"Hmm," said Gwen. "How long did this last?"

"Several years."

"And when you look back, do you wish you'd stayed in the church?"

"No, not at all. It was important for me to leave, so I could know what I missed and understand that I valued it."

"So is this just a routine story of repentance? You know, one of the ones they show in seminary classes, where a kid's in a rehab center and finally changes his life for the better?" There was an edge to her voice now, and I knew I had to tread carefully.

"Gwen, I don't see you as someone in need of rehabilitation. And no, you never come back the same, if you come back at all. What I'm trying to say is that you need to embrace the truths you find along the way, not push them away. If God exists, and I believe He does, then all of the goodness is part of Him. Just because it doesn't fit someone else's rigid view of righteousness, doesn't mean you should throw it away."

Gwen looked directly at me, her eyes soft as her voice had not been. "Thank you, Linda," she said, and restarted the car.

I guessed that was my cue to leave, though I felt like I hadn't done more than touch the surface of the question of her crisis of faith. I hoped I'd given her enough of a reason to trust me with more when she was ready. I got out of the car. I looked back from the porch; Gwen waved at me, then drove away.

I went into the house and found Kurt in the kitchen, making himself a peanut butter and jelly sandwich.

"How'd it go?" he asked.

I briefly told him about Gabriela and her children. I didn't feel it was right for me to share any of the questions Gwen had asked me about the history of the church or the literal truth of the Book of Mormon as a record of the American Indians.

"Do you really think Gwen is a good fit for the Police Academy?" Kurt asked as he pried open the peanut butter jar.

He must have talked to Brad about it. "I don't see why not."

"You don't think she's too . . . small?"

"That doesn't mean she's weak. I think it will give her purpose," I said. We all needed purpose, didn't we? And I assumed they'd teach her moves that could compensate for her physical size at the Academy.

"Maybe," Kurt said, stirring the jelly absently.

"What do you think we should send Samuel for Christmas?" I asked, hoping Kurt would go along with the abrupt change of subject.

Bless him, he did. "I have a few ideas. He might need some cold-weather clothes." It was true, Samuel hadn't had to go through the full Boston winter last year since he was in the Missionary Training Center in Provo for part of it.

"I suppose," I said hesitantly. I wanted to protect Samuel from the cold as much as any mother did for her son, but hats and gloves were such a boring gift. I wanted to get him something more personal, more fun.

"We could do the Twelve Days of Christmas for him and his companion," Kurt said. "Just send some little things every day."

I wasn't sure the mail system would cooperate with us, but I liked the idea. I could mix in store-bought items with homemade goodies. I wished I knew more about his mission companion, though.

"Why do you think he was transferred again so soon?" I asked. Samuel had written us an email on his last P-day (the once a week preparation day when missionaries didn't have to proselytize and could have a little fun and get laundry done). He'd told us that he'd been transferred to a new area. Then the next week he wrote that he'd been transferred again, on a non-transfer day, to a new companion. It was odd, but I was trying not to go into full-on mom-worry mode yet.

"I figure the mission president has his reasons," Kurt said, taking his first bite of the sandwich. Kurt hadn't skimped on the peanut butter, and I wondered how he could talk without pausing to unstick his teeth.

"You're not curious about what they are?" I asked.

Kurt shook his head and swallowed hard. "Inspiration strikes at strange times. And maybe there was a personality conflict that he had to deal with."

"You think Samuel had a problem with another missionary?" I asked. Samuel was one of the easiest people in the world to get along with. If there was a problem, the odds were that it was about Samuel serving a mission while openly gay, which was very unusual in our church these days. Gay missionaries had served for years, of course, but only secretly.

"I doubt it," Kurt said, then took another bite. "Really, the kids in his generation are much less likely to have a problem with someone's sexual orientation than in ours."

That didn't mean that none of them did, though. "Can you call President Cooper and find out exactly what's going on?"

I figured he would have better luck talking to another male priesthood authority in the church than a concerned mother would. Besides, we weren't supposed to call Samuel directly except twice a year, on Mother's Day and Christmas. May felt like a long time ago, and I was looking forward to Samuel's call soon. He could Skype us from a member's house while the whole family was here, and it would be like we were all together again. Almost.

"Linda, I really don't think we should worry about it," Kurt said. "Samuel is in God's hands. If the mission president decided to transfer him, that's his business, not ours. We should pray for Samuel to find those he's there to find. This isn't about him having an easy, comfortable experience. It's about him learning about how to put his own feelings aside and help others."

I didn't buy this logic at all. I wanted to know if Samuel was being persecuted. These days, the apostles kept insisting that gay people were part of God's plan, that they were loved and welcome in the church. As long as they were celibate, anyway, which was the path Samuel had chosen, at least for now. No one had any reason to tell him he was less worthy of membership or service than anyone else. It was just plain bigotry if they did.

I had to work to unloosen my jaw. "You don't still think that Samuel is going to be 'cured' of being gay if he's faithful enough on his mission, do you?"

"No, Linda, I don't think that," Kurt said. He looked away as he spoke, though.

"But you think he should marry a woman and try to become straight?" I pressed him.

"Linda, I don't want to argue with you about this anymore," Kurt said. "I just want Samuel to be happy, and I want him to have all of God's blessings. Right now, he's on a mission, and that means following the mission rules, including changing companions and locations without complaint when he's asked."

I knew all about following rules. I also knew about the price of following rules that were meant for square pegs, not round ones. I didn't want to see Samuel forced into a role that wasn't authentic to him.

"I want Samuel to be happy, too, Kurt," I said, sighing. "I'm just not sure where that will take him or the rest of us."

"Well, let's wait until that moment comes and enjoy the present," Kurt said.

It was a reasonable request, so I let the matter go. For now. I was still trying to live by what I'd told Gwen, about embracing all of the good and realizing that God was there in all of it.

CHAPTER 5

I got an unexpected phone call from Gwen early the next morning.

"Linda? I need you to come meet me." Her voice was clipped and urgent.

"Gwen? Where are you?"

"I'm at Gabriela's apartment." She gave me an address that wasn't far from the building the ward had been in—close to the freeway, on the less nice end of town. "Please, can you come over right now?"

"What's going on?" I asked, wondering if I should call Kurt or the police.

"Gabriela says she's been accused of embezzling money from the ward. She's terrified the police are going to come arrest her, and that she's going to end up deported with her kids left here all alone."

"Oh no!" I said, hearing Gabriela's panic through Gwen's voice. I couldn't imagine what it would be like to worry about your kids having no one to care for them. I didn't understand where the accusation about her taking money from the ward would even have come from, but I wanted to help the poor woman.

"I'll be there in twenty minutes," I said.

"What's up?" Kurt asked from his side of the bed.

I explained briefly.

"How could she have taken money from the ward? She can't even serve in an executive calling as a woman."

Mormon wards were very careful about who handled money. There were only a few men designated to take the gray envelopes that held offerings and tithing, and even then, they weren't supposed to open or count the money unless there was more than one of them there watching to make sure it was all deposited properly.

"Maybe she had access to one of the billing accounts at the grocery store?" I asked dubiously.

"I guess, but most of the time, people just get receipts and are reimbursed."

"Well, Gwen could be confused," I said. "I didn't talk directly to Gabriela."

"All right. Go on, then. I hope you can calm them both down. Let me know if you need anything," Kurt said and gave me a quick smooch on the lips before I left him there, still warm in his covers.

As I drove down the mountain and west toward the Oquirrh mountain range, the sun was high in a clear sky, and it felt more like early September than late October. Leaves were on the ground everywhere, and I could hear them crunch faintly under my tires as I drove.

I pulled into the apartment complex's parking lot, not far from the prison, which was destined to be moved as soon as the new buildings were finished in Tooele, west of here and far from any population centers. The first apartment building was not in good shape. Patches on the roof needed to be repaired, and the balconies seemed to be falling down. The siding was faded and looked brittle enough to be blown off in one good windstorm. It didn't look like there had been any maintenance in years on the yellow lawn or the unkempt scrubby pine bushes around the perimeter.

There were at least a dozen young children outside playing on an old rusted playset without any supervision, but I didn't recognize any of them as Gabriela's.

I went upstairs and knocked on the apartment door.

"Come in!" called Gwen from inside.

I turned the rusted knob and stepped in. There wasn't much there in terms of furniture, but the floor was spotless, and the kitchen was at least as clean as my own.

As soon as the children saw me, they came running toward me and yanked on my purse, asking for candy.

Gabriela glanced over at them, but I could see from her tear-streaked face that she was desperate.

"Thank you for coming, Linda," Gwen said. "I think the kids are hungry, and Gabriela is too worried to deal with them right now."

Did she have food in the house? I wished Gwen had warned me I should bring something over to feed the kids. I did have more candy, but that wasn't lunch. Looking in the refrigerator, I saw only milk. I opened a couple of cupboards as Gabriela rattled in Spanish to Gwen, who nodded and made reassuring noises. It made me uncomfortable to imagine being in a situation where I didn't have enough money to buy food for my children. Things had been tight in the early years with me and Kurt, but never *that* tight. And Gabriela didn't have a husband with whom to share the burden. She was applying for DACA, which meant she could end up being deported, too. And then what would happen to her children? I couldn't help but worry for her.

I found some cans of tuna in the cupboards, and although there wasn't any mayonnaise, I used margarine to stick the tuna to the homemade bread on the countertop. It was good bread, the gluten strands properly activated so that it held together instead of crumbling.

The children devoured the bread and made no complaint about the tuna fish lacking mayonnaise. They asked about more candy though, and I gave them what I had.

After that, I attempted to entertain them by performing various animal pantomimes. Their favorite was the elephant, which they had me do over and over again until Gabriela and Gwen were finished.

I could only hear snippets of their conversation, all of it in Spanish. The only part I understood was when Gwen gave Gabriela five twenty-dollar bills, crisp from the bank. It wasn't until we were out of her apartment and standing by my car that Gwen explained to me what was going on.

"She says that Bishop Hope demanded she repay money he gave her for food and medical bills last month," Gwen explained.

"Why would he do that?" I asked, because it seemed a matter of course that a bishop would offer to cover expenses in a situation like this, a single mother with three small children to care for. I wondered if that could have had to do with Gabriela's phone call at the church.

"He claimed that she hadn't turned in the proper receipts," Gwen said, rolling her eyes at me.

"Seriously? That seems like taking things a step too far." The Mormon church liked their record-keeping, but even the late

President Thomas S. Monson had been known for a quote: "Never let a problem to be solved become more important than a person to be loved." Wasn't that what was happening here?

"I can believe it of Greg Hope. It's all about what makes him look good," Gwen said.

I didn't give a hoot about the bishop at the moment. I cared about those kids. And Gabriela. "Should we go back so I can give her some money, as well?" I suggested. Kurt and I always had enough and to spare, and what else was money for but helping people?

"I told her we'd come back tomorrow after I talked to Bishop Hope about her situation. I promised her that I'd make sure he didn't call the police on her," Gwen said. "That seemed far more important to her than money right now."

I thought about the nearly empty refrigerator I'd opened, but sighed. "All right. Would it help if I got Kurt to call Bishop Hope and talk about the situation? Maybe he can get the stake president involved as well."

"Thank you. That will probably be better for Gabriela. Men in the church always listen better to other men," Gwen said sourly.

AT HOME THAT night, I asked Kurt if he'd contact the stake president about the money problem in the Spanish ward. I explained what Gabriela had told Gwen.

Kurt rubbed at his bald spot. "Linda, I can't do that. It's none of my business. Not to mention it's not within my realm of authority. Only the stake president can talk to another bishop about problems in his ward."

The sacred church hierarchy, of course, but I had prepared a counterargument. "You can talk about it as a problem for Gwen. She's a member of your ward, and she has questions about how money is being managed in that ward, where she has a calling. Wouldn't that work?"

Kurt gave me a skeptical look, but he promised he'd call and "feel out the situation." "Have you considered that you're assuming that Gabriela is telling the truth when she might not be?" he pointed out.

"Why would she lie?" I asked.

"Because she's desperate and needs the money," Kurt suggested. "But it might not even necessarily be a lie. Maybe she's just frightened and a little confused."

I seriously doubted that was what was going on. "You're taking Greg Hope's side because he's a bishop," I said.

"Well, I guess I do assume there's a reason he was made a bishop. He has to have served well in the past. So maybe I do give his side of the story more credence than hers."

I was boiling over with fury at this point. How were women supposed to be given credence if they were never granted positions of authority? But men didn't seem to see the problem, because they were never on this side of it. Even good men like Kurt couldn't see it.

"Seems like if you're a woman and you're not white, you're always going to be considered lesser in this church," I blurted out in frustration.

"Linda, I think you're too emotionally involved to look at this clearly. Whenever there's a woman you think is being oppressed, you blame the church," Kurt said.

"And there's a reason for that," I said pointedly. "Women are often abused by the system of patriarchy in the church and by the men within it who benefit from that system." I sounded like one of my own college essays on feminism, but I wasn't ashamed of it.

"Fine. I'll do my best. But bishops are usually in the business of helping people, you know."

"Then why is Bishop Hope threatening to call the police on her?" I asked.

Kurt had no answer for that.

He went to bed and I went online, trying to seek out an organization that might help an undocumented immigrant in a situation like this. To my surprise, I found a Facebook group called Mormon Women for Ethical Government, or MWEG, that had been around since late 2016. There were thousands of women in it, from every part of the United States. I couldn't see anything but the public posts, which were all about rallies to stop immigrants from being deported, fundraising to help defray the costs of court battles, and actions to send letters to our members of Congress to plead for them to reinstate DACA and stop ICE raids on working families. I asked to be added, then got to work putting together a care package of food staples—flour, sugar, oil, and canned foods—and hoped it wouldn't be received negatively the next time I saw Gabriela.

CHAPTER 6

The next day, Kurt came home and told me he'd had a meeting with President Frost about Gabriela and Bishop Hope.

"And?" I asked eagerly.

"And he said that Bishop Hope personally employs more than half the people in his ward at his business."

Kurt clearly thought this was a heroic effort. I wasn't convinced. "What does that have to do with the embezzling charge against Gabriela? That has nothing to do with his business." Whatever it was.

"He also said that the Spanish ward has been in the red for months, and the stake isn't sure they can cover the deficit. They're going to have to go to the regional level for more financial help, and President Frost sounded embarrassed about it."

This was probably information Kurt wasn't supposed to tell me, but he had anyway. I tried my best to feel grateful for that. "So Gabriela could be telling the truth," I said. "If the bishop is pressuring her to repay funds, he could have threatened to call the police."

"It's possible," Kurt admitted. "But at this point, we should probably let President Frost take over. He said he'd bring Greg

Hope and Gabriela together and negotiate a solution. He said that he probably needed to go over the rules again about what people needed to do to qualify for help."

It made me sick sometimes that we had people "qualify" for help when the Mormon church was so rich in assets, from cattle farms to stocks to buildings and property. During the Depression, the church had begun a policy of only giving help to those who were attending church and serving in callings, and they had to do extra service hours each week to repay the help in part. The same policy had been extended to the present, most of the time.

"Did he say he'd make sure she wasn't arrested?" I asked, thinking it was the very least he could do.

"Not exactly," Kurt said uncomfortably. "But he strongly implied it."

And that was probably as good as we'd get.

"What about Bishop Hope?" I asked, thinking about Gwen's negative impression of him. "Do you know anything about him?"

He shrugged. "Not personally, but it's Greg Hope, you know. The basketball player," he said. "From BYU."

It took me another minute to place the name with a face. And then I was astonished to realize I did know him, at least from TV.

"The guy from the car wash commercial?" If he was who I thought he was, he'd done a series of commercials for a local car wash where he had dribbled soap bubbles like basketballs and shot them at a hoop. The car wash had long since gone under.

"That was his first business. He's much more successful now," Kurt said.

"At making money or church leadership?" I wasn't sure what Kurt was trying to say here. I knew Mormon bishops didn't have to go to theology school or have any formal training. They just had to be considered worthy males who could handle the responsibilities of the job. In my mind, too many bishops were considered the "right material" if they were successful in business or were well known and well liked. It didn't make them morally upright, compassionate, or even good leaders.

"Back in the day, he had one of the highest-ever records of baptisms for a missionary in the church," Kurt said.

"What? I never heard about that." I was also immediately suspicious. I hated when people talked about conversions in terms of numbers. It made it seem like the church was some kind of sales opportunity, and the best missionaries were pushy salespeople. In my experience, good missionaries were more thoughtful and didn't press religion on people unless they were interested, but that usually didn't stack the numbers.

"I understand he baptized over one thousand people in his two years in Mexico," Kurt went on.

"That's ridiculous," I said. "One thousand people? That's ten a week. How long did he talk to each of them? Ten minutes?"

I'd heard some stories about what had happened in the '70s and '80s when the church was having incredible success in Central and South America. That missionaries had taken kids to the beach and promised them ice cream cones if they were baptized. Or made a detour after a basketball camp instead of heading for the showers after the game. Or baptized young women who thought they were going to be taken to the United States as brides. And on and on. It was a time when anything American was seen as desirable in poorer countries, and to take advantage of that was pretty low, if you asked me. It was definitely not a reason to give someone a leadership position.

Kurt shrugged. "It was what the church needed to grow there

at the time. They saw his success as proof of his obedience and leadership."

I saw it as proof of something else. "Is that really the kind of man who gets higher positions in the church these days?" I asked. What a legacy we were leaving for the next generation, if this was so. The members baptized so quickly in Central and South America were rarely active even just one month after baptism. I wasn't sure what the point was in counting baptisms like that if the wards and stakes weren't growing commensurately. How many people did the average ward in that area have in it on paper? Three times as many as a regular ward in the US? Ten times as many?

And then what happened? The real members in those wards were tasked with the impossible job of trying to track the members who had been baptized so hastily and try to convince them to come back to full activity in the church. It was a terrible burden to put on the already overburdened members in such a poverty-stricken area.

None of my sons had served in South America. Kenneth had gone stateside, like Samuel, but in New Jersey. Adam had gone to the US Virgin Islands, which he had loved because he could wear short sleeves all the time and all the baptisms were in the warm ocean, not to mention P-Day excursions to beautiful sightseeing spots. Zachary had gone to Germany, but had mostly worked with American servicemen or refugees from other countries, because native Germans weren't often receptive to religious messages, particularly American ones.

"I'm not going to sit in judgment about him. If he baptized a lot of people, that doesn't automatically mean he was scamming them," Kurt said defensively.

"You think he was so successful just because he was filled with the Spirit?" I asked, skeptical.

"It could be." Kurt had reached the point where he was only going to dig in further, so I gave up on this point. "And he married one of the women he baptized, after he was finished with his mission and had a chance to go back and date her properly."

I'd heard about missionaries marrying other missionaries, as well as members or investigators from their missionary years. These stories were usually told with a kind of winking amusement. Young men between the ages of eighteen and twenty were notoriously unable to avoid making romantic attachments of one kind or another. But when they involved vulnerable women in foreign countries, I was skeptical. But I tried to refrain from judgment, supposing this was one of the reasons Greg Hope had been called to be bishop of this ward.

I sighed. "Well, what am I supposed to tell Gwen? Or Gabriela, for that matter, about the threat to call the police about the theft?" I asked.

"Just tell them that it's all going to be fine. No one needs to panic about this. It's taken care of." Kurt had a great calming voice, but it wasn't working on me now.

"Are you sure Bishop Hope isn't going to call the police?" The kind of man who would baptize a thousand people in two years seemed to me all about rules and numbers.

"I don't see any reason why he would do that to a member of his ward about such a minor problem," Kurt said.

I thought about all the times Kurt had dealt with problematic ward members on his own without ever calling the police. He was probably right, that Gabriela was just exaggerating her fear here. It made sense, considering how stressed she must be with three little kids and her husband gone. But I felt a niggling sense of unease, since I didn't know if Hope was the kind of bishop Kurt was.

"Gwen's not going to want to go back to her without anything concrete," I reminded Kurt.

"Linda, try not to get Gwen too upset over this. I don't want this to become an issue between her and Brad."

Another issue between her and Brad, he must mean.

After Kurt left for work, I checked on my membership in MWEG, which had been approved. Then I posted to the Facebook page, asking a few questions about someone being deported for embezzlement from the church. The responses were all messages of confusion, since that wasn't supposed to be how monetary assistance from the Mormon church worked. Nonetheless, I was given some names and phone numbers I could call to ask for immediate help if something went badly and Gabriela did end up arrested. I took some comfort in that.

Then I packed my car with the food staples for Gabriela and drove over to Gwen's to tell her what Kurt had said. She met me at the door and her face was swollen and red, like she'd had a rough night.

"Are you serious?" she said, her voice ice-cold. "That's it? She's supposed to trust the bishop will do the right thing?"

Gwen knew the man better than I did, and she clearly didn't trust him. Did I think she was being paranoid, or did I take her word for his character?

"Whatever he gave to her, it's a trivial amount of money when compared to the whole ward budget, surely," I said, trying not to land in the middle somewhere.

"That's not how Bishop Hope sees it," Gwen said. "You haven't heard the promises he makes at church on Sunday to these families about the American Dream and the covenants God has made with the Lamanite people. All about if they have problems with finances, it's because they're not paying tithing."

I felt nauseated at the idea of people who had nothing in their refrigerators being asked to pay tithing. Blessings were one thing. Magic was another.

I told Gwen about the names and numbers MWEG had given me. "We can give them to Gabriela to call in a last resort situation," I suggested.

"And she's supposed to trust a group of Mormon women to help her when her Mormon bishop may be the one to turn her into ICE in the first place?" Gwen demanded.

I didn't think that was what it sounded like Greg Hope would do, but I could see her point. To anyone used to seeing Mormon women as those who were most likely to fall in line and obey orders from men in authority, it would be hard to see them as anything else. Was it possible for women to be both politically outspoken and faithful? It had been in the past in Mormonism, but I wasn't sure anymore. Were the founders of MWEG likely to end up in the same situation as Ordain Women, who had all been excommunicated or disfellowshipped? I hoped not.

"I can't bear to go over there in person with this news." Gwen stared at her cell phone.

"Do you want me to call her instead?" I asked, worried about the food I had in the car. Was now the wrong time to offer it? But how could I, in good conscience, just leave it there, knowing how hungry those kids were?

"No. That would just make it worse for her. I have to do it

myself." Gwen let out a breath and then pushed the number on the phone.

Gwen fake-smiled as if Gabriela could see her and then seemed to be trying to inject positivity into her voice. It didn't last long. I could hear the rush of Spanish on the other end of the line and then Gwen's face fell. She turned away from me and said a few words. More Spanish words on the other line in quick procession, and then Gwen was clearly on the defensive, saying "*Lo siento*" more than once.

In the end, Gabriela must have hung up on her, because Gwen called out her name a couple of times, glanced down at her phone, and put it away.

"What did she say?" I asked quietly.

"She said that she hopes we'll think about her children when she's in jail," Gwen said sadly. It sounded like she'd been hit in the stomach and could hardly breathe.

"I'm sorry," I said. Just because Gabriela wouldn't talk to the names on the MWEG list, that didn't mean I couldn't do it for her, though, did it?

"She also said she never wanted to speak to me again," Gwen said. "That was before she called me some pretty bad names—I didn't even recognize half of them. She said that the Spanish ward was clearly just an attempt to breed complacent workers who don't complain, who are so afraid they'd never demand more."

I wanted to ask about that, but now didn't seem like a good time. "Once she's past this, she'll realize it wasn't fair to blame you." If she did get past this. If she and her children were safe. Would they ever be?

But Gwen's expression was desolate. "Linda, Gabriela doesn't get angry easily, and she doesn't make promises she doesn't keep. She was my best friend in the Spanish ward, and I can't undo the damage I just did." Her voice caught on a sob and she turned away.

"Gwen, I know you're upset, but let's think about this for a bit." I didn't want her to despair. "There has to be another solution. Everyone is trying to help here."

"I'm tired of making excuses for Mormons," Gwen said tautly, looking out the window instead of into my face "I'm tired of waiting for them to catch up to the real world. It's like we're drooling infants being led by old white men who want to keep us that way. No one thinks for themselves. No one questions authority. We're told that our leaders speak with God, but if they do, why the hell doesn't He change things before it's obvious to every single person on the planet that the church is making a terrible mistake?"

"I don't know," I said dully. I had my own complicated feelings about all of this, and wasn't sure I could untangle them here.

There was a long pause.

"Do you really think He's out there?" she asked in a ragged tone, looking at me at last.

"I do," I said.

"Then why is everything such a mess?"

"I hate to say this, but I think it's mostly our fault. We blame everything on God, like he's the source of all evil. But we're the ones who glorify war and elect movie stars." I'd talked to her about politics before, and we were both pretty upset with the current state of the country.

"But church leaders are supposed to speak directly with God. You'd think He'd do better than this."

"Maybe He's doing the best He can with what He's got," I said.

She didn't seem appeased by these answers, and I didn't blame her. I also wished people would change faster than I saw them doing. But if others like Gwen left Mormonism, we would never do better.

I drove over to Gabriela's myself, but lost the nerve to knock on the door and simply left the big brown paper bag of food on her doorstep. I didn't need her to know who it was from. I just needed to know that she—and her children—could eat.

CHAPTER 7

On Thursday, I got Samuel's regular weekly email and found out he had been moved to yet another area. That made three transfers in two weeks, which was a definite signal that something was wrong. After rereading his email, I did my best to contain my motherly frustration and wrote back a quick note about how much I loved him and admired his dedication to the work. I thought about calling Kurt to talk about the email, because I knew he'd received the same one, but I didn't want to chance that I'd break down in tears. Then Kurt would play the "too emotional" card.

So instead I texted him:

There's obviously something going wrong on Samuel's mission. We need to contact President Cooper and find out what's up. Do you want to call him or should I?

We'd never reached out to a mission president directly before, but none of our other sons had faced the kinds of problems Samuel had. At risk of seeming overprotective, I had to intervene.

An hour later, Kurt texted back:

Samuel isn't a child. He needs to learn to manage problems on his own, not have Mommy and Daddy come swooping down to save him every time. If this is about him being gay, he needs to learn how to handle that, too. There will always be other members who are confused about how to react.

Fine. I'd given Kurt a choice, and it looked like I'd be the one calling President Cooper. It wasn't my fault he'd dismissed my justifiable concerns.

I looked up the Boston Mission Office online and called the number listed for President Cooper's office. I spoke to the secretary first and waited patiently for about two minutes to talk to the mission president himself.

"Hello? Sister Wallheim, is it? Elder Samuel Wallheim's mother?" There was a precision in his pronunciation that made me wonder if he'd ever been onstage or on television.

"Yes," I said.

"It's nice to meet you by phone. I suspect you're concerned about the number of times Samuel has been transferred lately?" He spoke so calmly that I steeled myself. I would not be dismissed with a few words.

"It just doesn't seem normal," I said. "Is there a problem of some kind that my husband and I should know about?" I hated bringing Kurt into this, but I knew it would go more smoothly if it sounded like he had condoned this call.

"No problem at all. Samuel is the ideal missionary. I feel very blessed that he was sent here to Boston. I've been personally inspired many times over by his giving heart and his sunny disposition, as has every missionary, member, and non-member who has met him," said President Cooper.

I had to admit, it was difficult to remain angry when someone said such nice things about Samuel. The way to a man's heart might be through his stomach, but the way to a mother's heart was through compliments to her children. "Thank you," I said.

"You and your husband deserve a big share of the credit for helping Samuel become the wonderful missionary he is today," President Cooper went on smoothly.

"I don't know if that's true. You know that children come to us as they are, and we can only have so much influence on them. I've always known Samuel was special." I hope it didn't sound disloyal to my other sons to say that. I didn't have a favorite, not really.

"God has been saving the best and brightest spirits, His elect children, to send in these dark days of trouble. Samuel was sent to you for a specific reason, and I believe he was sent here for a reason, too." There was practically a singsong to his voice now as he recalled the hymn "We Thank Thee O God For A Prophet."

I noticed that for all his talk, he still hadn't said one word about Samuel being gay. That bothered me, the way he was talking around my worry without naming it. Samuel had been very open about his sexuality since coming out, so it couldn't be that his mission president didn't know.

"Samuel's gay," I said bluntly. "I doubt that's a problem with the general population in Boston." Massachusetts had been the first state in the union to legalize same-sex marriage, after all. I'd looked that up when I'd found out Samuel was going there, and I felt strongly that it was the right place for him to be. Mormons get their mission calls through a process that we believe is inspired by God, where each applicant is looked at carefully and chosen for a specific mission by the Holy Spirit. I had never believed that more strongly than with Samuel's case.

"He has a special mission to fulfill here in Boston, and he's just started on that," President Cooper said, as if I'd mentioned his coming home.

"Yes, but I'm wondering if there's a problem with his fellow missionaries, especially the ones from Utah. Not everyone is necessarily accepting of homosexuality here," I said.

There was a long pause. Too long. I suspected that President Cooper resented my forcing him to talk about this openly. Well, too bad. I would make him uncomfortable if it meant finding out what was happening to my son.

"Have his companions complained because he's gay? Are they accusing him of not being dedicated enough? Or is it something else?" I said, since he still hadn't spoken.

President Cooper cleared his throat. "Ahem, Sister Wallheim. Please have faith that any adversity he's experiencing right now is God's gift of a refiner's fire for Samuel."

I knew that many people saw missions as more important for the character development of the missionaries than for the actual baptism numbers, but why should the character building come from conflict with his own companions?

"He may be facing some difficult situations, but he's doing it with God's grace. And we all have to try to be kind to those who struggle with understanding and love," Cooper said.

I felt a slow burn of anger. He was doing it again, trying to step around the issue—he still hadn't even acknowledged that Samuel was gay.

"Are you saying that his companions are homophobic?" I demanded pointedly. "Are they asking not to serve with Samuel?"

He cleared his throat again. "Sister Wallheim, I'm not going to pass judgment on any of these young men. They may not see the bigger picture, but they've also given up two years of their lives to serve God and His children, and we have to accept that for the gift of faith that it is."

"No, I don't," I said explosively.

He sounded confused. "What is that, Sister Wallheim?"

"I don't have to accept that they have good hearts or that they are showing faith just because they've committed to serving a mission. If they can't love Samuel and see that he's serving God right along with them, then I don't know what gospel they have faith in, but it certainly isn't mine. And it isn't Christ's, either. Christ sat with the harlots and the publicans and the Samaritans and the Romans, and I daresay he would have sat with gay men and women, as well." I'd become very articulate when it came to defending my son.

"Well," said President Cooper, drawing out the word for so long it could have been a psalm. "I know that as a mother, you have a certain point of view."

And he had a different point of view about who Christ was, what our role as Christians was?

My words were clipped now. "You can't say that these other missionaries are justified in their prejudice against him. What if this were about something else—race, class, gender? If they complained about someone being black, would you simply shuffle that person around to avoid conflict?"

"These young men work very closely together. It's best to keep them away from conflict as much as possible," said President Cooper, which I interpreted as a yes—he might well do the same thing if the issue was race-based.

I let out a sigh. I wished I knew more about President Cooper. Where was he from? Was he a businessman or a teacher? Was he a convert or born into the church? What about his wife and children? Did he have any close associations with LGBT Mormons? While he had plenty of information about my son in his papers, it wasn't a reciprocal arrangement. I could try to look him up online, but some people our age didn't bother making profiles on the internet.

"Don't lose hope, Sister Wallheim," President Cooper said soothingly. "Samuel is changing minds every day. He has made an enormous impact on many of his companions. There are a few who are unwilling to change, but they're in the minority."

"Thank you for your time, President Cooper," I said, and hung up.

I then did what I always did when I was angry and didn't have anyone to yell at. I went to the kitchen.

I loved making Christmas candies, and it was never too early to start. I began a batch of toffee, divinity, and caramels simultaneously. The divinity only required sugar syrup and beaten egg whites, which meant it went the fastest. The caramels needed little attention but an occasional stir, and they cooked slow and long. I buttered the toffee pot, then got the butter and corn syrup boiling. That should be ready to go right as the divinity was finished.

Kurt and I used to make edible gifts for the neighbors in our cul-de-sac. That was before he'd become bishop and felt obligated to give the same gifts to everyone in the ward, so as not to be seen as playing favorites. With two hundred families in the ward, I couldn't commit to making them all a plate of candy during the holidays. These would go to Samuel and whichever of the missionaries in Boston stuck with him for more than a few days.

Then I thought of Gabriela's children again, in need in a different way than Samuel, but with a fierce mother to protect them. I'd already left them some necessities, but they deserved special treats, too. So I saved half the candy for them, hoping I might see them again soon.

I managed to get the egg whites to crest perfectly into stiff peaks, then slowly added the boiling hot sugar syrup. When the mixture was light and fluffy as clouds, I mounded them onto waxed paper just as the timer for the toffee went off. The kitchen smelled divine—a mixture of butter, caramelizing sugar, and nuts. I usually made divinity with chopped walnuts, but this time I only had pecans on hand—I'd been stocking up for pecan pie at Thanksgiving.

I used the same chopped pecans on the toffee and already had them spread in the pan as I took the buttery mixture off the stove. I nearly burned myself on the handle before remembering to grab an oven mitt.

There is a pleasure in seeing beautiful, golden toffee spread itself out, hardening as it moves and still shining like a liquid even after it has turned to a soft-crack stage. I dotted chocolate chips on top and waited a moment for them to melt enough to spread, then sprinkled more chopped pecans on afterward.

When the boys were younger, they would fight over who got which pan to scrape at the bottom with a spoon. Now that they were gone, it was up to me. I licked at the toffee I'd collected in a spoon while it was still warm and liquid. It was delicious, but the real test would be if it broke up properly in the pan. Toffee was a precision art. If I cooked it for a minute too long, it would turn out too hard and tacky. If I cooked it a minute too short, it would be grainy and soft.

And I wouldn't find out until hours later, when it was too late to do anything about it. In the old days, the bad batches never went to waste because my sons hadn't been picky about

Christmas candy. That meant I'd had plenty of chances to practice until I'd become the expert I was now. I guess I'd have to
serve in the capacity of toffee-taster this year.

The caramel was waiting patiently for me, bubbling away.
Caramel was a candy I could eyeball. It wasn't that it was less
finicky, but I could hear and smell and see when it was ready. I
loved to watch the caramel thickening on my spoon, how it
dripped slowly, like a candle, back into the pot. It would be
another ten minutes until it was finished. I was glad I kept real
cream in the house, because caramel was always better when
made with cream instead of sweetened condensed milk. It was
richer and its color darker, more auburn than golden.

I poured it into a foil-lined, buttered pan—there was no such
thing as too much butter! Then I left it to sit and sat myself down
on the stool in the kitchen, relishing the ache in my muscles that
came from spending hours over a hot stove. My mind had found
peace somehow between the chopped pecans and the caramel,
and I wasn't quite so angry about my conversation with President Cooper anymore.

Yes, Samuel was facing injustice from other companions on
his mission. But he was strong enough to handle that. It was one
of the reasons I loved him so much. He was courageous and
honest, but also patient and loving. He wasn't easy to anger, as
I could be.

I let out a long breath and thought about how much I missed
him, this holiday season especially. And then I looked into the
heavens and sent a prayer upwards. Something along the lines
of: *You'd better send me extra blessings in Samuel's place this year,
because otherwise it's pretty unfair that he's gone on a mission to
serve You and we're both suffering as a result.*

With that done, I could admit to myself that the real reason I'd been so upset about Samuel's being treated badly on his mission was selfish. This was a reminder of how often I needed him around to help me deal with my own anger at the injustice in the world around me. And his being on his mission meant that other people were getting that blessing instead of me. Even if some of them didn't see what a reward his presence was.

Idiots.

I was reminded, too, of how privileged it was for me to worry about Samuel, who would come home in a couple of years older and harder but largely undamaged. He'd have enough food to eat and warm clothes to wear—and he was an adult. Unlike Gabriela's children, who might face far worse if their mother was taken from them.

I started to work on the dishes, filling pots with warm water and soap suds and unloading the dishwasher. I filled it completely with big pots and a few breakfast dishes, then asked for God's blessing to those I could not reach, and for His Spirit to guide me to those I could.

CHAPTER 8

Kurt and I were watching the late-night news together after our date night at La Caille, a fancy French restaurant a few miles away in Sandy that we only went to once a year. It had gone better than I'd expected; we'd talked about our children and grandchildren, making aspirational plans for their futures. But the breaking story was about the body of a strangled woman that had been found just two hours ago behind a dumpster at a local gas station in Draper. The police were asking for information from anyone who had been in the area during midafternoon, but they weren't releasing any details about the victim.

I didn't think much of it until a few minutes after we'd gone to bed, when my phone buzzed. I was tempted to ignore the call, but saw that it was Gwen, so I got up and hurried over to answer it in the bathroom for Kurt's sake, since he was already asleep.

"Did you see the news about the dead woman at the gas station?" Gwen didn't give me a chance to answer before continuing. "I think it's Gabriela."

"What? Why would it be her?" I asked. There had been no public clues given as to her identity.

Gwen ignored my question, sounding on the verge of hysteria.

"She's dead and her kids are alone now. It's my fault, Linda," she sobbed.

"How could it be your fault?" I asked. "You were only trying to help."

"All my fault," Gwen went on as if she hadn't heard me.

"Gwen, calm down—let's be reasonable about this. I'm sure it isn't Gabriela. Let's talk about this tomorrow, or whenever they release more information." Some sleep would probably help us both think more rationally.

"I'm going to the gas station now," Gwen got out. "Come with me or don't. I don't care." Her voice was the monotone she sometimes used when she was upset, and I knew I wouldn't be able to talk her out of this.

"All right, Gwen. Let's go make sure it's not Gabriela," I said. "Will you come and pick me up on your way?" I'd have to get dressed without waking Kurt, but I was willing to do that for Gwen.

"Okay," she said. "I'll stop by in a few minutes. Come out when I text you."

"I'll be ready," I said.

Gwen hung up and I went back to the bedroom. My clothes from the previous day were right on top of the laundry basket, so I just pulled them back on.

Kurt snuffled and turned over, but remained asleep.

I scooted out of the room and closed the door quietly behind me, then tiptoed down the stairs.

Should I leave him a note? I didn't want to chance the buzz of a text message waking him up. I also didn't know when I'd be back. I ended up scrawling a message on the whiteboard in the kitchen that we hadn't used since Samuel had gone on mission.

Before that, it had mostly been for magnetic games of one kind or another.

It was sneaky, I knew. I wanted to say I'd left a message and be able to point to it if Kurt got angry, but I didn't really want him to know I was leaving in time to intervene. I'd promised Kurt not so long ago that I wouldn't put myself in danger investigating murder cases, but this was different. How could I be in any danger? But I knew he'd still be angry if he found out.

After that, I waited at the front door, staring outside for five minutes until Gwen arrived. I hustled outside the moment she pulled up. Gwen's passenger door was unlocked, so I got in. I was less worried about Gabriela than excited for an adventure. But I also knew this was a bad idea. Sneaking around, getting in trouble—I guess I hadn't gotten that out of my system as a teenager. I'd been too busy following all the rules that a good Mormon girl follows, at least until my twenties.

"It's chilly," I said, tightening my coat around me.

Gwen mumbled something back, then circled the rest of the cul-de-sac and turned back onto the main street that would lead down the mountain. From the occasional light of street lamps, I saw her face was still stripped of makeup and splotched with red. Her eyes looked puffy from tears. She wasn't in a talkative mood. She had her brights on, which was fine since there were no cars for a couple of miles in each direction. All the good Mormons were home, asleep.

She drove down to the Pro-Stop gas station I'd seen in the news clips. It looked like it was still cordoned off. There weren't any flashing lights, but I could see a couple of police cars.

Gwen hadn't explained her rationale to me, but on seeing the gas station, my adrenaline evaporated, and I wondered if Gwen was right, if Gabriela was really dead. I suddenly wanted to drive off and climb back into my nice warm bed, but I knew it was a cowardly thought.

I could see one of the uniformed policemen was directing cars away from the gas station, a halo of frozen exhalations around his face.

"Gwen, I know you feel bad about what happened. But I still don't see what this has to do with you," I said as she pulled the car to the side of the road. "Even if it is Gabriela, we should let the police handle this." Even as I said it, I was aware of how much I sounded like Kurt.

She took in a jagged breath. "Listen to this." She got out her phone. Her hands were shaking, and she didn't have gloves on. One pink fingernail had been bitten to the quick, with dried blood around the cuticle. Her other fingernails weren't in much better shape. She touched a button and pushed the screen toward me. The volume was already set to maximum.

"Gwen? Hermana Ferris? Are you there? Please pick up. Please." It was Gabriela's voice, I was sure of it—her slight accent and cadence were unique. She sounded panicked, her voice all over the place—high-pitched, then quiet, then loud and then scratchy.

"I need help, Gwen. Can you meet me at the Pro-Stop gas station by the freeway tonight at nine or later? I'll wait there until you come. I really need to talk to you. I've made a terrible mistake, done something I shouldn't have."

A pause and some scuffling sounds in the background. A beep, then, "Please, Hermana Ferris. I don't care about myself. I only care about my children and their future. They're so young to be alone in the world." A choking sound, then weeping. "I know that

I was rude to you, that I said I never wanted to speak to you again. But please, please come and meet me. If you don't come, I don't know what I'll do."

A few shallow breaths, and the call ended.

Gwen's hands were shaking so much now that I was afraid she might drop her phone and break it. I took off my gloves and put a hand over hers so she had some human contact. Her hands were ice-cold, and she looked like death itself.

"When did you get that message?" I asked quietly. It wasn't conclusive proof that Gabriela was dead, but a definite sign she could have been the body the police had found.

I'd been close to violent death too many times in my life. I felt sick at the thought of the beautiful dark-haired mother I'd known never going home to the lively children waiting for her. The sound of fear in her voice as she'd spoken to Gwen was heart-breaking. If only . . .

Gwen said, her voice cracking, "A few minutes after I saw the news about the body at the gas station, I checked my phone. I'd been meaning to call Gabriela, but I was busy all day at work, then out shopping, so my phone was set to silent. I hadn't thought to check it. And now she's not picking up."

I kept hold of her hand, though it seemed there was no warming her more deeply. "This isn't your fault, Gwen," I said. "And we still need to make sure it's her."

Gwen pointed across the parking lot, and that was when I saw the familiar twenty-year-old Honda parked across the street. My hope for Gabriela's safety sunk to nearly zero.

"They're probably going to call it drug-related," Gwen said bitterly. "That's what they always call crimes against people who aren't white and rich."

I winced. "That's not true," I said, hoping it wasn't.

"No one cares if someone like Gabriela dies. They think she should have just been deported anyway. To most of them, she's not a real human being." I wasn't sure to whom she was referring—the police, Mormons, or the entire white population of the United States?

"They're not all like that," I said. But Gwen didn't seem to be listening. "Let's say a prayer for Gabriela and her children."

Gwen still didn't answer, so I closed my eyes and bowed my head to voice the words for both of us.

"Dear Father in Heaven, please comfort us and bless Gabriela and her children, wherever they are."

Gwen let out a gasp at the end, then yanked her hand out of mine. She slammed her left fist into the steering wheel twice. I could see the guilty tension in every inch of her.

Before she slammed her hand again, I caught it and tried to get her to look at me. "Gwen, this isn't helping. Maybe we should go check on Gabriela's children. Maybe she'll even be there with them." I didn't have the best feeling, but couldn't tell if that was a spiritual confirmation or not. Why not be sure about this before we decided on our next steps?

"Are you going to pray for a miracle?" Gwen asked, her voice as sharp as my carving knife.

Fine. That hadn't been helpful for her. "Look, Gwen, we're not getting anything done just sitting here. The police aren't going to let us walk around a crime scene. The best thing we can do is stop by her apartment. You heard Gabriela on that call. She was concerned about her children—first and foremost. She wanted them safe."

"Because that's what the church tells her," Gwen said

scathingly. "That she's a mother, and that's all that matters about her."

It stung a bit that she was so disdainful, but she was hurting, too. I wanted to tell her that she was loved, that there was still a place for her within Mormonism, but at this moment we needed to focus on protecting those small, vulnerable little ones. I guess it was hard for me to stop being a mother, too, because I couldn't stop thinking about making sure the little ones were all right.

"Let's go," I pleaded again.

"Fine," Gwen said. Her pale, shaking hands put the car into gear and we lurched off toward the other side of the freeway.

CHAPTER 9

A few minutes later, we came to an abrupt stop in the parking lot of Gabriela's apartment building. There were lights on in her second-floor apartment, but that was true of several others as well.

We walked up the stairs and knocked on the door. I desperately wanted to see Gabriela's face, but instead, a young Hispanic woman appeared through the narrow crack when the door opened. She looked about sixteen years old. "Hello?" she said nervously, but without an accent.

"Is Gabriela home?" Gwen said.

The young woman hesitated, looking nervously behind her. I felt enormous relief that the children weren't alone. This young woman must be the hired babysitter for the children, safely asleep inside. She must not be Mormon or she and Gwen would already know each other.

"We're friends of hers," Gwen said. "From the Mormon church. We were helping her get her papers for citizenship prepared."

The young woman hesitated another moment.

Then Gwen added, "Maybe she's mentioned me—my name is Gwen. Hermana Ferris?"

No response from the young woman.

Gwen went on, "Gabriela called me a few hours ago, worried about her children. I just wanted to make sure they're all right." The last words came out in a rush of muddled guilt and fear.

At this, the young woman undid the chain on the door and stepped out. She closed it behind her, but continued to speak quietly. "I'm Alma Rodriguez. Gabriela asked me to watch the children for a few hours, but she was so upset when she left, and now it's hours after she said she'd come back. I've got school tomorrow. But I can't leave the children here by themselves." She maintained composure as she spoke, but I could hear the undertones of fear in her voice. Poor girl. She was just a teenager, and stuck in the middle of all this.

"Gabriela didn't tell you anything about where she was going or why?" I asked, since Gwen seemed unable to speak at this point.

Alma shook her head. "I babysit for her all the time. My parents live just downstairs. They know her pretty well—my dad works with her."

I considered telling her that we'd take over with the kids, but with one glance at Gwen, I realized I'd better plan to follow her so she didn't get into trouble.

So I said as gently as possible, "Can you stay here and we'll see if we can find out what's happened to Gabriela? We'll try to be back before you have to head off to school, but at this point, maybe it's best if you sleep on the couch?"

"Maybe I should call my mom," said Alma.

I made a quick calculation about the likelihood that we would be back anytime soon, added to the question of Gabriela's demise. "I think that's a good idea," I said. Her mother could stay here until someone in authority came to relieve her and take care of the children.

Alma glanced at us once more before going back inside.

I turned to Gwen, feeling heavy at the thought of another funeral, another broken family, and another murder investigation in the small town where I lived. Why did bad things happen to good people? God wasn't answering that question any better now than he had the first hundred times I'd asked it.

"Back to the gas station?" I asked Gwen softly.

Gwen nodded and hurried down the stairs, knocking a knee loudly against the door at the bottom. On the way back to the Pro-Stop, her driving was shaky.

We parked a block away from the gas station, and Gwen opened her door. "I have to try to get in there," she said. "I have to do something."

I sighed. "All right. I'm coming with you." Maybe a bad idea like this was better with company.

We walked toward the uniformed policeman we'd seen before. He was waving away a driver as we approached. The driver swore and threw something out the window as he drove away. Ignoring him, the policeman turned to us as we approached. "Ladies, this gas station is closed. You'll need to go on to another one."

He looked so young. About the same age as Samuel, and without even a full beard yet, though maybe it was just the terrible light of the street lamp and the fact that his hair was mostly blond. My instinct was to give him a hug and tell him he was doing a good job, that his mother would be proud, but I didn't.

"How long is this going to be closed, Officer . . . ?" Gwen asked.

"Grant," he filled in. "Probably until morning. This is a crime scene."

"I'm starting the Police Academy down at UVU this year," Gwen lied, her tone masking the anxiety I'd seen at the apartment.

It was a bold lie, though not quite a criminal one. I knew she had only resorted to it to try to glean more information, so I played along.

Gwen craned her head as if trying to get a better look, though nothing of importance was visible behind the single strand of yellow tape. "I can't wait to learn about stuff like this."

"Well, it's a lot different in real life than it looks like on TV," said Officer Grant, a hint of superiority in his tone.

It played right into Gwen's hands.

"Hmm. Different how? I mean, I know you can't tell me any details, but I'd love to hear about your experience with this. There's only so much we can really learn from our textbooks," she said, leaning in slightly toward him.

The young policeman straightened up. Did he realize Gwen was married? Probably not. Her ring wasn't visible in this light, and the way she was acting, he could easily assume she was interested in him as more than a source of information.

He said, "Well, a woman's body was reported found by the clerk at the convenience store a few hours ago. I came with my partner to check it out. We confirmed she was dead and called the medical examiner and crime scene crew. Now my partner's talking to the clerk and looking through the surveillance tapes. I'm just out here, waiting for the detectives to come and finish securing the scene."

It was a nice, succinct rendition of the process as far as I'd observed in previous murder investigations from the outside. Except for divulging all this to us, he was doing his job well.

"Is the body still here?" Gwen asked, full of false eagerness.

"Yes, but it's been covered, awaiting the detectives' sign-off. It was shoved behind the dumpster out back." He nodded the direction of the dumpster, and I thought I could make out a shrouded lump near it.

I shivered at the thought that it could be the once-vibrant Gabriela, who had only worried about a better life for her children, even when she might have been in danger.

"Do they know who she was already? Do they have to fingerprint the body to find that out?" Gwen asked stiffly. Her façade was cracking.

"Oh, there's no problem there. She had identification on her. And if that wasn't enough, there was the car registration to match. I guess there aren't any relatives to contact, so they have to go to the ward instead," said Officer Grant, giving away his Mormon affiliation.

"No relatives?" Gwen asked. "Was she not from around here?"

"She lived here," he said. "But her next-of-kin was a husband in Mexico."

My heart dropped. The husband who'd been deported. I could only imagine him in Mexico, being contacted by the Utah police force only to hear that his wife had been killed. Would the children go back to him? They were American citizens, as far as I knew, but surely a parent in Mexico was better than the foster care system here.

"Mexico? Oh, I hope she isn't someone I know from the Spanish ward," Gwen said worriedly, putting a hand to her chest. "I do a lot of church work there."

"I really shouldn't tell you her name—we haven't even released it to the press. But you'll keep it between us, right?" He glanced around and took a step closer to Gwen. I think he'd forgotten I was even there.

"Yes, of course," Gwen said earnestly, nodding.

Officer Grant put a hand on Gwen's shoulder in an entirely inappropriate fashion, then said, "Gabriela Suarez. Do you know her?"

There it was, the confirmation I'd hoped would never come. I felt hollow. Gabriela was gone.

Gwen let out a low moan. I moved closer and put a hand on her arm, but she pushed me off.

Detective Grant saw me and his eyes opened widely as he suddenly became aware of how it looked for him to be whispering to a layperson at the scene like this. He stepped back and held himself straighter, apparently rethinking things. "If you knew her personally, I should get the investigating detectives to ask you questions. You might be able to assist in the case."

Gwen let her head fall. "No, we don't know her. Just a poor woman who was in the wrong place at the wrong time."

I almost spoke up, but I wasn't sure talking to the detective would be a good idea at the moment either. I didn't know how I might've wheedled information out of this young man, but I made appeals to people differently from Gwen, who was young and self-assured and attractive.

Grant cleared his throat and appeared ready to tell us to get going, but before he could, a tall, black woman in plainclothes approached from the gas station. "Officer Grant," she began, "why are you . . . ?" And then she trailed off as she recognized me.

Oh, no. It was Detective Gore, whom I'd gotten to know last year when a member of the bishopric had been killed in our church building. She'd spent a lot of time at my house, trying to understand the ins and outs of Mormon culture. She'd never been a member, which was clear then and now. I was nervous she might ask me something that would force me to incriminate Gwen for her, but her presence on the case also meant it would be wrapped up quickly by someone with homicide experience.

"Sister Wallheim, what are you doing here? This can't have anything to do with your ward, surely."

"No," I said meekly.

"Then you should move along. Murder scenes aren't open to the public, and the victim isn't here for anyone to gawk at," she said sternly.

Gore's characteristic bluntness was a relief this time. If she ever did figure out our connection to Gabriela and decide to question us, it wouldn't be lightly, and I was ready to go home.

But Gwen wasn't as eager to leave. "She wasn't just some nameless victim," she said, brow furrowed.

This was about to go downhill fast. Though the detective had barely spoken to us, Gwen didn't seem to trust Gore with a matter so precious to her, and she wasn't in the right state of mind to keep quiet about it. If this got messy and ended up with both of us at the station under the charges of misleading a police investigation, I'd have a lot to explain to Kurt, and all in the middle of the night.

"I'm the detective assigned to this case, and I don't need to justify my decisions to either of you," said Gore, glaring at Gwen.

I tried to act as mediator between the two of them. "Detective Gore, I'm glad to see you're on the case. We'll be on our way now; we didn't mean to interfere," I said.

But Gwen didn't budge when I tried to pull her back to the car. "I'm sure you'll investigate as long as the media's watching the case, then let it drop. Because you just can't stop illegal immigrants from dying, right? Unlike white citizens. Their names are in the news the moment someone can't get in touch with them."

"Gwen," I said, interrupting her, "this isn't the time." I just wanted to us both safely home.

"How do you know she was undocumented?" Gore said, her eyes narrowing.

"Just conjecture," I interrupted. "Sorry, she's sleep-deprived and worried about work. We were planning to stop for gas and parked when we saw the lights."

Gore looked like she wanted to press me, but then decided against it. She turned to Grant. "Officer, make sure they leave the premises."

"Yes, Detective," said Grant, moving toward us.

"We're going. My apologies," I said to Grant, pulling Gwen by the arm back toward the car. She didn't resist, though I could feel her breathing hard. I opened the door for her, and she climbed in. Then I went around and got in on my side. Gwen was sitting with her head bowed into the steering wheel.

"Let's go home," I suggested. "We're both tired." My mind was spinning with thoughts about Gabriela's husband in Mexico, her young children waiting in the apartment for her when she would never return, and the strange coincidence of Bishop Hope having threatened to call the police over her supposed embezzling of church funds.

Back in the car with me, Gwen started the engine and cranked up the heat. She backed out of the parking spot and pulled away, but she didn't go far. She circled the block, then headed back to the gas station, parking just out of Grant's line of sight.

"Gwen, what are you doing?"

She got out her phone. "Wait here," she said. She didn't try to justify herself. She didn't even seem to hear me. Before I could try to talk to her, she got out of the car, leaving the keys in the ignition and the heat on full blast.

The police cars were on the north end of the gas station, by the dumpster, but we were now on the south end. She ducked behind the big sign, then dialed a number on her phone. It was noisy on the freeway overpass and I couldn't hear anything.

What was she doing?

I watched as she crouched down, listening for something. She dialed a number on her phone again, and this time there was a long silence on the freeway. Apparently that was enough for her to hear what she needed.

She half-crouched, half-crawled her way to the neglected grass and bushes behind the convenience store, closer to where the police were.

I should have done something to stop her. But she'd moved too quickly, and now anything I did would just draw more attention to her, which could jeopardize her future at the police academy. And the truth was, I'd once tried to take charge of getting justice for a victim—one I'd known far less well. I'd been relentless, and followed instinct instead of advice. If Gwen was set on this during her process of grieving, sticking around to make sure she didn't get herself into too much trouble might be more effective than trying to stop her.

My heart was in my throat as I watched her turn back and move rapidly back toward the car. If Officer Grant turned around at any moment, he'd surely see her.

But then Gwen was at the car. A truck pulled past us up to the front side of the gas station, which was just enough of a distraction that Gwen could get into the car easily. When she slammed the door shut, I cringed and looked at Officer Grant, but neither he nor Detective Gore seemed to have heard the noise. They'd moved toward the new vehicle on site.

Gwen and I both sank in our seats for a few minutes, trying to remain invisible.

"What were you doing out there?" I asked.

"Just looking for something," she said, neglecting to say whether she'd found it or not.

"That was dangerous."

She let out a laugh of reckless abandonment mixed with real fear.

I shook my head, wondering if I'd ever done anything so impulsive. Maybe on my first case, but I'd learned since then.

When I dared look up again, I saw Detective Gore walking out to talk to a man dressed in a jumpsuit, probably a crime scene investigator.

"I think it's time for us to go home," I said, hardly recognizing my own voice because of the harshness in it.

Gwen patted something in her pocket and started the car. Soon we were heading back up the hill to our neighborhood. Safe. At least for now.

I mulled over whether to press her again about what she'd found. When she stopped in front of our house, I finally said, "Did you find something of Gabriela's?" I remembered the time I'd unearthed something related to an investigation and kept it from the police. I hadn't known for certain that it was evidence, but I had known I should have called them. This was far worse— Gwen had taken an item straight from an active crime scene.

"What could I have found that the police wouldn't have already?" she asked with an edge. "They've said they're doing such a good job. It would be impossible for them to miss anything, right?"

"Listen, Gwen. Do you remember that murder case in our ward? Carrie?"

She nodded.

"Well, I found something when I was poking around her place. I should have turned it into the police right away. It would have helped them find the truth sooner than they did otherwise. I've always felt guilty about it."

"It's not the same with Gabriela," Gwen insisted. "She's not a pretty white woman with money and a typical Mormon family."

I sighed. I couldn't force her to tell me what she was hiding, not unless I was willing to get Detective Gore involved. And I wasn't—yet.

I shook my head and got out of the car, but before closing the door, I said, "Gwen, call me if you want to talk, all right? I know this is really hard on you. Just—give me a chance. I can help." I meant with whatever she'd taken from the scene.

But as Gwen looked up at me, I saw the sharpness in her face and knew she wasn't ready to talk. "I don't need your help with this, Linda. I'm planning on going to the police academy, not just playing detective, okay?" she said.

Well. She'd just dismissed all the experience I'd had with murder as amateur work. She'd said it deliberately to hurt me, and it had. I could forgive her for that, but it made me worry about something else. Had Gwen been abused for so long that she hadn't learned to trust anyone? I hadn't seen this side of her before, but if she was treating Brad the same way, that must be hard on him, too.

I watched as she drove off. Maybe I should have said another prayer, but after Gwen's reaction last time, I didn't. We told so many stories as Mormons of the wonderful miracles, big and small, that we saw. But what about when there was no miracle? What about the floods and famines and wars where God didn't intervene? I thought I'd spent the last thirty years figuring that out, but right at this moment, I felt no closer to the answers, no closer to seeing God's love for all His children.

CHAPTER 10

I checked my watch as I closed the front door and saw it was
just past 3 A.M. I heard a noise in the kitchen and poked my
head in. Well, so much for sneaking back to bed.

Kurt was wide awake, sitting at a stool over what smelled like
a cup of my favorite Strawberry Daiquiri Teavana herbal tea. It
was a strange sight, since as far as I knew, Kurt didn't like herbal
tea and thought it was a bit too close to breaking the rules of the
Word of Wisdom to indulge in it. He didn't think a bishop should
be seen drinking something that gave the "appearance of evil"—
not to mention, this particular flavor was cocktail-inspired. From
what it looked like, though, Kurt was not so much drinking the
tea as stirring the teaball and watching it as it slowed and
slowed, then stopped.

"I suppose you didn't see my message?" I said as I walked in.
I took off my coat and put it on the chair next to Kurt, the one I
wouldn't be sitting on. I put my gloves and hat there as well.

"Message?" Kurt said.

I pointed to the whiteboard, but it was covered by the door
of the cupboard he had left open. I closed it. "See?"

His eyes widened briefly, then he shook his head. "Not much
of a message," he said.

"I didn't want to wake you. You get so little sleep these days," I said. Did it sound as much like an excuse as it felt? I felt a little guilty about following Gwen into a vigilante murder investigation, but I felt responsible for her. I knew Kurt wouldn't understand this protective reflex.

"What did Gabriela need so desperately in the middle of the night?" Kurt asked.

"She's dead," I said bluntly. "She was the woman whose body was found behind the dumpster at the gas station on the news. Gwen was devastated and needed to talk about it with someone." I was careful to omit any mention of the police and hoped he wouldn't ask how we'd found out the victim had been Gabriela.

Kurt digested this for a moment. "She couldn't have called in the morning?" He was clearly upset, but I think he was trying to tone down the dial on his outrage.

"Gwen was close to Gabriela, and I wanted to be there for her," I said, resentful. And I did believe God wanted me to be there for her as her sister in the ward. It wasn't my fault she had taken things so far tonight.

Kurt shook his head and stared at the whiteboard message. "It really didn't occur to you to wake me up and tell me what was going on? I thought we were trying to stay on the same page and keep lines of communication open with each other."

"Kurt, I was trying to be there for Gwen." It was true. I had no doubt things would've been worse if she'd gone over to that Pro-Stop alone. She might have made the same progress with Officer Grant, but who knew how far she would've escalated things with Detective Gore?

"Maybe Brad could have helped with Gwen. She's not your problem, you know."

So she was Brad's "problem"? What did that make me, Kurt's "problem"? I took a long breath to calm myself. Kurt probably hadn't meant that the way I'd heard it.

Well, maybe not. "It was the best I could think to do in the moment," I finally admitted.

Kurt let out a breath. "Fine," he said. "What now?"

I thought about calling one of the names from MWEG, but I wasn't sure they'd be interested in getting involved in a murder investigation. I was pretty sure these were lawyers who specialized in immigration, and that wasn't an issue for Gabriela anymore.

"The children!" I said. They were still in the apartment with the babysitter or her mother, unaware of what had happened at the gas station. While they weren't in danger of being deported, that didn't mean they were safe. "How long until DCFS gets there and starts the process of placing them with a family? What about their father?"

"Good question." I could see the wheels turning in Kurt's mind. Mormon bishop wheels, more efficient than most. "I'll see what I can do to make sure their transition is easier, at least. The stake president should know what's going on. He can suggest a ward family to do fostering while it's needed. What's the address?"

I wrote it down for him, along with the names and ages of the children involved.

It might sound ridiculous, but I felt sad I hadn't thought to bring candy with me before, to have the babysitter pass along. Now I'd never have a chance to give it to the children, once they were in foster care. And so much for that care package I'd dropped on their doorstep.

Kurt got out his phone and started dialing as I went upstairs.

From our bedroom, I could hear Kurt turn on the dishwasher. Then he went into his office and closed the door. How many nights in the last two years had I spent alone up here, listening to Kurt's nighttime rustlings in that office? This might have been the only time I actually knew what he was doing in there. That should have made it easier for me to sleep, but it didn't.

About an hour later, he came up to bed. I was still cold from the time I'd spent outside in the middle of the night, and I curled around him. Kurt didn't pull away; he kissed the top of my head and stroked my hair until I warmed up and finally fell asleep.

It wasn't until morning that we talked about the calls he'd made the previous night.

"What happened with Gabriela's children?" I asked.

"President Frost sent someone to check on them, but DCFS had already come and taken them to a temporary shelter."

I felt sick at the thought of those children with complete strangers. Had they been told the truth about their mother while only half-awake?

"He asked to be updated on their status, and DCFS said they'd keep him apprised of the situation. Right now, they're working on the assumption that the father is out of the country and can't take custody immediately, so they'll be placing all three children in foster care, ideally in the same home." Kurt's monotone made this sound like something he had recited over and over again.

"Ideally?" I said skeptically.

"Linda, you know what that means." His voice was back to normal now. "They'll do their best, but they can't guarantee a family will be able to take in three young children this close to the holidays."

Because people were too busy with their own families during the holidays. I thought for a fleeting moment of asking Kurt if we could take them in, but I didn't. The last time Kurt and I had talked about foster children, he hadn't been enthusiastic, and I knew that was partly because we'd been dealing with so many of our own marital problems. I wasn't sure those problems had entirely gone away, even if they seemed small in comparison to the needs of Gabriela's children.

And to be honest, taking in three preschool age children seemed daunting to me. For the first time, I felt like an old woman. As adorable as those three faces were, I couldn't imagine exerting the amount of physical labor that caring for them twenty-four-seven would require. Or rather, I could. All too well.

"All right," I said, still feeling guilty. I was itching to call Gwen. "Someone should try to get in touch with the father."

"I'm sure law enforcement officials will take care of that," Kurt said.

"And that's good enough for you?"

Kurt sighed. "Linda, what exactly is it you think I should be doing here?"

"Well, if he and Gabriela were married in the temple here, then he's probably active and attending a ward in Mexico. Can't you look up his records somehow and find out where he is?" The Mormon church recorded every date, every address, every ritual, every name. We had databases of databases.

"I guess I can talk to President Frost about that," Kurt said.

"And you'll talk to the father personally so he knows what's going on?" I pressed.

"Linda, even if I could get hold of him in Mexico, what would

I say? He's going to be distraught when he finds out his wife is dead and his children are alone in this country in foster care."

I could tell Kurt had put himself in this man's shoes all too easily. He was a father, too. "You can give him some reassurance, at least. He needs to know that the children are going to be well taken care of until he can get custody," I said.

I could see Kurt struggling to contain his frustration. "But he can't do anything."

And of course, as a Mormon man, Kurt struggled to understand the point of anything that didn't involve a checklist of tasks to be completed. We talked about comforting those in need of comfort, but if it didn't involve food or shelter, it wasn't his forte.

Kurt went on, "You know that he can't legally return to the country, and I'm not about to encourage him to break the law. It's against church doctrine."

The Twelfth Article of Faith recited by Primary children everywhere:

We believe in being subject to kings, presidents, rulers, and magistrates, and in obeying, honoring and sustaining the law.

This innocuous-sounding article had been used to excuse German Mormons who had colluded with Nazis. It justified signing up to fight in wars you didn't believe in, obeying corrupt political leaders, and so on. It also allowed the church to send missionaries to countries where the regimes were, well, less than ideal. But the spreading of the gospel was the most important goal, wasn't it?

"Promise me you'll talk to him, father to father," I pressed.

He let out a breath. "Linda, I'll make sure he's notified through official church channels and that he has someone to stay with him for a while to help him deal with his grief. But that's all I'm promising." His posture was defensive now, and I felt guilty about my insistence.

Kurt had five hundred people under his care in our ward already. Asking him to take on more than that wasn't fair, even if I would gladly have taken on the duty myself if my position had afforded it. It was healthier for Kurt to mark the kind of boundary lines that I seemed unable to draw.

"Did you talk to Brad?" I asked after a moment.

"I did," Kurt said.

"And?"

"He's concerned about Gwen's behavior, but he also knows he can't control her. She's not a child, and he doesn't think she wants to listen to him right now."

I waited for Kurt to assign me the job of outreach, to talk her down from the ledge, but he didn't. He didn't seem to think it was a great idea for me to spend too much time with her right now. And maybe he was right—Gwen and I were all too similar in certain reckless ways. We fed off of each other sometimes, instead of leading each other to safer choices.

CHAPTER 11

I slept poorly the rest of that night. I woke up around nine and made some fresh Strawberry Daiquiri Teavana tea of my own, but even with extra cream and sugar, it didn't help me feel better. I tried to play the piano to soothe my mind, but when that also provided no relief, I called Anna, my closest friend in the ward, and asked if she wanted to go on a walk.

"I was just about to call you, Linda," she said. "The weather is so perfect. We've got to enjoy global warming up here in the Arctic."

She meant it as a joke, but I didn't laugh. Sometimes politics came between us, but I was trying not to let it happen so soon. "I just thought it would be a good chance to talk," I said.

"What happened?" asked Anna, who knew me too well. "Is something wrong with Samuel's mission?"

"Yes," I said, almost relieved to talk about that instead of Gwen and Gabriela. "He's been transferred three times in two weeks."

Anna's voice was soft. "But that's not it, is it?" She could have had a job as a drug-sniffing canine, I suspected.

"No, not quite," I said. "I'll tell you all about it while we walk, all right?" And maybe about what I'd already mentioned, as well.

"You always do," she said serenely. "And we can have tea

and cookies at my house afterward. I have a new batch of pumpkin cookies I originally made for trick-or-treaters, but hardly any of them came."

During my growing-up years, my mother had hated Halloween, which she thought of as a Satanic celebration. But around here, religious objection wasn't the reason there were so few trick-or-treaters these days. Parents just didn't want their kids out in the dark, even in a local neighborhood. That was why we'd started the ward Primary Halloween party, so kids could still dress up and have fun and eat spooky snacks without parental concerns.

Ten minutes later, I was at Anna's house. The scent of cinnamon, nutmeg, and cloves hung in the air. If anyone was a better baker than me in the ward, it was Anna. Was I ever jealous? Maybe a little. But not just about the cooking.

Anna always looked like she had gone for a makeover the day before. I swear she could pass as a movie star. She must have had sixteen different chic coats she cycled through for our walks. I was lucky if I could find a single coat that didn't make me look like I'd put on fifty pounds over the winter.

"So what's happening with Samuel?" she asked as we headed out.

"He's apparently dealing with some homophobic companions, and the mission president is moving him around until he finds some Mormons who actually remember the Savior's command to love their neighbors as they love themselves," I said sourly.

I could have been more tactful about it, but I realized after I'd said it that some part of me was testing Anna to see if she was really on my side—and Samuel's.

She closed the door behind her and said, "I'm sorry you're having to deal with this, Linda. But it sounds like the mission president wants what's best for Samuel if he's moving him around to protect him."

I stiffened at her words, which could mean almost anything. "He's making excuses for hate," I said.

She grabbed an elbow and steered me down the walk. "He's the mission president for all of them. He's supposed to help them all be better. Do you think he should just send home every missionary who has a problem with homosexuality?" she asked.

Maybe not, but some real punishment and a dose or two of shame might have had some effect on the problem.

We started walking. I almost turned the wrong way and had to keep up with Anna's quicker feet. We had a brief look down into the valley from up here. It wasn't the lush view of green trees and lawns that we got in the summer. Late fall in Utah was depressing, and here the trees looked like skeletons, their only colors gray and black and brown.

"Maybe he's trying to show the Savior's love to everyone, and this is his way of doing it," Anna suggested quietly, looking around us. Not that anyone else was on the streets around here at the moment. We were too late for the morning runners, and the only people I saw were the ones in cars, probably headed out to shop.

"Maybe." I was willing to concede the possibility, but I was still angry at the man. My prayers at night were for Samuel, not his mission president.

"We have to pull people along the path sometimes, give them a spoonful of sugar as encouragement to change," Anna said.

"Why can't people lead? Take a strong stance and demand others follow?" I asked.

"Like Christ did? Punishing anyone who doesn't live up to the proper standards?" Anna said mildly, glancing back at me with eyebrows raised.

"Well, when it came to the money-changers in the temple, Christ didn't mince words," I pointed out. "Christ got angry about real evil all the time. He wasn't always Mr. Nice Guy."

"Maybe not, but the rest of us aren't perfect. We're just trying to do the best we can," Anna said, going breathless as we headed up the big hill.

I tried to take this chance to lend her some compassion. LGBT issues had been on my radar since my first marriage to a man in the 1980s who'd turned out to be gay, but other Mormons were still playing catch-up.

"Anyway," I said as we reached the top of the hill and turned back.

"But there was something else bothering you, wasn't there?" Anna asked again. She tugged her gloves on tighter.

No reason to drag this out. I'd decided to trust Anna for now. "Gwen Ferris was attending the stake's Spanish ward, and one of the women she befriended was killed last night. Her body was found behind a dumpster of a gas station by the freeway." I felt horrible saying it aloud again.

"The Pro-Stop killing," Anna said. She must have seen it on the news, too.

As we went back down the hill, I briefly outlined the details for Anna and told her about Gwen's citizenship workshop. But I neglected to mention that we'd gone to the scene of the crime last night.

"Gabriela's husband was deported last year, so she was the sole caretaker of their three children, all preschool-aged," I said. "It's terrible."

"Ah," Anna said.

"What does that mean?"

We made a turn and had to hurry to get out of the way of a car that was coming up the street, so it was a long moment before Anna said, "I know you're struggling with this woman's death."

"You're going to tell me this isn't my problem," I said, once we were safely back on the sidewalk.

"And you're going to say it is, because everything is your problem," Anna said, shaking her head.

What did she want from me? I threw up my hands. "Well, I can't just turn a blind eye!"

"I didn't suggest you tell three tiny children to fix their own problems," Anna said, reaching over to brush something from my face. She showed it to me. It was a bit of leaf that had gotten caught in my hair. "But you don't have to do it all yourself. The children are getting help, aren't they? DCFS? Foster care?"

I pulled away from her and started walking again, wondering if Anna had already heard about this from someone else. No, that wasn't fair. Kurt wouldn't have told anyone, and there was no way word would've spread so quickly otherwise. She was just echoing the standard Mormon view, and I started to understand Gwen's complaints more clearly about how our community of white Mormons tended to see the world in ways that protected them and their privilege. But the way I read the Book of Mormon, we were supposed to be sharing our houses of worship with the poorest and remembering that no one was more beloved by God than the meek and lowly in heart.

"I watch someone like Gwen, who's so full of energy, and so frustrated with how slowly the church changes. And how many problems there are that don't seem to be on anyone's radar. How can she stay when she's told to be quiet and wait?" I asked.

"But it's only Gwen you're worried about?" Anna said, her tone arch, though she didn't turn to show me her expression.

How far were we from her house? I was just about ready to be finished with this walk. "I had my crisis of faith thirty years ago, Anna." I'd come back to Mormonism since then, warts and all. Why did she have to question my motives about getting involved in this case?

"I see," Anna said. "And since you've had one faith crisis, you can't have another?"

She didn't get it. "This isn't about me," I insisted.

"You and Gwen have a lot in common," Anna pressed. "Maybe that's why you're so concerned with her situation right now."

"Maybe some things in common," I admitted. I hurried up toward her house, which was now in view.

"I think you see Gwen as who you might have been, if your life had taken a different path. Maybe you're a little jealous?" She spoke as if to the fencepost, completely neutral, but I knew it was a pretense.

"I'm not jealous of Gwen." If I'd wanted a career, I could have had one, but I'd chosen to raise a family instead. I was content with my path.

"I'm not sure you see the danger in the path Gwen is on. I don't know her well," Anna said as we finally came back to her driveway. "But the few times I've listened to her in Relief Society before she stopped coming, I've been very concerned about her. She's pushing the limits of what's proper within the church, and more than that, I've gotten the sense that she likes making people angry. She feeds on it. I don't think that's a good thing, Linda."

Was she warning me away from Gwen, like I was at risk of catching some perceived contagion? "It's fine, Anna. I'm just trying to help her." I waited for her to open the door for me even though it wasn't locked.

She reached for the door, but didn't open it. Instead, she stared at me long and hard. "I know you are, Linda. You think you can help everyone, but sometimes the best thing to do is to help yourself."

"That seems like a selfish way to look at the world," I said.

"It's not selfish. It's survival. You deserve to be able to protect yourself," Anna insisted. She opened the door, but now I was the one who didn't go inside.

"What is it precisely you think I'm in danger of?" I asked.

"Another faith crisis. And leaving the church," Anna said, nudging me in.

"Anna, I already told you I'm not having another crisis. And I'm not leaving the church." The Mormon church was my world. It was my family. Well, most of my family, since my son Kenneth had left.

"Then why are you spending so much time with someone on her way out?" Anna asked quietly.

I thought about this before answering with the truth, which was that I liked Gwen and so many of her ideas.

And then I realized where these accusations were coming from. I wasn't the one who was jealous of Gwen—Anna was. I'd been spending more time with Gwen than my dearest friend. Why? Was it because I thought of Gwen as the daughter I'd never had? Or because Gwen took risks and voiced some of my own doubts about Mormonism in words I might not dare to use? Ones Anna certainly never would.

As we walked up the entryway into the kitchen, I said, "Anna, Gwen needs someone. She isn't close to anyone else in the ward."

"Maybe she should look at her life and think about why she has so few friends, then," Anna said so bitterly that she sounded more like Gwen than ever before.

"Gwen is still in her twenties—practically a child, compared to us," I said, grinning a little at the joke. "But she's a bit lost, and I'm trying to help her," I continued, the warmth of the house and the smell of the pumpkin spices making me take off my coat and hat.

Silently, I admitted to myself that maybe there was more to it than that, a confluence of things that drew me to Gwen. Her husband in the bishopric with mine, her closeness in age to my daughter Georgia, who'd died at birth, and something else that was hard to explain. Her willingness to call out injustices, even when she knew she was up against a system that didn't want to hear them, made me wonder when I'd become so subdued and obedient.

"If you say so," Anna said. She didn't mention Gwen again as she got out the tea and the cookies.

"These are incredible," I said, taking a bite of the delicious crumbly pumpkin cookie. It was true, but also was a way to shift the conversation to something less contentious and personal.

"Do you want the recipe?" Anna asked. An offer of reconciliation—Anna didn't often share her recipes.

"Thank you," I said. "That would be lovely."

She wrote it down for me, and then we drank the hot Caramel Truffle Teavana tea I'd gotten her for her birthday last month. I wondered for a while what it would be like if it were caffeinated and no one cared whether we were following the Word of Wisdom in every sip and bite. What if Anna and I could just be ourselves without wondering if we were obeying God's word and doing the best we could to get back to the celestial kingdom? Would our relationship be the same? Would we still be friends at all?

Maybe Anna was right about my connection to Gwen exacerbating my problems with Mormonism.

"How about next Wednesday?" she asked as I left.

"Sounds great," I said. I thought about asking her if she wanted to join MWEG with me, but wasn't sure she would care about it. The politics of the women in the group were all over the board, but I suspected Anna wasn't as concerned about the current administration's policies as were others in the group.

CHAPTER 12

I got a call later that night. From Gwen, of course. I glanced around to see if Kurt was nearby, then stepped out into the garage to answer it, just in case.

"Hi, Gwen," I said, closing the door behind me. It was cold in the garage, and I wished I'd thought to bring a jacket, but I was stuck in just the long-sleeved shirt I'd been wearing in the house. "Anything I can do for you?" I asked.

She hesitated, then said with a sigh, "Linda, I have to confess something to you."

Kurt was the one who was supposed to hear confessions, not me. But I was pretty sure this was about what she'd taken from the crime scene, so I waited.

"I found Gabriela's phone. On the grass by the Pro-Stop."

I wasn't terribly surprised. Still, stealing evidence was pretty bad. The police would need this, and now that I knew Gwen had it, I had to talk her into giving it to them. "I see," I said, counting breaths as I tried to be the grown-up.

"I called it until I heard her ringtone. I don't know what's wrong with the police—how did they not think to call her number like I did?"

Probably because they assumed the crime scene was secure

enough that they didn't need to worry about it being taken. They'd have been focusing on the body and witness statements to begin with.

"It's further proof to me that something is wrong with this investigation," she said.

That again? "I'm sure they'd have found it soon enough. Gore is competent and thorough, not to mention unbiased," I said. "But you distracted Officer Grant, you know."

"That's no excuse," Gwen said.

I could imagine Detective Gore saying the same thing to him. "You could have offered to call her number for them," I said.

She grunted. "Like they would have accepted any help from me. They just wanted me out of there."

"Well, we were civilians with no place in an official police investigation," I said. And we were both probably too close to the victim.

It might seem hypocritical of me to criticize Gwen for doing things I'd done, but it was the opposite—I was trying to save her from making the same mistakes I had. I'd also assumed the police were incompetent in the past, but I'd learned otherwise, especially when it came to Detective Gore.

I edged closer to the other side of Kurt's truck. "Gwen, you've got to turn that phone in to the police. Holding onto it could impede the investigation," I said, hoping Kurt wasn't listening from the other side of the garage door. He wasn't someone who made excuses for breaking the rules.

"Linda, it barely had any battery left, and the screen was completely cracked. I fully charged it and replaced the screen with a kit I bought online."

Very industrious of her. Even so, I highly doubted the police would be grateful for her efforts.

"Do you want to come over and see what's on it?" she asked. "I'm trying to figure out her password."

It seemed like the only chance I had to get her to listen to me was talking to her in person, so I relented. "All right. I'll be there in a few minutes."

"Brad's not home," Gwen said. "I'll leave the door unlocked." She hung up before I could respond.

I went back into the kitchen and stood there, trying to decide what to tell Kurt. He was in his office at the front of the house, so I knocked lightly and opened the door.

"I'm going over to Gwen's for an hour or so," I said. I hoped it wouldn't take longer than that to convince her that the best thing she could do for Gabriela was to turn the phone over to the police. Whatever her obligation to her friend, she could fulfill it best by going through the existing lines of authority, not taking too much on herself when she didn't have the training or the status. Or did that sound too much like I was talking about the church? Maybe that was why we both tended to flout authority—we were ordered around by it too much on a daily basis.

"Are you sure that's wise?" Kurt asked.

"No," I said, too honestly.

His eyebrows rose. "You want to tell me what it's about?"

I couldn't. It would feel like too much of a betrayal. Kurt had so often kept information from me after a confession. Now it was working the other way.

"She just needs to talk," I said. "She's angry."

Kurt stared at me for a long moment like he knew I was lying. He probably did. What kind of marriage did we have if my lying was such a regular occurrence that he had a ready expression for when it was happening?

"Linda, just think for a few minutes about what's important, all right? That's all I ask," he said at last.

"I will," I said, and blew a kiss at him.

As I drove to Gwen's, I thought about what we each had to lose here. The risks weren't really much different from in previous cases, but I was much more aware of them now. I could end up exchanging my comfortable life with my family for a jail cell. Scandal, even if only attached to me, could threaten Kurt's position as bishop. If we were convicted of anything, Gwen and I could both lose our church membership. She could be forsaking her marriage, as well as her chance to attend the Police Academy. She could probably afford the fines, but she wouldn't be able to buy her way out of a prison sentence.

I could call Detective Gore right now. She'd give us a stern lecture about how Gwen should never have taken something from an active crime scene, or at least should've turned the phone over when she found it. But Gore would let us go with that—I hoped.

Still, I didn't call. I understood Gwen's position too well. She was desperate to find the answers herself here. She felt guilty for not doing better by Gabriela before, guilty for being so privileged.

I opened the door and walked in. "Gwen? It's Linda," I called.

"I'm back here!" she responded.

I followed her voice to the small kitchen area, where she had Gabriela's phone on the countertop. I perched on the tiny barstool next to her and watched as she showed me the new screen she'd put on the phone.

"See? Working perfectly now," she said, and turned it on. "We just have to figure out her password." She wrinkled her forehead and punched in a few numbers, but the phone buzzed a rejection. "That was her last name in numbers."

"Are we really going to be able to just guess her password?" I asked. I wondered if someone would be able to guess mine, which was Georgia's birthday and the first three letters of her name. It was probably a bad one, but I'd used it for years.

Gwen said, "Hackers do it all the time. They say it's pretty easy, because most people use the most obvious things as passwords. They have to remember them, so they do what's easy."

Right. But had Gwen known Gabriela well enough to guess hers? Too many incorrect tries, and the phone might shut itself down. "Gwen, we really should give this back to the police," I said delicately. "They'll be able to get into it and find the important information on it."

Gwen glared at me. "If the police take this, then how do we find the real murderer?"

"I told you. We can trust Detective Gore. I've seen her work cases before, and she won't let anyone sweep anything under the rug. Besides, you don't want to do anything to sabotage your future career."

I could imagine Gwen alongside Detective Gore—an older, less impulsive Gwen. I hoped she stayed out of trouble long enough to get there. I just had to make sure she put her emotions to the side and thought her next steps through logically. Right— because I'd always been so great at that.

Gwen tried another password and swore out loud when it didn't work. She started pacing. "I need to think like Gabriela. Her kids mattered so much to her. I keep thinking the password has to be one of their names or birthdays, but I've tried all the combinations I can think of."

I mulled it over for a moment. "Do you know their full names?" I asked. "First and middle?"

"Middle . . ." Gwen turned to me, her whole face alight. She typed something new into the phone and set it on the table. "That's it, Linda!" she said. I could see all of Gabriela's apps now and wondered whose middle name had been the right one.

"Let's see what's in here," Gwen said. She scrolled through Gabriela's most recent calls first. On Friday, the day Gabriela had died, there had been calls from "Work," from "Luis," from "Carlos Santos," and from "Bishop Hope."

"Luis? In Mexico? I guess if she has an international calling plan, it might not be too expensive. But who's Carlos Santos?" Gwen murmured to herself.

"She has Bishop Hope's number in her cell phone?" I asked, wondering how many of the members of our ward had Kurt's. Mormons did tend to call their bishop in an emergency, sometimes even before 911. We were trained to think of the church as the backup to every plan.

"In case of emergency, probably," Gwen said absently.

I pulled up the "Work" number and typed it into my own phone, then hit dial. In a moment, I was talking to a woman who thanked me in a soothing tone for calling "Celestial Security," then asked me to leave a number so that someone could get back to me during regular business hours.

"Celestial Security," I said out loud. "What's that?" The word "celestial" was clearly intended to target Mormons, since we used it to describe the highest kingdom in the afterlife. Did Bishop Hope own a bank or securities investment company? I'd gleaned from Kurt that Gabriela had been on his payroll, and wondered what she'd done for the company.

I'd have to go home and look up Celestial Security on the computer. I could try it on my phone, but reading anything on a phone was getting to be more of a problem for me every day, and I was too vain to carry reading glasses with me everywhere.

"We should go back to the apartment," Gwen said. "We can look around and see if there's anything there that will help us figure out which Carlos this is."

It sounded like she knew several from the ward, but there was no guarantee this one was any of those.

"The police might have gone through and gathered evidence from the apartment already," I said. Not to mention, it might still be cordoned off—what if we ran into Detective Gore or Officer Grant again?

"Maybe," Gwen said. "But they could have missed something we might see."

"Why do you think we'd be better at this than the police, who have the training and resources?" I asked.

"Because we knew Gabriela. And because we actually care about this," she said.

She wasn't going to back down on this. I could practically hear the guilt in her tone, involuntarily recalling Gabriela's phone message.

"Fine, I'll go to the apartment with you," I said with a sigh. I debated texting Kurt, but decided against it. It would only strain things further between us, and possibly between Kurt and Brad as well. I noticed Gwen didn't bother to stop to write a note or text for her husband, Brad. Maybe we'd both be back home in time that no one would ask what we'd been doing.

CHAPTER 13

As I suspected, Gabriela's apartment was locked, though there wasn't yellow tape anywhere, as this wasn't a crime scene. I listened for noises inside, but heard nothing.

"We have to get in," Gwen insisted.

"How?" I said, folding my arms and staring at the door.

Gwen jiggled the handle again, then shook her head and went back down the stairs.

I followed her, assuming we would get into the car and head home. Instead, she went around to the other side of the building and started climbing up the fire escape. Surely that wouldn't work . . . would it?

I watched nervously as Gwen made her way up the outside of the building from floor to floor, surprised at how much more agile she was than I. The effects of age were not on my side when it came to physical feats of prowess like this. Clearly her training for the Police Academy was going well for her.

When she got to right floor, she used her elbow to break the living room window to Gabriela's apartment. I winced at the sound, hoping no one had heard the break or the subsequent clearing of the shards. I didn't see or hear much to indicate the neighbors were home, but I hurried back around to the front side of the building and up the stairs again, huffing and puffing and cursing Gwen's better form as I went.

I knocked on the door, and after a long moment, Gwen let me in, and except for a couple of cuts on her hands, she seemed fine.

"This is breaking and entering," I said. "What if someone calls the police?"

"Even if they do, you really think the police will bother coming here?" Gwen asked with a marked certainty. "If they send a car around, it'll just be to make sure there's no gunfire. They'd never arrest two white Mormon ladies like us, just trying to check on a friend who isn't answering her door."

I sighed. "I can't believe we're doing this."

Unexpectedly, she smiled and put her hand on my arm. "Linda, I know this is the right thing for Gabriela. Please trust me."

And in that smile, I didn't see Gwen. I saw Georgia, my little girl. And I knew that I couldn't stop myself from seeing Gwen as a daughter figure and wanting to be closer to her, even in circumstances with such high stakes for us both.

If I didn't stop Gwen, that meant I was committing to joining her. And maybe that was what I wanted, anyway. I was also invested in finding out what had happened to Gabriela, and if the police had already been here, what could it hurt?

The apartment was different without the children. It should have felt bigger, but instead seemed painfully small. There was a child-sized couch in the front room, but no television, and the carpet was worn enough that I could see through to the cement foundation in spots. It was spotless, though. I could imagine Gabriela vacuuming and picking up after her children in a constant effort to keep the place clean.

In the kitchen, Gwen started looking through cupboards one

by one. I noticed as I passed her that the highest cupboard had cleaning supplies and a childproof lock on it. I'd done the same thing with dangerous chemical products when my boys were younger.

I'd noticed the first time how bare the refrigerator was. Now I saw the cupboards were much the same. Pantry items included beans, rice, and corn flour. The white flour and sugar and oil I'd dropped off were there, along with baking powder and a keg of salt. Gabriela had clearly done all of her cooking by hand. There wasn't a single box of store-bought cookies or crackers. No cold cereal, no microwave popcorn, no potato chips or Pop-Tarts.

But I was wasting time. Who knew how long we could safely poke around here? I went down the short hallway into the single bedroom. Inside, I could see a portable crib set up in the corner, as well as a toddler bed. There weren't any other beds in the room, just sleeping bags with mattress pads under them, which I assumed were for Gabriela and her oldest child, Lucia.

I had to sit down for a moment to process the sadness that weighed on me at this realization. Gabriela had been a caring, attentive mother. She'd made sure the children had a babysitter whenever she went out. She'd made sure they weren't hungry, as well as she could. But there was such a difference in our circumstances. She lived only a few miles from my house, and yet, I lived in luxury in comparison. I had a year's supply of food in my basement. I had extra beds in my house, empty rooms full of furniture I never used.

When I was able to get to my feet again, I explored a little more. I noticed a pile of clothing in the opposite corner of the bedroom. I assumed it needed washing, but when I picked everything up, a pair of scissors dropped and I realized after checking that one of the small pants had a needle with black thread stuck into it. The other pants had already been mended with careful stitches.

It made me feel kinship with her again, and reminded me of how often my boys had split out the knees of their pants as children. I'd heard other parents talk about handing clothes down from child to child, but I'd never managed to get even one pair of pants to last that long with my boys. Knees were split, hems torn to shreds, pockets ripped, and grass stains everywhere.

And then there was the Saturday night problem, when the boys brought me their Sunday shirts and pants for mending. Because of course they hadn't noticed any problems the Sunday night prior, when they'd taken them off. So I'd spent years of Saturday nights sighing as I mended clothes, wishing my sons didn't look like such ragamuffins at church.

A part of me wanted to finish this mending for Gabriela while I was here, a favor from one mother to another, but of course that made no sense. I doubted that DCFS would come back to take any of these clothes for the children. The foster parents would probably get them new things instead of keeping these reminders of tougher years with their mother, who was gone.

I stood up and left the clothes on the floor, reminding myself why I was here. I was trying to find any evidence that might have led to Gabriela's murder. I opened the closet next to the small window and on a shelf above a sparse collection of her dresses and blouses on hangers, I saw a shoebox. I pulled it down—it was far too light to contain shoes—and opened it to discover a stash of letters from Luis. I felt a pang of guilt for invading her privacy, but brushed it aside. I told myself any information about

Gabriela's life might help me understand her better, and thus figure out who had killed her.

The first letter I opened was postmarked from Colonia Industrial in Ozumba, Mexico.

I tried to read the letters, but they were written in Spanish, so I couldn't tell what they said. I scanned through them anyway, and saw the names of the children mentioned more than once. I hoped that meant that Luis had been a caring, involved father, at least as much as he could be from out of the country. Apparently, he'd communicated with Gabriela often.

I noticed that the newer letters were postmarked from Salt Lake City. That was odd. Maybe he'd given them to a friend who traveled back and forth regularly?

"Linda, come here!" Gwen called from the bathroom, interrupting my thoughts.

I went in and saw the medicine cabinet gaping open. Inside were only children's aspirin, a bottle of children's cough medicine, and a tube of bubble-gum flavored children's toothpaste. No adult over-the-counter medications of any kind, no prescriptions. Four toothbrushes sat in a divided cup on the sink. I assumed that Gabriela must have used the bubble-gum flavored paste herself as well, since there wasn't any other kind.

But that wasn't what Gwen had called for me to look at. She was sitting in front of the open cupboard beneath the sink, where there seemed to be the financial documents I'd been looking for.

"I thought she said she didn't have any receipts," Gwen said as she handed me a plastic basket with mail inside that was as carefully ordered as the letters from Luis had been. There was a bill from a nearby doctor's office where Gabriela had taken the children in July, and a matching bill from the local pharmacy.

There were her utility bills, her receipts for gas for the last several months, grocery bills, and even a record of her rent payments.

So what was the accusation of embezzling about?

But then things became even more confusing—and intriguing.

"Look at this," Gwen said with satisfaction, handing me the last three months of bank statements, which showed regular payments of $1,000 a month from Celestial Security and another $1,000 a month from The Church of Jesus Christ of Latter-Day Saints. The former must have been her salary. But why had she been getting regular payments from the church in the same amount?

If these statements were right, Bishop hope had been giving her regular payments, which made the whole embezzlement story stink to high heaven. Whatever Bishop Hope had been doing, it wasn't proper church protocol, especially since he'd claimed he'd only given her money to pay her bills. If anything, he should have been the one to get in trouble, not Gabriela.

And then it struck me.

"Did you just swear?" Gwen asked.

I guess I had. Had Gabriela been trying to get someone to look into what was going on? Was that why she'd called Gwen for help?

"Does Kurt give out that kind of money every month?" Gwen asked.

I was sure she already knew the answer to this. "No, never," I said anyway.

Bishops were supposed to give vouchers for free food from the Storehouse or temporarily pay bills for specific things, but never make regular payments without oversight like this. The idea was to help people become self-sufficient, not to make them permanently dependent on church welfare.

I wished Kurt was here so I could see his reaction to these bank statements and ask him to make sense of the accusation that Gabriela had been embezzling church funds. But of course, he would doubtlessly have been roaring at me and Gwen to get out of the apartment, which was getting colder by the minute because of the window she'd broken.

"He couldn't possibly be getting that much in fast offering every month from our ward. And why would he give this to Gabriela when there were other people in just as much need?" Gwen asked.

"He was getting money from the stake from other wards' fast offering funds," I said, thinking back to what Kurt said about his conversation with President Frost.

"What did Gabriela think of Bishop Hope?" I asked, hoping she had a bead on that.

Gwen hesitated, then said, "She said he paid his employees on time every month."

My eyebrows went up at this. Damning by faint praise? "Anything else?"

Her eyes narrowed as if just realizing this might be important. "She also said his children were well behaved and his wife was very kind."

Which meant nothing, really.

Gwen continued, "Now that I think about the two of them at the church together, she never spoke to him. I think she might have even gone out of her way to avoid him a few times. And maybe she wasn't the only one in the ward who did that. I interpreted it as shyness and an attempt to cover up his lack of Spanish language skills, but it could have been something else."

Yes, it could well have been. An avoidance was almost as telling as a direct connection.

"Are you ready to go?" Gwen asked, standing up and closing the medicine cabinet. Then she looked at the basket of mail at her feet.

I bent over to push it all back where it had been, but Gwen stopped me, picking out the latest bank statement and tucking it into her coat pocket.

I made a disapproving sound.

Gwen walked toward the door. "It's not like the police are going to notice it's missing. If they even bother to come here."

I glanced back at the broken window as we stood on the threshold.

Gwen paused a moment and turned around. "I guess I'll leave some money in the kitchen drawer to cover the broken window." She did this, and then we locked the door of the now-drafty apartment as we walked out, heading back to Gwen's car.

CHAPTER 14

Kurt wasn't awake when I got back, and by the time I was up, he was already at the church for his early Sunday morning meetings with the bishopric and other leaders of the ward. I'd have to talk to him about Gabriela's bank statements when he got home.

I checked on where Luis had sent his letters to Gabriela from, Colonia Industrial in Ozumba. To my surprise, I discovered that this was a hotspot of the "Third Convention," a group of native born Mexican Mormons who, in 1936, had demanded that a native born Mexican be appointed as the leader of their area. They were excommunicated and seemed almost extinct, though later were rediscovered, defiantly rejecting the authority of the mainstream church but adhering to other parts of Mormonism, including the Book of Mormon and the moniker of "Lamanites." I had no idea if Luis had ever been part of them, but it seemed unlikely, given that he and Gabriela had been sealed in the Salt Lake Temple. Just another part of the strange history between Mormonism and Mexico.

I walked to church on my own, as I'd gotten used to by now, and went into the Relief Society room with its nice padded chairs. This week's lesson was by Yolanda Jones, a biracial woman who defied the white Mormon stereotype. She taught from a talk by Chieko Okazaki, the first Japanese American member of the General Relief Society Presidency, a woman who had been a firecracker through the 1990s.

I could see some of the other women shift uncomfortably in their seats as Yolanda talked about the reality that less than a quarter of Americans lived in a traditional family, with a mother at home with the children and the father working as a provider. Gabriela certainly fit into the non-traditional demographic, though it hadn't been her or her husband's choice for her to live as a single mother.

Yolanda went on to say that all families should be protected and valued by the church—families with single women at their heads, families with grandparents, even families that looked different. Yolanda didn't directly mention same-sex families, but she glanced at me as she trailed off, so I was pretty sure that was what she meant.

There was a long quote by Okazaki in which she used different types of quilts to talk about life and faith:

This style is called a crazy quilt. Some pieces are the same color, but no two pieces are the same size. They're odd shapes. They come together at odd angles. This is an unpredictable quilt. Sometimes our lives are unpredictable, unpatterned, not neat or well-ordered.

Well, there's not one right way to be a quilt as long as the pieces are stitched together firmly.

Sometimes it felt like my plan for my life had been a different kind of quilt, but that it had turned at some point and other people had started adding and taking away pieces. I'd just kept on making the quilt, and what was wrong with that? My family was still wonderful, and I refused to accept that Kenneth's leaving the church or Samuel's sexuality damaged the quilt in any way. It was just a different texture than I'd thought we were getting, but the quilt still kept us warm. Maybe it was all the more beautiful for being a little surprising.

I walked into Sunday School, but it was being taught by the teacher I didn't like who made constant comments about the evils of the current world that were not-so-vague references to same-sex marriage. So I ducked out and went into the foyer.

I was the bishop's wife, and I wasn't going to my meetings. I was hanging out in the foyer and pretending to listen to another ward's Sacrament meeting when I was really checking my phone for messages from Gwen, who hadn't responded. Was she back at the Spanish ward today, or getting into more mischief about Gabriela's murder case?

I managed to make it through the day's Sacrament Meeting, which was about genealogy and how we should all be doing more of it so that we could baptize our ancestors and make sure they could move from "spirit prison" in the afterlife to "spirit paradise" as they waited for the resurrection. I had nothing against genealogy or temple work, but at the moment, I was more worried about how Gabriela's children were doing and the next step to take in finding her murderer.

After church, I hurried home and got a casserole in the oven for whenever Kurt was finished with his bishoping commitments. While the casserole cooked, I spent some more time poking around online, this time to learn about Bishop Hope's company, Celestial Security, where Gabriela had been working. It was an electronic security business based mostly in Utah—one that seemed to be thriving, based on its sleek website and large social media following. Customers paid a lump sum up front to have the electronic hardware of a pricey selection of systems installed, but it looked to me like most of the money the company made was from the monthly monitoring fees.

It appeared the business had been running for about four years and had plenty of celebrity advocates. The site was plastered with photos of Greg Hope with Senator Orrin Hatch, Senator Mike Lee, Senator Harry Reid, former President George W. Bush . . . not to mention Mormon Church President Thomas S. Monson and his counselor Dieter F. Uchtdorf, as well as former BYU quarterback Steve Young and BYU basketball standout Danny Ainge. There was one with Donny and Marie Osmond, too, but that looked like it had been taken when Greg Hope was barely out of his teenage years.

As I clicked through, I found that there were plenty of ways to join "the Celestial Security team." The site mentioned a vague fee for a "full training and documentation package" to begin a lucrative career selling security systems to your friends and family members. It sounded to me like a classic pyramid scheme, though of course, the fact that there was a real product involved technically made it legal. What was this called? Multi-level marketing?

I looked at some of the testimonials listed. Each was accompanied by a photograph of a smiling family in a lavish home. The families all struck me as "Mormon" in subtle ways. I couldn't necessarily spot the lines of their undergarments, but they all wore modest clothing: pants to the ankles, shirts to the elbow, high necklines, and no visible tattoos, body piercings, or double-earrings.

Every family was also nuclear—a father, a mother, and their children lined up in a row. No same-sex married couples, no summer-winter relationships, no single mothers. Unlike the varied quilts Chieko Okazaki had praised, these were clearly meant to be perceived as perfect, intact Mormon families. The wedding rings were visible on all the parents' hands, and the women and girls wore their hair long and perfectly styled, with makeup to a T for women and girls over the age of twelve.

Was there objectively anything wrong with using a "clean" Mormon image for a business? Plenty of Mormons sold their products to other Mormons. It was a quiet but tightly knit network. I'd heard non-members complain about not being able to sell car insurance to Mormons because they weren't Mormon themselves, and that loan services handled by Mormons were more likely to be patronized by other Mormons.

And that didn't even begin to cover the large number of independent "home businesses" that Mormon women ran, selling everything from children's books to kitchen tools, vacuums, and oils. Mormons assumed that other Mormons wouldn't cheat them. And even if they did, charges were rarely filed. Money didn't matter in the long run, right? It was only useful for getting us to the next life, by being given away to good causes and to the church itself.

Kurt eventually came home, and we shared the cheesy casserole.

After dinner, I left the dishes where they were and put a hand on Kurt's arm as he headed into his office. "Can I talk to you for a minute?"

"Of course," he said, sitting back down on his stool.

"Greg Hope's business, Celestial Security—have you heard of it?"

"He's not still doing commercials for car washes?" joked Kurt.

"No," I said, refusing to smile in response. I explained what the business sold and then told him about Bishop Hope's payments to Gabriela, omitting the part about how I'd obtained the information.

"I see," he said, looking troubled.

"That's not normal, is it? For a bishop to give someone direct deposits like that for month after month?"

"I don't want to second-guess another bishop," Kurt said. "Maybe there was a good reason for the arrangement. Bishops have to do their best in difficult situations."

I wasn't attacking him, but Kurt always took it that way when I criticized another church authority. I had to be careful. "Why do you think he might have given her that much money every month?"

"He might have thought he was paying for regular medical costs. Or I don't know, legal bills, if she was trying to get DACA status. Could be anything," Kurt said.

"But she didn't say anything about having a lawyer at the workshop I helped Gwen with." And surely she would have mentioned it if she was already getting help. Gwen had started at the beginning and Gabriela had seemed to be paying careful attention.

"She could have misunderstood something," Kurt said.

Okay, but what? This was so frustrating. I took a breath. "Do you think you could call President Frost again to ask about this? I'm concerned about what's going on in that ward, and I think someone needs to look into it." Someone who wasn't a woman with no official standing in the church.

"Linda, you're poking your nose into other people's business again. Leave it be. You and Gwen should both walk away from this. The police are investigating. Let them do their job." Kurt licked a finger he'd run around the edge of the plate. He must have liked the casserole. Too bad I hadn't made it myself, though I doubted the credit would've helped me persuade him.

"I want to trust that everything is right here, Kurt, but there are too many signs otherwise," I said, trying to make my voice sound meek and pleading.

"Linda, you're always assuming the worst of people, especially men in the church. Not every church leader is selfish, scheming, and abusive." He looked me straight in the eye, and I knew I hadn't been able to manipulate him into softening.

"I know," I said. "But you and I have both met a few bad apples who're enough to make the barrel stink."

"That doesn't make us all bad, though," he said defensively. "And you and Gwen sometimes sound like those Ordain Women agitators who just want to stir the pot. They think women want even more responsibilities in the church than they already have? More work heaped on them, when all the women I talk to complain that their husbands aren't doing enough to help at home?"

I sighed. This wasn't an argument I was willing to have right now. Someday perhaps, I would want to talk to Kurt about why women complaining about their husbands not being home was part of the point here, that the whole structure of men being in charge left women holding the short end of the stick and even missed the reality that sometimes men were better at home and women would be happy to swap wrangling kids for leadership positions. But now wasn't the time.

"Gwen and I just want to know what was going on with Bishop Hope and that accusation of embezzlement. Even if it has nothing to do with the murder, the Spanish ward needs to be properly managed, and I don't know if Hope is doing that," I said as calmly as I could manage, but I knew that Kurt wouldn't think it was my place to demand anything. It wasn't my ward, and even Gwen, who had been called to it, should be using the "proper priesthood channels" to deal with any of her concerns.

"Linda, what you should be concerned about right now is the effect this surreptitious investigation is having on Brad's marriage. He's doing his best to love his wife and show patience with her. But that's difficult if she's intent on humiliating him in front of everyone in the ward."

"Humiliating him? How?" What was Kurt talking about? Nothing Gwen had done had had that effect on Brad. No one in our ward knew anything about what we'd done at Gabriela's apartment, and I certainly wasn't going to tell them.

"It's clear to everyone that she's completely out of line," Kurt said.

Out of line—meaning that Brad was supposed to be in control of her, like she was a misbehaving child or a pet? "And have I been humiliating you the last two years you've been bishop?" I asked sharply. I had no interest in Kurt seeing me as a piece of property, not in this day and age.

Kurt didn't say anything, which was probably wise. He knew when I was angry enough to spit fire.

I stomped off and started the water running in the bathtub upstairs. It was very, very hot, just the way I liked it. I soaked for a good long while with the door locked and thought about all the chores I needed to get to. But those weren't for Sunday. Sunday was a day of rest, so I was resting, damn it!

By the time I got out of the tub, I'd planned to go straight to bed, but Kurt had still not gone to sleep. He had a contrite look on his face as he put up his hands. "I'm sorry, Linda. It wasn't fair for me to dismiss what you said about Gabriela's bank statements. I've thought about it, trying to figure out any good reason for monthly payments from the ward like that, and I just can't come up with anything."

Well, I wasn't above enjoying an "I told you so" moment.

"Thank you. Now what?" I said, hoping he would confer with me on next steps.

Instead, he said, "I'm going to look further into the whole thing," he said. "Tomorrow, while I'm at work. I can put out feelers to some of my corporate contacts and see if I can find anything out about Celestial Security. I'm also going to call President Frost again."

My knot of resentment dissolved. "Thank you," I said. This was the Kurt I knew and loved. It was nice when this Kurt came home from church, rather than the other Kurt my husband sometimes had to become to survive being a bishop.

CHAPTER 15

Monday evening, I got a call from a number I didn't recognize. When I answered, I heard Samuel's voice.

"Hi, Mom," he said.

"Samuel!" I waved at Kurt, who'd just gotten home from work and still had his coat on. I was so relieved to hear from him! But I felt an immediate sense of dread settle over me. Why was he calling out of the blue like this? Mormon missionaries had to follow strict rules about calling home. This wasn't just to chat. Something had to be wrong.

"What's going on?" I asked.

"Mom, I'm fine. Prez told me that was the first thing I had to tell you—President Cooper, that is. He said to say I was fine and you're not supposed to worry about me. They're taking good care of me, him and his wife."

I let out a long breath. "Okay, good," I said, suppressing my initial panic that there might be a medical emergency.

"He said you were upset about the transfers I've been going through, and that you needed to hear my voice to know that my mission was going all right," said Samuel.

He sounded happy. He sounded—well, exactly like the son I loved so much and had sent off with trepidation to the MTC almost a year ago. He didn't sound discouraged or hurt, or like he'd been beaten down by the rejection of his companions. He was as upbeat and warm and loving as always.

But I wondered if there was something beneath it. I knew missionaries were encouraged to send home emails about the good things that happened during their trips, not about anything negative. This phone call might be more of the same.

"Where are you?" I asked.

"At the mission office."

Was President Cooper standing right next to him? Listening in, making sure he was saying all the right things?

"Are they transferring you again?" I asked. There were other reasons he might be at the mission office—sometimes missionaries worked as support staff for the president. It was often seen as a promotion of sorts to be designated an "AP," an assistant to the president. But I knew from my other sons' mission experiences that it could also be a way to keep an eye on difficult cases.

Samuel said, "No, Mom. President Cooper just asked me to check in with you after tracting today."

I checked my watch. We were two hours behind Boston, which meant it was after 10 P.M. his time—that seemed pretty late. Was everything really fine?

"Sister Cooper fed me and my companion dinner with all the office APs. She made homemade rolls and lasagna and green beans; it was awesome."

I pictured Sister Cooper standing there as well, eavesdropping.

"Not as good as your food, obviously," said Samuel.

I could practically hear him grin at this.

"Especially not your rolls."

I relaxed when he said this, knowing that Samuel was too well behaved to have said such a thing if the woman herself was listening in, even if it was true. "Well, I've spent my whole life perfecting them," I said. I was proud of my homemade rolls. I brought them to every church event we went to, and people always gushed over them. I hated cheap, stale, store-bought rolls—they were just plain nasty, a waste of gluten.

"So mission food is good, then?"

"When we eat at the mission office, it is," said Samuel.

I tried to remember what we'd talked about when he'd called on Mother's Day back in May. His companion had been around, and the call had been from a member's home, so we hadn't discussed anything personal. Was there more privacy here for an honest conversation?

"So what happened with the transfers?" I asked. I wanted to hear Samuel's side of the story I'd already heard from the mission president.

"Mom, it's no big deal. One of the transfers was an emergency because two companions got into a really bad fistfight. They had to be assigned new companions immediately, and the prez trusted me to help with that. I was actually really honored that he chose me."

All right, that explanation I could believe. Mission companions were largely luck of the draw. The mission president was supposed to be inspired to put certain people together, but it didn't always work out that way when there were a hundred missionaries who had to be assigned in partnerships. They spent twenty-four-seven with the other person, sometimes for months on end, trying to work out their differences while knocking on doors and spreading the gospel. I'd often heard it could be trying.

I'd never gone on a mission, though. Back when I was the right age, girls were encouraged to get married at a young age. So I was—both married and divorced before age twenty-one. But I'd heard plenty from my older sons about their missions, and how impossible some companions were. Just as often, though, their companions were wonderful and ended up being lifetime friends.

"And the other two transfers?" I asked.

Kurt had come closer to sit by me and made a face as I asked this. I ignored him—had he thought I'd skirt around the truth with my own son, whom I was so worried about?

After a few moments of hesitation, Samuel said, "Well, the one after that was tricky because he eventually admitted he was gay, too, and he'd been suicidal for years, trying to keep it hidden."

I felt a pang in my chest at this. I'd clearly nosed my way into something painful. I suspected Samuel had asked President Cooper's permission to tell me about this. People thought that a mission was a great chance to get out of Utah and to see more of the world's culture, but it often didn't turn out that way. Mission culture and the insistence on staying with your companion at all times meant it was often the most regressive part of Mormonism.

"He tried to work it out with a mission psychiatrist, but after a week, he asked to be sent home."

How awful. I couldn't stop myself from worrying that if he'd felt he'd had to hide himself for so long at home, this wasn't a real solution for him long-term. But then again, Samuel hadn't said the boy had come out to his family yet, either. Maybe it wasn't safe for him—which meant it would be awfully tricky to contact him or get him any help, as I wished I could do. I sent a prayer heavenward and decided I'd ask Samuel later if he had any updates or knew of ways I could help.

"And the last one was just a jerk, Mom," Samuel said without me prompting him. "He told me the first time we met, months ago at a zone conference, that he would never be my companion because I'd be kicked out of the mission by then as unworthy. When we got put together, I assumed that the mission president had talked to him and that things would be okay, but apparently not. He refused to sleep in the same apartment as me, to speak to me, to eat at the same table as me."

My breath caught at this. I'd assumed such open prejudice was a thing of the past.

"Anyway, I finally called the prez after a few days. My companion was walking three miles every night to sleep at a member's house and went out tracting on his own in parts of downtown Boston, which was dangerous. I wasn't trying to get him in trouble."

Of course not. "Samuel, no one thinks this is your fault."

He let out a long breath. "Well, some of the other missionaries probably do. But there's nothing I can do about that. I tried my best with him, and the mission president decided to transfer me anyway."

I was shaking with anger at this point, and Kurt had come even closer to put a hand to my back. He patted me gently, rhythmically. I was sure he could feel the angry, anxious heat pouring from me. But I was trying to prevent Samuel from realizing how angry I was.

"Anyway, I'm with two other missionaries now and they're both great. They don't have any problems with me being who I am. And it's really fun being in a trio." He sounded enthusiastic, and I hoped it was real.

"Good," I said.

He went on, "I just wanted to make sure you know that I'm fine. Better than fine—I'm great. I'm doing the Lord's work and feeling His blessings every day. I don't want you to worry about me, Mom."

I wanted to reach out and hug him, to tell him how much I missed him. Samuel had always been the kid who made people feel better, who put others before himself. It was why I missed him so much, and why I knew he was a good missionary.

Unfortunately, being so open and vulnerable would also cause him pain. Pain I couldn't take on myself, even if as a mother, I felt it was my job. It was time to let go of the strings. Samuel had to stand on his own now.

"Thank you for calling," I said. "I'm so proud of you." I was struggling not to cry at this point, knowing he was about to hang up. I knew I should be happy he'd called at all, because this was outside of the usual rules.

"I love you, Mom. I miss you and Dad, but I'm doing good work. I'm sure this is where I'm supposed to be," said Samuel.

"I love you, son," Kurt said, coming in close to me so that Samuel could hear.

I realized then I should have put Samuel on speakerphone for the call, but I hadn't thought of it, and to be honest, even now that I had, I was glad I'd kept it private. I was selfish enough to want to keep the conversation just between me and Samuel.

"Love you, too, sweetheart. Goodbye," I said, and held the warm phone to my ear for another minute after he had hung up.

Then I looked up at Kurt. "Did you call President Cooper to ask for this?" I asked.

Kurt reddened slightly. "Maybe."

I kissed Kurt on the cheek. "Thank you," I said.

I cried after that, but it was all right, since Samuel couldn't hear it.

CHAPTER 16

I got a phone call from Gwen at around 9 A.M. Kurt was already gone, so I didn't have to deal with his questions or unsolicited advice.

"What is it, Gwen?"

"Linda, I'm calling to ask if you'd be willing to come with me to the police station," she said soberly.

"Really?" I was surprised but heartened by the request.

"Yes. I realized they need Gabriela's phone. Giving it to them is the right thing to do, and I shouldn't have put it off for so long."

I felt an enormous wave of relief. I wondered if she had had an epiphany about this on Sunday at the Spanish ward, or if she'd talked to Brad about it.

"I was thinking that we could go talk to that detective you said you knew and trusted. The one from the crime scene?" Gwen said, her voice getting softer.

"Of course," I said. "Her name is Detective Gore. And this is a good idea, Gwen. You won't regret it."

I didn't want to delay this in case she changed her mind, so I offered to drive and went over immediately to pick her up, and off we went.

I drove to the police station and walked Gwen in. At reception,

I asked to speak with Detective Gore. For a moment, I was worried she wouldn't be in. Should I have called in advance? This was during regular business hours, right? But she could easily be out interviewing witnesses or doing other legwork on this case or another one.

But after a moment, the woman at reception told us that Gore would come "as soon as she could" and showed us to an interrogation room with only a table and a few folding chairs. "You can wait here," she said, closing the door behind her.

We could have sat in the regular waiting area, but all right. I wondered if the dark glass opposite us had someone on the other side, but why would anyone be watching us?

"Gwen, I can do the talking if you want," I said while we waited.

"I think that's a good idea," she said, looking nervous now that we were here.

It was only minutes later that Detective Gore herself came in. She nodded at me and sat down across from us, offering some brief pleasantries.

That is, until I started explaining why we were there and Gwen set Gabriela's phone on the table. I could see the detective's expression grow progressively angrier as I explained. The promise I'd made to Gwen about her not regretting this now seemed impossible to keep. Gwen's stare was fixed on the door, rather than either me or the detective.

"You did *what*?" she asked as I explained that we'd cracked the password and found out whom Gabriela had called the day she died.

"I realize it wasn't exactly orthodox—" I began.

"You stole an important piece of police evidence. In a murder investigation. Knowingly," said Detective Gore. She directed this only to Gwen, which didn't seem fair to me. For all she knew, I was the one who'd done all this. She knew that I'd been guilty of similar indiscretions in the past. But it had been Gwen who'd verbally attacked and insulted her back at the gas station, which Gore clearly hadn't forgotten or forgiven.

"We're sorry," I said, attempting to draw her attention back to me. "That's why we brought the evidence in."

Finally, Gore turned back to me. "You're sorry? That's all you have to say?"

I hadn't prepared for this. What else could I say, really? "We made a mistake, but we're trying to rectify it," I said.

"Do you have any idea of the damage this might do to our investigation? How you may have delayed us in finding important information? What if the prosecution ends up being unable to use this evidence at trial because the chain of custody is compromised? What if the murderer walks free? What if they kill again?" Gore demanded.

I cringed.

"If the phone was so important, why didn't you find it? I picked it up hours after the murder. You're making excuses so you can blame someone else for not doing your job," Gwen quipped.

What was she doing? I barely resisted the impulse to shush her.

Detective Gore stood up and took a couple of steps closer to Gwen, looming over her so there was no way to avoid looking at her. "No one tells me I don't do my job. No one," she said in a low voice.

Gwen swallowed but tilted her chin upward. "Gabriela

deserves justice just as much as anyone else," she said in a steady, quiet tone.

"The way you get justice is to trust the police. We get justice for victims. It's our job. That's the way it works," Gore said.

"I've been a victim, and I can certainly say the police are just as likely to protect the perpetrators as they are to help the victims," Gwen said.

I realized as she spoke that she was talking about her own past. She'd gone to the police when she was sixteen and told them about her father's abuse. They hadn't believed her any more than her own bishop had. It was her word against her father's, and he'd been a stake president at the time. Everyone chalked it up to her being an angry teenager, out to get revenge on her father for setting too strict a schedule for her.

"Gwen, Detective Gore isn't—" I tried to say.

But Gore interrupted me. She pointed a finger at Gwen, her volume rising. "You don't ever tell me that I'm not fighting for victims. Do you understand me? My stepfather murdered my mother when I was eleven years old. I spent ten years making sure he served justice. I will always be seeking justice for victims. It's why I became a police officer." I could see a single drop of sweat slide down her forehead as she spoke.

I was cowed into silence by these two women's histories of violence.

Gwen had also gone quiet. "Please, just look at the evidence on the phone," she asked softly. "Don't waste any more time shouting at us."

Detective Gore looked skeptically down at the phone. "I have no idea if this has been altered. If you've added to it or erased from it. I have to get the techs to work on that—I can't do it myself."

"We didn't—" I started to say.

Gore dismissively waved a hand. "What you say doesn't matter. What matters is what a good defense attorney will be able to imply that you might've done."

There was a long silence. I'd known it had been bad to let Gwen hold onto the phone, but I had to admit, I hadn't thought through all of the implications. It was one thing for us to be prosecuted for something like this, but if it meant Gabriela's killer went free, how would either of us live with that?

"I have little reason to do this, but let me assure both of you that we are close to an arrest. As for the phone, we had just this morning tracked it to your house, Mrs. Ferris. We were investigating the possibility that you were involved in the murder, or that your husband was. When we'd cleared him, we were going to move on to you."

For the first time, Gwen blanched. She shook her head. "Brad didn't have anything to do with this. And I didn't kill Gabriela. I was trying to help her."

Gore's expression was stony. "Help her? Who appointed you her savior?"

Gwen just grimaced.

Gore pressed the point. "You don't know how often I see this. Bored, privileged white women with nothing better to do in their lives than poke around in police matters. You think that because you've always been well off, that you can see what other people need and give it to them. Well, you're not the saviors of this planet. You don't know anything about police work, and you should both stay out of it."

I was humiliated. I wanted to apologize again, but there was no point. Detective Gore had made it all too clear what she thought of what we'd done.

"I was only trying to help," Gwen said, looking down at her hands. She was on the verge of tears now. Finally repentant, as Kurt might say.

But Gore was in no mood for sympathy. "Trying to help? Because you know so much more than the professionals? What in the world made you think you should try that? Too many CSI episodes, or too many Miss Marple mysteries? Did you just think that it looked easy, so you didn't need any training to do it?"

I was pretty sure that this was also directed toward me. Coincidentally, I had watched almost every iteration of CSI and read just about all of Agatha Christie's novels.

Gwen's face had gone very pale by now. "I was—I'm planning to start the Police Academy at UVU in January. I feel—called to it."

I wished I'd warned Gwen not to mention her ambitions. I wasn't sure Gore could stop her career before it started, but why take the risk?

"You feel 'called' to become a police officer?" Gore laughed aloud at this, and not in a friendly way. "You think your Mormon God wants you to be a police officer, so you jumped the gun and started messing around with my murder investigation? No, that doesn't excuse you." Gore looked over at me and shook her head. "Real detectives don't get on their knees and pray to some god for the answer to the question of who committed a murder. They don't assume people are good or bad based on their temple recommend status."

Her words made me suspect that her resentment of

Mormonism went far beyond this one case. It also made me wonder why she remained here in Utah. A woman with her credentials could surely go anywhere she wanted.

She continued to dig at Gwen. "You wouldn't make it two months at the Police Academy. Personally, I'd bet on less than two weeks. It'd be too much work for you, work that's too dirty and beneath you," she said scathingly. "No inspiration or scripture reading involved."

Gwen let out a gasp, and I knew Gore had really hurt her.

Satisfied with Gwen's reaction, Gore crossed her arms and stared at us coldly. "Mrs. Wallheim and Mrs. Ferris, I want you both to leave this station right now, and I want to make sure that neither of you ever poke into an investigation like this again. It's not safe for you or for anyone else involved." She walked to the door and held it open for us.

I stood up and walked out with Gwen, trying to suppress my own hurt that Gore hadn't called me "Linda" or "Sister Wallheim," as she had when she'd trusted me to help her before. I supposed that I deserved to be just "Mrs. Wallheim" now.

CHAPTER 17

We walked back to the car together.

"You were right," Gwen said quietly as we both sat there, waiting for the heater to kick in.

"Well, don't get used to it. I'm wrong plenty," I said, trying to make her feel better.

"Do you think I should just give up on the Police Academy, like she said?" Gwen said dolefully as I pulled away from the station.

I felt like this was all my fault. I should have made Gwen turn in the phone earlier and taken the heat from Gore myself. I had been trying to make things better, but had made them worse instead.

In a soothing tone, I said, "No, of course not. Detective Gore was just angry. You should do what you feel called to do, Gwen. Spiritual promptings are important."

In the silence that followed, I turned up the road to our neighborhood and caught a glimpse of the beautiful Draper temple against the drab colors of the winter mountain beyond, which still had very little snow on it. Mormons had taken this bleak landscape and made something of it. We were supposed to be reminded that this history proved that we mattered, but I didn't feel it right now. I only felt depressed.

Gwen eventually said, "I didn't mean called like that. I didn't mean that I thought it was what God wanted me to do." She sounded defensive.

"Okay," I said, holding out for more.

"I just meant that I felt it was right for me. Even nonreligious people talk about that—finding the thing they were always meant to do, the thing that finally makes sense of everything they've been through in their lives."

I tried to think of the right thing to say to her. "Gwen, if you're saying you don't think of yourself as Mormon anymore, you can just come out and say it. I already know you're a good person; whenever you talk about the Police Academy, it's about helping the people who need it."

"I can't just bottle up all my questions and problems with the church. I can't be a good soldier this time," Gwen said after a moment.

I put a hand on her knee. "You don't have to be. You can leave if you need to, but you can also stay on your own terms. I, for one, think it's refreshing when we have people talk about their doubts in church." I wouldn't get so bored or walk out as much, for one thing. We'd had the same lessons, heard the same canned answers to scripted questions in our correlated manuals. Everyone felt like they weren't good enough, but was afraid to admit their real issues because they'd become the "problem" soul everyone talked about and pitied.

Gwen looked up at me. "It's not just questions. I need more than someone telling me to go to God and ask for answers. I need more from the church, period."

I did, too. For all the rules, sometimes it felt like there was a depth missing in Mormonism, like it had stopped being about saving souls and showing Christ-like love, and had become a church of checklists. Going to meetings, raising your hand, reading scripture automatically, saying the same prayers, fasting on the days you were told to, wearing the right clothes and voting the right way. If only I could have conversations like this at church. But people like Gwen tended to leave for their own protection. And who did that leave behind?

"We need you there. We need someone to push others," I said. But if that was true, why wasn't I doing the pushing? Instead, I also walked out of those meetings, sitting in the corridors.

"I don't think they can bear to know the real anger I'm feeling. They'd all run away screaming." She laughed, but with pain behind it. "I've never been a proper Mormon woman, not from the beginning. And now, with me going to the Police Academy, I'm so far in left field, they don't know what to do with me."

"Mormon women aren't just one thing," I said. "They never have been and never will be. Just read the old journals of Emma Smith and Eliza R. Snow." The two women had both been strong and both had been married to Joseph Smith, but it was hard to think of two more different personalities. "And what about Emily Richards and Martha Cannon? And Emmeline Wells and Zina Young? And Sarah Kimball?" I searched my mind for names from the Mormon suffrage movement from the 1890s and beyond. Utah had been one of the first states to grant women the vote.

"That was a long time ago," Gwen said. "It doesn't seem like women are seen in the same way now."

"But you didn't hear Yolanda Jones's talk on Sunday about Chieko Okazaki," I reminded her. "It was so great. She was so inclusive and feisty."

"And she was released a few years after she was called, while all the men stayed in place," Gwen reminded me, rubbing at her eyes.

Yes, that was true. Mormon women weren't paid for their leadership positions, and their main priority was supposed to be their families, so they only served in executive positions temporarily instead of permanently like the men. And they only had authority over women and children. It came back to this again and again. You might not have to be the same Molly Mormon, but if you weren't, you didn't go far. And if you were, you only went a little bit farther.

"But things are changing," I said. "There's Ordain Women and other groups—"

Gwen shook her head. "All the original leadership of Ordain Women were excommunicated or pushed out. The new leaders have turned down the volume completely, waiting patiently to be heard. And the other movements around women's power are ridiculous. Women wearing pants to church? Like that's a way to get power. And women praying in General Conference? That's what we think will make men see women as equal?"

That was a pretty damning evaluation of people who were doing good work to change things. But Gwen had a good point, that they weren't changing the organization of the church itself. It was hard to get men to see the problem when they were convinced that the existing patriarchal power structure came from God. If you didn't even ask the question, how could you get an answer?

"I don't think this is all the problem of Mormonism. Or God. It's just the world we live in. Most of us are so used to breathing this air we don't even think about it." That was my best attempt at explaining it to her.

"I know," she said sadly. "But if we're the one true church and God is speaking daily to the prophet and the Quorum of the Twelve, then why are we facing so many of the same problems?"

I didn't have an easy answer for that. "Because people move slowly. God works with us as flawed mortals," I said.

"Maybe I don't want to work with God anymore. It seems to me that faith takes up so much energy," Gwen said. She gestured down at the valley below us. "There are a lot of people out there who are suffering—they've given up on God, too. Maybe they need someone in a position of authority who will listen to them. If I can't do that in the church, maybe I can do it on the police force."

Years ago, I'd felt like believing in God again had given me new energy, but I didn't want to argue with Gwen. I knew good people who were atheists, including Kenneth. Gwen had to follow her own path.

"Leaving means a ton of paperwork," I said in a halfhearted attempt to make her laugh. You had to write a letter with very specific legal language, or the church just sent more missionaries or a bishop to talk you out of your decision.

She frowned slightly. "I know paperwork very well from Zions. I think I can handle that part."

"Of course you can. I don't doubt you," I said, too exhausted to explain the joke.

She leaned forward, resting her head in her hands. "Linda, I know I made a mistake with Gabriela's phone. I shouldn't have stepped onto that crime scene. Detective Gore was right to yell at me. In fact, I'll remember that, in case I ever need to do the same thing to someone like me, who means well but isn't thinking straight."

I sighed in relief. "I guess that's some good that's come out of it, then."

To my surprise, when I pulled up in front of her house, she didn't get out. I'd figured she'd be eager to get away from me and any reminder of what had just happened at the police station.

"Brad is really angry with me," she said instead, looking down at her hands. Her nails were chewed and uneven.

"Because he suspects you don't believe in God anymore?" I asked, trying to get to the heart of the real problem, not just the symptoms of her odd behavior when it came to this murder case.

Her voice was small and sad. "Among other things. He says I've changed, that I'm not the same person he married nine years ago. He says I've changed and he hasn't."

I snorted at that. "No one who is married for so long survives without changing. In fact, the longer you're married, the bigger the changes are." I'd seen plenty of changes in Brad myself. He'd become stronger when he learned what had happened to Gwen in her childhood, and more open-minded. Being in the bishopric had made him more aware of the problems other people had. And that was just the beginning.

"No, I think he's right," Gwen said. "I mean, he's changed, obviously, but not as much as I have, and I'm sorry about that, but I can't turn back time and go back to being someone who isn't me anymore. He really did fall in love with a different person, and I'm not sure he'll be able to fall in love with the person I am now."

"Well, that's the challenge of any lasting marriage. We all have to figure out how to keep falling in love with the person our spouse becomes. How to find new things we have in common."

I thought about how often Kurt and I fell back on the children we had together—something Gwen and Brad might never share. Was anything as powerful as the binding weight of children? Perhaps not, which could be the reason the church had had so much success with the message "Families Are Forever."

"Or we don't," Gwen said simply. There was less sadness than acceptance in her tone.

Was this it, then? Would she and Brad get a divorce? Brad would be removed from the bishopric without a temple sealing, but be free to find a new wife who could have children and who would be more committed to the church. But if he thought he could find someone who wouldn't change, he was sadly mistaken. I wondered if I could get Kurt to talk to him about the real lessons of a lasting marriage, the compromises that had to be made.

"Brad is a good man," I said, not ready to give up on their marriage. "Even if you think he hasn't changed as much as you have, that's no reason to dump him."

"Dump him? He's the one who wants to dump me," Gwen said, her anguish now clear. "I'm not faithful enough for him, apparently. The only thing I can do for him now is let him find someone else."

If she was acting in what she saw as his best interest, then there was still hope for them. While I'd seen the way he'd looked at her worriedly at church and how he'd shut down during her fight with Shannon Carpenter at the Trunk or Treat, I didn't think he wanted to give up. He was just figuring out how to adjust to an increasingly tricky position.

"Gwen, Brad might be struggling with who you're becoming, but that doesn't mean you're being kind to him by letting him go. I think he's trying to love you better. Try not to fault him for that—he's just lost his grasp on who you are now and needs help figuring out what you need."

She let out a long breath, on the edge of a sob. "I think we're too far apart now to ever come back together. And I don't know if I want to be with someone like that anymore, anyway."

I thought of the end of my marriage to Ben Tookey, my first husband, more than thirty years ago. He'd been in denial about being gay, and our marriage was a disaster in many ways, but I'd still loved him and wept at the end of our relationship, even though I'd been the one to pursue a divorce.

But Gwen and Brad's marriage seemed different to me. The Ferrises had weathered so much difficulty already. This couldn't compare to the rest, surely. Kurt and I had been through a lot together, too. We weren't in perfect harmony at the moment. Maybe we never would be. But I wasn't going to throw it all out because of that.

"Maybe you should give it some time," I suggested, though I wasn't sure Gwen was listening.

"Yeah," Gwen breathed out. "Time." She got out of my car.

I let her go at that, waiting to drive off until she had walked into her house and closed the door behind her.

CHAPTER 18

I opened my door the next morning to find Detective Gore there, waiting for me. She hadn't called to warn me in advance and after what had happened yesterday, I was nervous that this was going to be a further harangue.

"Can I come in?" Gore asked, not quite meeting my gaze.

I hesitated a moment, then led her into the front room. She'd been there several times before, and I couldn't help but think of the times she'd made sure things came out right. I wanted her to trust me again.

"I wanted to talk to you privately," Gore said. She sounded cool and collected, unlike yesterday. She hadn't come here to apologize, surely? It was Gwen who'd been on the receiving end of most of her anger.

"Anything I can do to help," I said. "Especially after what happened with Gabriela's phone. I didn't know it would cause you that much trouble."

"I'm glad you said that." Gore smiled. "I do have something to ask you." She sat down on the couch across from me.

"All right. Go on." As long as it wasn't testifying against Gwen in court, I was in.

"I wanted you to help me understand the Spanish ward here.

I could have asked some of the other detectives who are Mormon, but I worry it would look like I was belittling their religion."

So there were boundaries she couldn't breach at work. I was glad she trusted me enough to ask difficult questions. It meant we were friends again, at least of a sort. Gwen would be able to better explain how the Spanish ward worked differently than a regular Mormon ward, but if she'd wanted to talk to Gwen, she'd have said that. I figured that with the phone incident, Gwen wasn't on the top of her list for trusted Mormon contacts.

"I'm not in the Spanish ward myself, but I might be able to help clarify some things," I said.

She met my gaze now. "My first question is—why is there such a thing in the first place? I mean, it looks from the outside like you're trying to keep certain people corralled in a lower tier or something."

I winced. "That's not the purpose of it. It's trying to meet people where they are."

Gore raised her eyebrows at this. "Seems like people are divided on racial lines."

"They're not racial," I said. "It's linguistic." But I knew that wasn't necessarily true. It was cultural, as well. "People choose for themselves if they want to be in Spanish wards or not. No one makes them stay if they want to move to an English speaking ward." Even as I said it, I knew it didn't sound right.

"Well, I've been reading up about the Mormon church in Mexico," Gore said, making it clear she had done plenty of research and had her own agenda here. "Do you know the history?"

"You mean about Mormon polygamists fleeing to Mexico to escape prosecution here in Utah?" I asked.

"Yes, that, to begin with. Until I was looking it up, I thought that the Wilford Woodruff Proclamation banned polygamy for all Mormons," Gore said. "Like, in 1890."

I winced. "Yeah, uh, not quite." The Proclamation was meant to sound like that to the law enforcement officials who were arresting polygamists and confiscating church property, and to make Utah look ready to become a state to the federal government back in Washington, D.C., but it was also clear to Mormons that the actual language of the document allowed polygamy to continue anywhere it wasn't illegal. For a while, that included Mexico and Canada.

"But it turns out there was another Proclamation against polygamy in 1910, was it?" said Gore.

I nodded again. This wasn't information that the average Mormon knew. It certainly wasn't taught in our Sunday School classes. Some very prominent Mormon families lived in Mexico as polygamists for decades after it was illegal in the United States. The Romneys, the Browns, the Pratts.

"There was a revolution in Mexico in the early 1900s and a bunch of Mormon polygamists came back to the US then."

"Yes," I said. Though there were plenty of Mormons who were still practicing polygamy secretly in Utah anyway. Polygamist marriages had continued to happen in temples in Utah and even been sealed by apostles of the church. But the polygamists in Mexico weren't as used to being secretive about it.

"The LeBarons were also part of the Mormon settlement in Mexico, did you know that?" Gore was watching me very closely.

I knew who the LeBarons were. They had started up various splinter groups from other small polygamous groups. One was called something about the Church of the Fullness of Times.

And they'd fought amongst themselves, killing rival leaders, until they were jailed and stopped in the 1970s. It wasn't a great time to be Mormon back then. The horror was spread all over the national newspapers, as if the average Mormons had something to do with it.

"Is this really what you came to ask me about?" I was uncomfortable now.

"I just think it's interesting that there are so many groups that come out of Mormonism where people follow a single supposed prophet without question," Gore said.

"Splitting groups after a change in leadership is hardly unique to Mormonism. You see it lots of other religions. And in other groups, too."

"All right, but what about Greg Hope? What do you know about him?" Gore asked, apparently finished with her questions about Mormon history.

I shook my head. "Probably as much as you do. I've never met him."

"Oh." She looked disappointed. "I thought you would have a better sense, since your husband is a bishop too. Don't bishops get together to talk about church matters and make decisions about their wards?"

I was pretty sure she had us confused with Catholics. The Mormon "bishop" designation is very different. "I don't think Kurt has met Greg Hope, either. We've only seen him on those car wash commercials."

"I understand he was a bit of a celebrity," Gore said. "Still is, among the rank and file of Mormonism."

I shrugged. "He was a basketball player at BYU. But it was probably his mission to Mexico that made him a bishop. Kurt told me he baptized over a thousand people in his two years there."

Gore coughed. "So that's a lot for one mission, then?"

I nodded. "It's probably a record."

But I didn't want to go on about it, since I wasn't sure it was something admirable. It was one thing to critique the church to other members, and another to do it to a non-member. "Back then, the church was growing very quickly in Mexico." This was a different history of the Mormon church in Mexico, after the polygamists had left and the missionaries came back to preach to the native population as "Lamanites," the people of the Book of Mormon.

"So that's why he's a bishop for the Latino population here? He has the charisma necessary to keep people coming back week after week?"

That wasn't exactly the way that I'd put it. "I think it's his general leadership qualities." Why was I defending this choice when I didn't trust it? Sometimes it was so frustrating to see how deeply ingrained my deference to leadership was, even when I thought I'd rooted it out.

"But he's in charge of the whole ward, and he's supposed to get them to pay tithing to the church every month, right? And to keep them from complaining that there aren't any higher church leaders who are Hispanic to represent their own interests?"

There was a newly called apostle who was from Brazil, but I didn't want to go into that with Gore. I wanted to say that we were still young as a church, still teaching leadership to those of other countries, but I was afraid of how colonialist that sounded. "I like to think he's trying to help them get along in the world we live in," I said.

Gore gave me an appraising look, like she'd never met me before. "You really see it that way?" she asked. "You think he's on a mission from God to civilize them or something like that?"

"No, no. Not like that. Just . . ." I trailed off, unsure where to go from here. Gwen had made me realize just how problematic the whole idea of "Lamanites" was. Yes, they were supposed to be the dark-skinned descendants of a branch of Israel who were destined to come to power in the Americas. But why did their skin have to lighten in the latter days, and why did they have to acknowledge the Mormon church as the one true way to God before being "saved?" I didn't know if I believed that at all anymore.

"What do you know about Bishop Hope's business?" Gore pressed.

I shook my head, getting the sense that she hadn't really been interested in talking about Mexico or the Spanish ward except as they related to Greg Hope. "Nothing. I mean, I've read a little about it online. He sells security systems." I didn't want to tell her what I really thought yet, since I didn't have any reason to have such a negative opinion.

"Did you know his staff is almost entirely made up of members of his ward?"

"I—I'd heard that," I said cautiously. "He helps them." I hoped that, though I didn't really believe it.

Gore sniffed loudly at that. "Helps them," she echoed. "Sounds more like he's helping himself to amass wealth while keeping his workers firmly beneath him in every sphere."

That was probably something she wouldn't have said to anyone else. "Do you think he had something to do with Gabriela's murder?" I asked. Was that why she was really here? Did she think I could offer insight on his personality or his role in the ward?

Gore stiffened. "Not necessarily."

I stared at her.

"I'm just asking about Bishop Hope because I'm trying to understand the dynamics of the ward Gabriela was in. How people related to each other there, so I can understand more clearly who might have benefited from her death." She was trying her best to be vague.

"Well, if you want to know more about how the Spanish ward works, maybe you should talk to President Frost. He's over the whole stake," I said.

"I remember President Frost. No, thank you," Gore said, glancing at the door. President Frost had stepped into one of Gore's previous cases and given Gore the impression he covered up for other Mormons in power. Given that level of perceived trustworthiness, I could see why she wouldn't go back to him.

"Then maybe Kurt could help? He's not home right now, but you could talk to him another time. Maybe if you came back at night?" I said, softening. I really didn't think I could help her in the way she wanted.

"Can you give me his number at work?" Gore asked instead, and put it into her phone as we spoke. Then she stood up and got ready to leave. Apparently I'd given her what she wanted about Hope, though I wasn't sure what it was.

"What about Gwen?" I asked. "You're not going to charge her with anything, are you? About the phone?"

Gore shook her head as if this was unimportant. "We're moving on. This is about Gabriela, not about your friend," she said, skipping even Gwen's name.

"Well, thank you," I said.

She walked to the door. "Greg Hope really isn't a friend of your husband's?" she asked one more time, her hand on the knob.

"No, not at all."

She nodded, walked out, and drove off.

I asked Kurt that night if she'd contacted him.

"Who?" he said.

"Detective Gore. You remember her from that other case?"

"Oh, the black woman detective. She's good, isn't she?"

"I think so," I said. "Did she contact you today? She came over to talk about Bishop Hope and the Spanish ward."

"Did she? Interesting," Kurt said.

What a strange answer. He didn't want to know more? "Well, she might contact you later. She thought you and Bishop Hope were friends because you're both bishops." I grinned at this. "Like how people outside of Utah think that if you're Mormon, you must know all the other Mormons."

"Well, I'll help her if I can," Kurt said, scratching the back of his head.

CHAPTER 19

L ater that week, I was still puzzling over Gore's visit and her questions about Bishop Hope. I looked online for more information, but I couldn't find anything else there. I ended up deciding that I was just going to have to see it for myself. I called Gwen to ask if she wanted to go with me and pretend we were interested in getting into sales. That seemed the best way to find out what I wanted to know about how the business worked. It wasn't in any way illegal, either.

I didn't tell her about Detective Gore coming by the house. I still didn't know what to make of it and didn't want her reading into it.

"You've just made my week," she said enthusiastically. "When can we go?"

That struck me as suspicious. "What about your job at Zions?"

"I quit," Gwen said.

That was a surprise. "Can you afford to do that?"

"I was going to give notice next month anyway, once I started the Police Academy. And we have savings. We'll be fine financially," she said casually.

"Have you told Brad?" I asked, because Kurt would surely

have passed that information along if he knew, and Brad would have told him.

She said nothing, which was answer enough.

There was nothing I could do to force her to communicate with her husband. I certainly couldn't step in for her. "All right, I'll drive," I said. "Pick you up in thirty minutes?"

"I think if we want a real sales interview, we'll need an appointment. I'll call and set them up, OK?" Gwen said and hung up. Clearly, she was as eager to figure out this piece of the Gabriela Suarez puzzle as I was.

I looked down at the sweatpants I was wearing and decided I'd better put on something more professional if I wanted to look like I was really trying to get a job at a home security company. I glanced through my closet and wished that I had something other than everyday casual clothes and the dresses I wore to church. I didn't really have anything that resembled business attire. It wasn't as if Kurt's job ever required me to entertain people. Anything he wanted me to attend with him as bishop was best done in Sunday attire.

In the end, I threw on one of my darker dresses without a big flared skirt and hoped it would work. I carefully put on some lipstick and ran a brush through my hair, then brought out the gel that my daughter-in-law Willow had showed me how to use for Adam's wedding years ago, which I hadn't bothered with since then. It made my hair look slightly less poofy.

I smiled at myself in the mirror. Good enough.

I hurried out to the car and went to pick up Gwen. She was dressed in a navy suit, far more appropriate for the occasion than my dress. Probably the outfit she would've worn if she'd been headed to work at Zions.

"So, I'm hoping to figure out if this is a scam," I said. "What about you?"

She gave me a funny look. "Linda, it's obviously a scam. We just have to figure out how big it is and how they get people to sign up for it—breaking arms, threats, or just plain old American lies."

I thought about Gabriela. She'd never talked about her job, but had clearly received regular payments for something.

It took about ten minutes to drive to the address I'd already put into my phone, down to the freeway, then up two exits and past the Southtowne Mall.

The Celestial Security property was extensive and high on the mountain. It looked almost like a palace with its white stone façade and incredibly lavish landscaping, including a waterfall near the building entrance, where we waited to be admitted.

The front door was opened by an attractive, slim woman wearing what looked like a gallon of foundation in addition to her very red lipstick. She looked up at me and said, "Ladies, it's so good to meet you both."

"We have appointments," Gwen put in.

"Ah," said the made-up woman. "May I have your names?" She looked down at an expensive electronic version of an appointment calendar.

We gave them.

"Well, I'm Serena Matthews," said the woman, tucking the electronic calendar under one arm and holding a limp hand out to me. "Come in and we'll get you started. We're so excited to meet you and invite you into our special family here at Celestial Security. This is a day you'll never forget, the first day of the rest of your life."

Wow. That was putting it on pretty thick.

"Come right this way. We have special, individualized sessions for each of you, with someone who can answer all your questions and give you the attention you deserve." She walked us inside, asking about our children—this was a misstep for Gwen, but was quickly glossed over. Apparently they hadn't checked our backgrounds.

Despite myself, I felt relaxed and well disposed. If this company was a scam, it was a very good one.

After this, we were offered a dazzling array of herbal teas, hot chocolate, Snapples, and sodas, as well as some expensive cookies and cupcakes that were "ordered in fresh every day." Gwen refused, but I eagerly tried a couple, since I figured I might as well enjoy myself while I was here. She gave me a bemused look, but I took pleasure in deciding that my own cookies were better and these cupcakes were over-frosted. They looked very pretty, but not enough care had been taken on the inside, a metaphor perhaps for the entire Celestial Security business.

When I'd dabbed at my lips with a napkin, Gwen was sent off with another attractive, heavily made up woman behind a door that was identical to the one Serena Matthews herself took me through.

"What a wonderful stage of life you're in, a grandmother still active enough to enjoy her family. And this festive time of year must be so full of joy for you," said Selena. "I'm envious. You've put all that work into your family, and now the investment is paying off!"

I didn't like to think of my family as that kind of investment, but it was still flattering to hear.

Selena gestured to a tan and beige floral couch for me to sit on. The room around it was big enough to comfortably fit my entire extended family. It sounded like there was white noise being pumped in, too, so no sounds from outside would impinge on the quiet, peaceful experience.

I felt a tingling sensation as I looked up at the elaborate chandeliers, then the white upholstered chair next to me, and the pale wooden desk Serena sat behind. Her black pencil skirt was the only thing out of place here; otherwise, this was very much a replica of the celestial room in the temple, the room meant to embody the peace and serenity that we would feel on entering the highest level of heaven within Mormonism.

The celestial room was also the central room of the temple that every endowment room led to. Two hours of scriptural explanations, as well as lessons on the signs and symbols necessary to be admitted to heaven, all led to the passage into the celestial room, which was the place families who had been separated by gender before were able to reconnect.

When Serena spoke again, it was in a hushed tone that couldn't possibly be unintentional. She sounded just like a matron at the temple, though I wondered if other people consciously noticed these parallels. "Are you ready for me to introduce you to the most important financial commitment of your life?" she asked.

This again reminded me of the temple questions, asking if anyone wanted to leave before they made the commitments to the Mormon church and to God that happened inside the temple.

"Yes," I said, feeling my stomach clench. The consequences of disobeying temple covenants had once been mimicked in graphic detail by all the participants, including cutting your own throat and disemboweling yourself. That had since been taken out and replaced with a simple promise to keep things secret. No matter how much I was willing to play along in general to get the information I wanted, there was no way I was going to swear an oath like that here.

I'd always thought that the secrecy of temple ordinances was a little overdone, that young Mormons who went to the temple for the first time should be given more of an explanation of what would happen and the specific covenants they'd have to make. But this imitation of temple trappings and ambience to sell a product and make money for Bishop Hope made me furious.

Why hadn't someone who'd been here already told church authorities about the temple trappings? I knew that if Kurt saw this, he would blow his top about how inappropriate it was. Though once I thought about it, it seemed that someone had walked a careful line to avoid doing anything that was excommunicable. There were no all-seeing eyes, no moonstones and sunstones, no hand signs or direct cribbing from the words of the temple ceremony.

"We're honored that you've come to us for help in your next stage of life. We want to give you what we have learned works best for most of our family members on the path to success. We're sharing that with you now." Serena pushed a button and a screen came down—very much like the film screen in the temple, hidden behind a curtain.

There was a short five-minute feature about the security system itself, though it didn't seem particularly special to me. Of course, the film showed each window of the house being surrounded by an angelic light, and the garage and front doors suffused in a golden glow as soon as the electronic monitoring device was activated. Someone had done a lovely animation of the power streaming from the device to each point of entry, and the music was a nice Bach concerto that I recognized from the orchestra in my college days, when I played cello.

When the film was over, the screen was retracted and the lights came back on. I found myself blinking a little at the sudden change, a feeling that was not unlike what happened when I stepped out of the temple and back into the real world on a hot summer's day.

"And now you're back with me," said Serena.

"Yes," I said.

She leaned over the desk and handed me a tablet. "You're ready for stage two now," she said.

I stared down at the tablet, but the images looked like nothing so much as a digital flipchart. I thought about when Bishop Hope had gone on a mission. Late 70s, when flipcharts had been in fashion. No wonder he thought they were the best way to convert people to his business.

Serena said soothingly, "Now, you'll be inviting other people to join our wonderful family here, so you want to start by making sure that the client knows you're on their side. If possible, you'll want to meet with both the husband and the wife so that both feel fully included in the decision-making process, and so you can answer any questions they may have.

"Be sure to keep them positive about the prospect of our family benefits. We want what they want for their family. We want their health, happiness, and peace of mind. We want them to know that their family is one-hundred-percent safe when they are with us, because their family is our family, and families are forever."

She had the Mormon code down pat. It disturbed me a bit to realize how often we as Mormons were told to do certain things to keep our families protected. Pay tithing. Fulfill our callings. Follow the prophets of the church, no matter what. When the same language was used for a business, it made me expect the worst. I felt like I was at a used car dealership inside of a temple. It was very strange.

"Now, Linda, you start in our suggested presentation here, with something that no one can disagree with." Serena leaned forward and swiped to the next screen for me, which showed a family standing in front of a home—a far nicer one than Kurt and I owned.

Every family deserves the gift of Celestial Security, the banner across the top of the photo declared.

Serena looked up at me.

I was trying to remember how this was all supposed to make me feel. Committed, convinced, calm. Ready to put money down. "Of course. How could anyone not want the best for their family?" I asked.

"And make sure to always use the names of both clients as often as you can. It makes them feel like you see them as individuals, and further makes them feel part of our tight-knit family. Can you see why I would do that, Linda?" said Serena.

"Sure," I said. Then I added, "Serena."

She nodded at me, not noticing my sarcasm. "Good." She swiped to the next image on the tablet. "What price can you put on the safety of your family?" she asked, reading verbatim from the line at the top. This time, the graphic was black and white, showing a house both on fire and flooded at the same time.

She swiped again. "What price can you put on peace of mind?" she read from the next screen, which depicted a man and woman in bed together—fully clothed, of course.

"What price indeed," I murmured.

She read another screen, "Your family's kingdom is worth all the money and time you can put into it, to keep it safe." The image this time was of a castle in the clouds, the family all in white clothing with green accents. Everyone wore a gold crown.

I shifted in my seat, uncomfortable with the subversion here of the temple promise to commit all our time and money to God's kingdom.

Then there were the mathematical graphics to prove how "easy" this was to afford compared to a car or student loans.

When you could buy a car for the price of your home security system, something was wrong. I didn't have a security system in my home at all, and if I did, I would never have paid this much for it. But the truth was, Serena made it very difficult to say "no." It was like a missionary discussion, where the only answers were affirmative, so of course you'd join.

"Well, Linda now we're ready for the big question." She swiped the tablet again.

Are you ready to invest in your eternity? it asked.

I shivered involuntarily at a couple's wedding picture, clearly taken in front of the Salt Lake Temple. There was no attempt to hide the HOLINESS TO THE LORD sign or the spires at the top. Moroni with his trumpet was on the highest spire, and the temple grounds were clearly visible.

"Our average sales consultants make up to ten thousand dollars a month," Serena went on in the same Muzak tone. "But I think you'll be surprised to hear that the only investment we're asking from you today is three thousand dollars."

I suppressed a choke at this, but Serena didn't seem to notice.

"For that small investment, you'll be joining our family, and you'll get all of the perks that come with that. Of course, we'll start you with your own security system and monthly payments. Then, as a salesperson, you'll be invited to our quarterly lunch, a chance to talk to everyone who is involved in this great endeavor. And if you sell extra, you will of course be invited to other special events, with special guests you will be very pleased to meet."

"Like who?" I asked.

"Oh, I couldn't tell you the names directly, but I assure you, they are very important people. National figures you'd be happy to have your photo taken next to." She made a gesture, drawing my attention to a photo behind her head I hadn't seen before. It had Greg Hope in the front with Supreme Court Justice Neil Gorsuch, and in the back were about a hundred other people. I strained to find Gabriela Suarez in the group, but it didn't look to me like there were any Hispanic people in it, not even Hope's own wife. All white faces, white shirts on the men, pastel dresses on the women.

"We treat our family very well. We want them all to know how much we value them and all they do to help us continue to grow and move forward in the industry," Serena said with her perpetual smile. "With your first investment, you will begin to build your own clientele and if they also join the family, you'll receive additional advantages because they're working for you, as well as for the rest of us. It's such a small amount of money when you consider all the possibilities, don't you think?"

Serena went on, caught up in her own spiel.

"There will be a small yearly commitment fee after that, and of course, occasional fees to help pay for new sales materials as they come out, and for the training meetings you'll come to in order to help you achieve your goals," said Serena, playing the part of a Stepford wife perfectly.

She paused and I knew I had to say something, but I wasn't about to tell her I'd write her a check. "That sounds very promising," I tried.

She seemed to only hear encouragement. "Wonderful, Linda. All you need to do is sign here," she said, pushing over a multipage document to me. Had that been next to her the whole time? She'd already opened it to the final page with a line for my signature.

I wished I could go through the whole contract for informational purposes and take photos of it with my cell phone, but I suspected Serena wouldn't allow that.

"I'll have to think about it," I said.

"What is there to think about? This is the way to a new, more celestial life for your family. How can you say no to that, Linda?" Her tone was pure saccharine, as if she wasn't pushing me to transfer thousands of dollars in one stroke of the pen—not to mention whatever else was in the small print that I hadn't had time to pick through.

I wanted to get out of here, and badly. I felt like I'd stepped through a mirror into a world where everything good was bad and everything bad was good. They said that the way Satan worked was to counterfeit the good, and that seemed to be exactly what was going on here.

I said, "I'm sorry. I can't make this financial commitment on my own. My husband and I have committed to always consulting each other before we sign a contract." It was true that we had agreed upon this, mostly so that we could say it to pushy salespeople.

Serena seemed to beam at me as if this was exactly what she had most wanted me to say. "Oh, your husband. Of course, you don't want to do anything without consulting him. Why don't we make an appointment for some time later in the day when he can come back in with you? I'd love to do the presentation again with him involved. He sounds like a wonderful man."

I had said absolutely nothing about Kurt, but wondered if him being an accountant would turn her off. I smiled faintly. "I'll talk to him about it at home tonight," I said, making no promises.

"Good, good. I can call you in the morning. But just for my information, is your husband still employed full-time? Or has he retired?" she asked.

I was slightly offended at her assumption about our ages. We weren't so close to retirement age, were we?

"He's not retired yet," I said tightly.

"Well, let's go ahead and schedule that next meeting for the weekend, then," she said, pulling out the tablet again.

"I'm not sure what his schedule looks like, but I'll call you." I had no intention of doing that. Kurt would be furious if he found out that I'd come here and pretended I was interested, just to get more information about Gabriela Suarez. And Bishop Hope.

Serena leaned forward, holding eye contact in an uncomfortable way. "Oh, no need for that. We'll make sure to call you, Linda. We keep track of everyone who's in our family, and you're already one of us now." After that, she led me back out to the front room and offered me a box of fancy chocolates. I took two, and savored the mint truffle and raspberry crème. I was deciding whether to head back to the car and wondered if Gwen had already finished her presentation when I heard a raised voice from the room next door.

Gwen came out a moment later, her tone angry and demanding. "I wanted to know about Gabriela Suarez, that's all. She told me about your company in the first place, and I thought she deserved credit for bringing me here."

The woman who'd been Gwen's own Serena came out after her, followed by what looked like a security guard, a man dressed in plain clothes who was about six-four, three hundred pounds, and Samoan. A former BYU football player that Greg Hope hired using his connections to the sports programs there?

"Oh," said my Serena, and yanked the box of chocolates from my hands. "You need to leave immediately," she said.

So much for being part of the family already.

Gwen and I were escorted off the premises and had to drive away before they stopped following us.

CHAPTER 20

I stopped the car after I'd driven about half a mile from the parking area of Celestial Security and let myself catch my breath.

"Well," Gwen said from the passenger seat. "That was telling."

"It was disturbing," I said. I rubbed my free hand up and down my other shoulder to reassure myself that I was in the real world, in my own body.

"Yeah, I wish I could take a shower," Gwen said. "There's something very wrong with that place."

It was true. "Why do you think people sign up for that package? All that money, and you just keep paying."

"I don't know," Gwen said. "It doesn't make any sense to me. I mean, I can see how Celestial Security is making money off selling the sales kits to their consultants, but I don't understand why people would pay so much extra for what seems like an ordinary security system."

"Maybe because it feels so Mormon?" I said.

Gwen shook her head. "And that makes their product worth ten times as much?"

Maybe. In my experience, Mormons could be manipulated by anyone who pretended to have a connection to the church, and the trappings of the temple would have made it that much easier.

"Are their customers just stupid?" Gwen suggested. "And don't understand how real companies work?"

"More like people who are used to believing what they're told and assuming that anyone in authority is looking out for their best interests," I said tartly.

Gwen blinked at that. I guess she hadn't heard me vent enough about my own problems with Mormonism yet.

"I've seen a lot of multi-level marketing stuff go through the ward. Amway, Mary Kay, Nu Skin," I said, shaking my head. There was always a new product being sold, but the method was the same. Mormons have big circles of friends in their wards and are used to "bearing testimony." They invite people over under the guise of throwing a dinner party, then ambush everyone about the latest product.

I'd never gotten into selling, but I'd bought a lot of things at parties from friends in the ward out of obligation or guilt.

"You missed doTerra and Nature's Sunshine," Gwen said. Those must have been newer ones I hadn't heard of yet. "And Noni Juice, Jamberry, XanGo."

"I hate the idea that con men come to Utah just to make money, but it works. We're easy pickings," I said. Mormons could be so gullible. I'd heard non-Mormons say that if you believed an angel came and delivered gold plates to a fourteen-year-old boy, you'd believe anything.

It wasn't always fake miracle products, either. There were a ton of fake investment schemes that Kurt had heard of through ward members. Some complained about being robbed, and others tried to convince him to buy in.

Because he was an accountant, Kurt had training in discerning good investments from bad ones and was never taken in. But he spent hours in Sunday meetings at the church trying to explain to people why they shouldn't invest in one cockamamie scheme or another. And he was sometimes blamed for it when they did it anyway, against his express recommendations, because he hadn't explained his reasons well enough for them to understand.

"If people think they can make money without doing work or taking any risks, they're bound to be fooled," Kurt said when I asked him about it once. "It's the greed that's ultimately behind the schemes. Ignorance is part of it, but if they weren't so greedy, I think they'd be able to listen. They think they're special and they deserve something for nothing. Like God wants His special children to be rich."

Mormons said that God wanted us to be happy, but that wasn't the same as being rich. I thought again of the ideal Zion society in the Book of Mormon, where there were no rich or poor among them, everyone just sharing what they had. That seemed a far cry from what we were living in now.

"They're definitely hiding something," Gwen said, drawing my attention back to the here and now. "They freaked out when I brought up Gabriela as part of the sales force. I assumed that was what she did, and figured mentioning her name might be a special in. But instead, it was like I'd thrown a grenade in there."

"So she wasn't in sales?" I asked. We still didn't know what the monthly deposits had been for, or whether they had to do with her death. We were just guessing they did.

Gwen sighed. "I wish I'd waited longer before saying anything about her. If I'd just gone with the program and signed up for a sample sales kit, I might have gotten the chance to ask the other employees about Gabriela."

"You have an extra three thousand dollars lying around for that? Wouldn't Brad get mad if you spent that much without consulting him?" I asked. Kurt certainly wouldn't have been happy if I'd blown that kind of money on a ruse like this. I couldn't have hidden it from him, since he had equal access to our accounts.

Gwen arched an eyebrow. "I have my own bank account—I always have. I have my own money saved up, and I can use it on whatever I want without consulting Brad. I don't understand women who don't have their own bank accounts. Why would you want to be dependent on someone else for every penny you spend?"

I tried not to feel stung at her judgment. From my perspective, it was strange that she and Brad didn't share finances. What kind of marriage was it when you didn't share everything? When you didn't make your decisions together?

A modern marriage, I supposed. It was hard for me not to think that this was one of the problems at the heart of Gwen and Brad's marriage. They were too separate. They didn't need each other like Kurt and I did.

"Now I can't go back to that same presentation. They'd recognize me. Do you think we could find someone else in the ward who would be willing to do it for us? Maybe if I paid them for it?" Gwen asked.

Anna popped into mind, but there was no way I'd ask her to do this for me. And I doubted she would, even so.

"Maybe I could try a disguise?" Gwen said. "I could cut my

hair really short and not put on makeup. Wear casual clothes. Slouch a little."

"No," I said. "That's not going to work, Gwen. And even if it did, it would take weeks for you to be able to start asking questions, and you would probably still end up being kicked out anyway. You'd be out the three thousand dollars for nothing."

Gwen went silent for a few moments. "I hate this. If I were a police officer, I could demand access to bank records and look into their finances. I could make them tell me what Gabriela's job was."

I wondered if Gore had already been here. "Maybe we should talk to Detective Gore again and tell them what we know about Celestial Security's payments to Gabriela," I suggested.

Gwen made a raspberry noise at this. "She's not going to pick up our lead. She doesn't trust us."

I stopped short of telling her about Gore's visit. She'd certainly been interested in Bishop Hope. But she'd stopped short of telling me she was looking into his business, rather than just personally and religiously. Gore always held her cards close to her chest.

"I'm sure she's already looking into things here. Maybe we should let it go," I said.

"When she might have been corrupted already? A big business like this, she could have been told to just ignore it by a friend of Hope's, focus on other leads," Gwen said.

"If you think the police are so easy to corrupt, why do you want to join them?" I asked.

"To change things from inside," Gwen said easily.

I shook my head. "Gore is a good detective, Gwen." She'd proven that more than once.

"You talk to her, then," Gwen said.

"And what are you going to do?"

"Figure things out myself," Gwen said bitterly.

That didn't sound good. "Gwen, don't be unreasonable. I want you to promise you'll tell me if you're planning to do something," I said.

She pressed her lips together and refused to promise anything. After a few moments, she said, "You're not my mother, Linda. So you can stop acting like it."

Well, that hurt, but this was the danger of me having taken Gore's side. "Fine. I'll take you home, then," I said. She was right. She wasn't my daughter, and I couldn't force her to do anything even if she were. Being a mother sucked sometimes.

CHAPTER 21

Kurt texted to say he was coming home early from work, and I started to plan a nice evening together for just the two of us, hoping to repair the damage I'd done by neglecting him for this case too many times already. I made fish tacos for dinner, the first time in ages I'd tested a new recipe. I thought they'd turned out pretty well, judging by their smell and appearance. The bright-purple cabbage stood out against the shredded carrot and the deep-green cilantro, and the fish was nice and flaky—I'd snuck a bite before putting the tacos together.

I jumped a little when the garage door slammed shut, but didn't have the sense of impending doom I probably should have, given what I'd spent the afternoon doing.

"Linda, what in God's name did you think you were doing at Celestial Security today?" Kurt roared.

I put down the plate of tacos and wished I'd nibbled more than a single piece of fish, because the conversation was one that clearly wouldn't end any time soon. Most likely, by the time I got back to these, they'd be soggy, and it was always a shame when good food was wasted because of an argument.

"I went to apply for a sales consultant position," I said,

answering the question directly, even if I knew it wasn't what Kurt wanted.

"I know you don't actually want a job there, Linda, so don't try that garbage with me," Kurt said angrily.

"You don't know that. I've been thinking about getting a job since Samuel graduated," I said. It was mostly true.

"I know that if you were going to get a job, you certainly wouldn't get one at Celestial Security, which you only heard about because of Gabriela Suarez's death. You have no interest in home security systems, and you hate those kinds of sales schemes. You'd rather do just about anything than ask people to buy stuff."

This was all true. Even though he was shouting at me, it was comforting that Kurt knew me so well. "Gwen and I went to find out what we could about the company Gabriela was working for. We wanted to know what she did for them," I said as calmly as I could manage.

"Gwen Ferris went with you?" Kurt demanded.

"You didn't hear that part? Kurt, who did you get your information about this from?" I asked. Had someone reported me? If they had, how had they known I was Kurt's wife?

Kurt looked down at his hands, and I could see him trying to rein in his emotions. He hated being angry, especially with me. "Bishop Hope called me an hour ago," he admitted.

So that's why he'd come home early. "He was angry about me being there?" Only me and not Gwen? Had he recognized my name when he'd checked over things for the day? Did he keep that careful track of the daily workings of the business?

"He couldn't understand why I had sent my wife over to poke into his business concerns when, as a fellow bishop, I could have just asked him for any information I wanted," Kurt said. "Linda, it was supremely embarrassing."

Typical Mormonism. Instead of speaking directly to the woman involved, call up her husband to complain to him about her "embarrassing" behavior.

I pushed away my questions about Greg Hope calling Kurt about me and focused on what was more important. "Kurt, there's something sketchy going on over there." I should have called him when I'd first gotten back to tell him about the creepy temple vibe. But now Greg Hope had been able to tell his version of the story first, and anything I said now would be brushed off. I wished that my husband would assume the best of me, but maybe I hadn't given him reason for that in the last two years of poking my nose into murder cases.

"Linda, if there is something weird happening there, it's not your place to dig into it. You're not a detective. You have no training. You don't just . . ." Kurt sighed. "I'm just afraid for you. I love you and I—I want you to be safe." His anger had drained away, and now he was leaning against the other side of the counter as if he'd deflated. He looked like he might sink into the ground without support.

This was moving at a faster pace than I'd first thought, which was good news for the tacos. "I want that, too," I said, remembering that this was what he'd been saying since last year, and that I'd agreed to do better.

I patted the stool next to me and Kurt came over. To set an example for him, I lifted one of the tacos up and took a big bite. The sauce dripped out onto my hands and then down onto the plate. Its flavor was delicious, and I had to admit, the messiness seemed apropos of the current state of our relationship.

Kurt watched me eat the entire taco before reaching for his own.

We didn't talk again until he was done eating. He looked like a new man by then, and I wondered if he'd forgotten to eat the lunch I'd made for him that morning. He was always grouchy when he was hungry, even if he refused to admit it.

"Making me good food isn't going to end this argument," Kurt said softly when he was finished. "You keep putting yourself in danger even after promising me you'd stop. You're so focused on getting information you forget about your own welfare."

That might have been true other times, but at Celestial Security? "Surely you don't think I was in danger at Greg Hope's company," I said. "Not unless you're worried about me blowing our Christmas budget on an overpriced security system." I was trying to inject humor into the situation, but Kurt was not amused.

"Linda, that's not what I mean. What if—well—someone had felt threatened?" Kurt was acting strangely now, and I didn't know why. Was this just about Celestial Security, or did it have to do with the fire that had almost killed me a few months ago?

"By me?" I said, waving at my squat figure. They might have been annoyed by me, but threatened?

"Linda, I want you to promise me that you won't do anything like that again. Stay away from Celestial Security, all right?" I noticed an involuntary twitch in his right eye, which seemed like a bad sign. I'd never seen that before.

"I'm sorry," I said, trying to sound suitably repentant. And I was sorry I was causing him such stress, which I'd never meant to do. "But Gabriela Suarez deserves not to be forgotten."

"That's why we have police investigating her murder," Kurt said.

I knew that. I'd defended Detective Gore to Gwen myself, but now even I had my doubts as to whether the murderer would be found. The news hadn't mentioned Gabriela since the night she'd been called an unidentified corpse behind a gas station dumpster.

"I'm serious. I want your promise about dropping this. It isn't your place." His tone was urgent and his face flushed.

"Kurt, you don't get to give me orders. I'm doing the best I can, and there's no reason to think I'm in actual danger." Greg Hope wasn't Stephen Carter. It felt like Kurt was just being controlling now, not protective.

"Linda, I'm doing this for your own good. You need to listen to me this time."

"And if I don't?" I asked stubbornly. I regretted it as soon as I said it. What I should have done here was give him the chance to de-escalate.

"If you don't, well . . ." There was only a moment's hesitation before he said, "I'm going to have to call both you and Gwen in for a disciplinary council."

It wasn't at all what I'd expected, and it made me wonder what was going on in his head. I wished I could be more sympathetic to him, but he was using his position to bully me, and I wasn't about to put up with that.

A disciplinary council was usually a first step to excommunication, though it didn't always lead there. Sometimes you got off entirely innocent. Sometimes you were only disfellowshipped.

But excommunication was a drastic measure. It meant removing your name from the records of the church, canceling your temple blessings, your marriage sealings, and every promise for the next life that Mormonism offered. It would sunder me from Kurt, and from my children. Not to mention make it impossible for me to take the Sacrament in church meetings, and disqualify me from holding any calling or even speaking in church.

"You're going to make me and Gwen stand in front of a church court because we're trying to get justice for a dead woman?" I echoed, sure he would take it back once he heard how it sounded.

But he was as stubborn as I was and I saw him swallow and clench his jaw. "Linda, you need to listen to me. I know more about this situation than you think. I'm trying to do what's best for everyone here."

Because he'd spent ten minutes on the phone with Greg Hope, he thought he knew more than Gwen and I did? It had to be more than that, but why wouldn't he just tell me?

"I'm pretty sure I know better than you do what's going on at Celestial Security, and if you think the right thing to do is to try to intimidate me, I wonder if you've ever met me," I said, and walked right out of the kitchen and up to our bedroom. But there were reminders of Kurt's possession of this place everywhere and I didn't want that.

So I stomped down to Samuel's room, then realized the bed was unmade, and I stomped back to the linen closet to get sheets and a quilt, as well as a pillow case. I threw all the bedding onto the bed and then stared at it. It was hours too early for bed.

I waited for Kurt to come in later that night to try to reopen the conversation, but he didn't. And that was odd. He wasn't an arrogant man; he never had been. Something was going on—something that was making Kurt act differently, and I didn't like that I had no idea what it was.

CHAPTER 22

The next day, I remained in Samuel's bed until I heard Kurt leave the house. It was the first time in our married life that I could remember not making him a lunch for work, but I had nothing to say to him that wasn't more of the same from last night.

My cell phone rang just as I headed down for breakfast.

It was Gwen. "Luis Suarez is in Salt Lake City," she said.

It took me a moment to realize she meant Gabriela's husband. But Gabriela had told us he'd been deported. Had she lied to us, or had Luis somehow found his way back into the country? Then I thought about the recent letters I'd seen from him with the Salt Lake City postmark. I'd thought they must have been posted by someone else, but apparently I'd been wrong. I wondered how he'd gotten back into the country after his deportation.

"How did you find him?" I asked.

"I copied all the numbers from Gabriela's phone before we turned it in to the police. This morning, I called the number she had for him and he answered," Gwen said breathlessly.

Gore would be furious about this, but it probably wasn't technically illegal in and of itself.

"I asked him if he had heard about Gabriela's death, and he

said that someone from the church had already contacted him," Gwen went on.

That had to have been President Frost's work. Did he know that Luis was in Salt Lake or had he just assumed that he had kept his old cell phone number?

"How long has Luis been back?" I asked, trying and failing to remember the date from the letter. Kurt had wanted me to keep out of this, but his threat was going to have the opposite effect of the one he wanted.

"I didn't ask him that," Gwen said impatiently.

"I think we should let the police deal with this," I said, aware that I sounded all too much like Kurt had last night.

Gwen made another of her raspberry sounds, which seemed to summarize how she felt about most of my advice lately.

"I'm going down to talk to him and thought you might want to come. You said you'd come with me, no matter what." There was a long pause that made it obvious she was withholding something.

"What's going on?" I asked when the silence continued.

"Well, I may have exaggerated our role a bit to him," Gwen said.

"Exaggerated?" I echoed.

Gwen took a breath. "I told him I was with the police and this was part of the official murder investigation, following up on their initial interview with him."

"Gwen!" The shout was involuntary, though I tried to tone it down. "That's more than an exaggeration." Now she really had moved into illegal territory. She said she wanted to go to the Police Academy, but she kept doing things that could get her kicked out of it. Did she really think no one would find out? If

Detective Gore caught her, there was no reason to think she wouldn't report her and ruin Gwen's plans for her future. What would she do then? She'd already quit her job at Zions.

"I had to take the chance, Linda," Gwen said. "This is for Gabriela. Will you come with me?" she asked softly.

I could hardly let her go down alone. For one thing, I had to make sure that Gwen didn't jeopardize the police investigation in some way. She seemed too hotheaded right now to be concerned about the potential backlash for Gore, but I could keep a cooler head.

"All right," I said.

"I'll be right over," she said eagerly.

I didn't leave a message for Kurt. That would only incriminate us. I felt shaky and a little nauseated as I waited for Gwen to pick me up.

She drove us to a Rose Park address that turned out to be a mobile home park. I didn't know Salt Lake City very well, but this was clearly not the nicest part of town. The houses were too close together, there was graffiti on most of the walls, and the trees and bushes I saw looked pretty badly cared for.

Gwen made sure to lock her car doors after we got out, and we looked around cautiously before moving toward the numbered mobile home that matched what she had written.

It was the middle of the day, I told myself. What could possibly happen?

There was a crash nearby, and Gwen and I both jumped two feet in the air and looked at each other.

"I'm sure it was nothing," I said out loud.

"Yeah, nothing," Gwen said.

She knocked on the door of the mobile home, and we waited

for a couple of seconds before it opened and a Hispanic man who looked to be in his late forties answered the door. He had graying hair and a bit of a stoop.

"I'm Gwen Ferris. We spoke on the phone earlier," Gwen said too quickly for me to intervene and try to protect her. "We're here to talk to you about Gabriela's death." Her tone was clipped and businesslike.

Was that how she thought police officers talked? After a moment, I realized it was an uncanny imitation of Detective Gore and struggled not to smile at the thought. Did Gwen know she was doing it, or was it unconscious? Probably the latter, given her opinion of Detective Gore.

"I'm Linda Wallheim," I said earnestly when Luis looked at me. Would it matter at all if I could say I hadn't lied about being part of law enforcement?

"You want to come in?" he asked. His English was nearly unaccented.

"Yes," Gwen said, pushing against the door.

Luis stepped back, and we were soon in a living room that looked like it was mostly boxes, with no furniture other than folding chairs around a card table near the kitchen.

"I already told the other officers everything I know. Gabriela and I weren't living together anymore. I hardly saw the children," Luis put in. He didn't look upset, despite the loss of his wife just days before. His eyes weren't red or swollen. I admitted the possibility that he was someone who wouldn't let himself break down with emotion because he was trying to be strong, but he looked so coldly neutral it was hard not to be suspicious.

"Why wouldn't she let you see the children?" Gwen asked. "What had you done?"

He put up his hands defensively. "Nothing. I did nothing to the children or to her. I already told the other police officers that."

This conversation was a bit awkward, since Luis assumed we already knew what he'd told Gore or whoever it was who had come to interview him before. Somehow Gwen was trying to make sure he didn't guess how ignorant we were, since then he'd know we weren't the police and send us away.

"You know we could report you to INS again and you'd be deported a second time. Or incarcerated. Is that what you want?" Gwen demanded.

I flinched at this. After Gwen's complaints about the police treating immigrants unfairly, it seemed like she was being deliberately cruel to this man. Did she think he deserved it simply because he was male? Maybe so. I wasn't sure she saw her own prejudice there, though.

"No, of course not," Luis muttered, cowed.

"Then tell us the truth. Why weren't you and Gabriela back together?"

"We were having problems," he said. "In our marriage. She was unhappy with me. I worked too much and she said I didn't bring home all the money I earned. She said I owed it to the children." His chin had lifted a bit in defiance at this.

I'd seen how poor Gabriela and her children were, how desperate for food. It was hard for me to feel sympathy for Luis if he'd been standing in the way of more security. No wonder Gabriela had thought of him as a bad husband.

"We know you're lying," Gwen said, her voice low and threatening. "You might as well tell us the truth so we can consider you a cooperating witness."

The official-sounding language seemed to work on Luis. He glanced away, ashamed. "I've been back in the country since September, not two weeks like I said before."

"And?" Gwen said, pressing him for more. "What else?" She was automatically treating everything he as he suspect. Again, I wondered if this was simply how she thought the police acted.

Luis hesitated, then said, "I wasn't out of state driving the truck, like I said before. When Gabriela was killed."

"I know that already," Gwen said shortly in a tone would have made me believe her if I hadn't known it was all fake. "So where were you?"

"I was here, looking for a better job. But I swear to you, I never went anywhere near Gabriela or the children." He was clenching and unclenching his fists and shifting back and forth, a bundle of nervous energy.

"And how can you prove that?" Gwen asked.

He threw up his hands. "I don't know. I was alone! I'm by myself most of the time. How was I supposed to know anything was going to happen to her?"

I felt sorry for him, but I was also trying to understand what kind of man he was and what his relationship with Gabriela had really been like.

"Did you call her that day?" Gwen demanded.

He thought for a long moment, and I could see a small tremor on one side of his face. He was genuinely frightened of us, and I felt terribly guilty for this whole charade. Had Gore seen through him? Was she still investigating him? If so, were we ruining things for her? That was a real possibility, not to mention her finding out we'd been here, impersonating police officers. We needed to leave sooner rather than later.

"I don't remember," he said finally. "I might have, but if I did, it was about the children. I was trying to get her to let me take them for the weekend. They're my children, too." His tone was just short of whining.

My pity for the man ended. Gabriela had been a good mother, of that one thing I was sure. She'd also been struggling to keep her children fed. If she thought Luis was bad for them, there was a reason for that.

"I thought you said the only problem was you not earning enough money. If that's the case, there's no reason for Gabriela to keep you from the children," Gwen said.

At this, Luis simply looked away and refused to answer.

I looked at Gwen, trying to communicate to her that it was time to go.

"Were you angry with Gabriela?" she went on.

"I was angry with her, but I loved her. Why would I kill her?" he insisted.

"Maybe you had a fight and you did something in the moment that you regretted later?" Gwen suggested.

He shook his head firmly, but I had no idea if I believed anything he said anymore.

"All right, why don't you tell me about Carlos?" Gwen said.

The other name we'd seen on Gabriela's phone. It was just another guess on her part, but apparently it hit the mark.

Luis's face suffused with red, and he turned to the wall and slammed a fist into it. The loud thump was enough to make me flinch. When he turned back to us, his hand was bruised and bloody, and he held it close to his chest, so it must have hurt, but the expression on his face was still anger, not pain.

It seemed this was the real reason Gabriela had kept him from the children and had thought him a bad husband. He was clearly violent.

"You knew about Carlos and Gabriela, then," Gwen said. How had she put together that there was something going on between Gabriela and Carlos? I hadn't thought of that. Then again, Gwen had seen Gabriela a lot more than I had. Maybe there was something in their interaction that had just clicked in her head.

"She told me that there was someone new in her life," Luis said, his voice low and rough. "When I came back and wanted to live with her and the children again. He ruined everything."

"And you were angry. You went up to her apartment to talk to her about it, but she insisted you go to the Pro-Stop gas station nearby so the children didn't hear you yelling." Again, this was all Gwen's guesswork. But it didn't make sense of the message Gabriela had left for Gwen, did it? Why wouldn't she have just said her ex-husband was back in town and was threatening her physically if that was what had happened? Why be so mysterious and vague?

"No, I never went to talk to her in person. I told you, I was here all that day. I spoke to her in the morning, and she told me she would talk to me next week about visiting with the children more regularly."

That sounded extremely suspicious to me.

Gwen said, "I don't think so. You argued about her relationship with Carlos, didn't you? She's your wife, married to you in the temple. She's sealed to you. She belongs to you, and so do the children."

Gwen seemed to be goading him, which I thought was an extremely bad idea, considering what he'd done to the wall. I'd wanted to get out of here for some time now, but she wasn't paying attention. Luis was distracting her.

His fists and jaw clenched, he said desperately, "She said she wanted a divorce. I didn't want a divorce, but she said she could get one because I'd abandoned her and the children. Even if I didn't want to leave them, even if I was back in the country."

I had no idea what the legalities of divorce in such a situation would be, but if Gabriela had wanted one, she could probably have gotten one. Her Mormon temple sealing wouldn't have made much difference in a legal matter.

Finally, Gwen looked at me and I motioned to the door urgently. She sighed. "Did you kill your wife, Mr. Suarez?"

"I didn't kill her. I loved her," he insisted.

What else could we do? It wasn't like we had the power to arrest him or hold him in interrogation. We'd have to leave that to the real police officers.

"We'll be back to talk to you again," Gwen said, pointing at him.

Luis looked away and said nothing.

We let ourselves out of the mobile home.

We sat in the car for a few minutes before Gwen started it.

"That was dangerous," I said.

"I know. I was terrified the whole time," Gwen said. She put her head down and took a few big breaths, then settled a shaking hand on the steering wheel. "I felt like I had to do it for Gabriela."

"Well, I don't think you have to keep putting yourself in danger like that," I said. And yes, I could hear the echoes of what Kurt had said the night before. But Greg Hope was not Luis Suarez. And as soon as I thought it, I knew that I was making unfair assumptions myself. That Greg Hope was a white-collar criminal, so he wouldn't hurt me, but Luis, a Mexican immigrant, would.

Gwen shook herself from left to right, then took a couple of deep breaths and moved forward.

"What did you think of his story?" she asked in a cool, professional tone. "Do you believe him?"

"I don't know what to believe at this point," I said, watching to see if there was more emotion beneath the surface than she cared to show. With her history of trauma, I couldn't imagine that witnessing violence like that was easy for her.

Gwen absently jingled her car keys in her hand. "Well, I guess we should head home," she said.

CHAPTER 23

We were headed back to the main road when Gwen said, "I can't believe Gabriela was having an affair. Do you think we should go talk to Carlos Santos now that we know about him and Gabriela?"

I sighed, not at all sure we should trust Luis on this. But of course Gwen wasn't going to give up that easily. "Do you even know where he lives?" I asked.

"Yes, since he's in the Spanish ward." She glanced through the LDS app on her phone and said, "He lives in the same building as Gabriela. Which would have been very convenient for them."

It seemed like a snide thing to say, and made me think again about Gwen's own implicit racial biases.

"Let's not pretend to be police officers this time," I said, since I clearly wasn't going to be able to talk her out of this.

"You think if we just tell him we're nosy friends of Gabriela's, that will make him want to open up about an affair?" she said sarcastically.

"I just think we can ask questions without lying." We could let him draw his own conclusions about who we were, as long as we didn't do anything illegal.

"All right, fine, we'll try it your way this time," she said with heavy skepticism and kept driving.

After Gwen parked, we climbed up to Carlos's apartment on the second floor. She knocked on the door.

It was immediately answered by a very handsome man in a white shirt and tie who could have passed as a Mormon missionary, except for the fact that he didn't have the traditional white-on-black nametag. Instead, his nametag was black on white and read CELESTIAL SECURITY instead of THE CHURCH OF JESUS CHRIST OF LATTER-DAY SAINTS.

"Hi, do you remember me?" Gwen said cheerfully.

He gave her a blank look, which I guess meant she hadn't made an impression on him at the Spanish ward.

"Well, I'm Hermana Gwen Ferris from the ward. This is Linda Wallheim. We need to ask you some questions about Gabriela Suarez," she said. Her manner made it sound official, but at least she'd taken my advice about not impersonating the police.

Carlos hesitated. "I have a few minutes before I have to get to work," he said.

Tall with muscular shoulders, he had a large Roman nose and a strong jaw, piercing eyes and long, framing eyelashes. He seemed male-model-perfect. I could see why a lonely young woman might've been tempted into an affair with him.

We sat down on his living room couch, which was made of brown leather and seemed new. Though this had the same floor plan and square footage as Gabriela's apartment, his seemed in much better shape. The carpet was less worn, as were the kitchen flooring and appliances.

"You work for Celestial Security?" Gwen asked.

"I do. I'm a sales consultant."

And he was just heading off to work now—I guess it made sense that he kept evening hours, since there would be no point in knocking on doors during the day when everyone was out. On the coffee table, I could also see a tablet like the one Serena Matthews had used on me. I repressed a faint shudder at the thought of the fake temple décor of the head-quarters.

"How long have you been working for them?" Gwen asked, still sounding quite official.

"Three years now."

"And are you happy with your position in the business?"

"I've been promoted twice and I'm making a very good living now, so yes, I'm quite happy," Carlos said.

"Was Gabriela also in sales?" Gwen asked.

I hadn't thought there was another way to find out this infor-mation, but obviously, there was.

"No," Carlos said.

"What did she do at Celestial Security, then?" Gwen pressed.

"Well, she wasn't in sales," he said again.

I could see Gwen looking away, too embarrassed to ask directly about the affair, so I jumped in with, "Did you know that Gabriela was afraid of being accused of embezzlement by the bishop?" I said. This was a part of the case that still didn't make any sense to me.

Carlos went rigid in response. "What?"

"She called us a few days before her murder and said that Bishop Hope was threatening to call the authorities about money the ward had given her," I explained. I still didn't know who she'd been talking to when I overheard her at the church talking about "Obispo Hope," but it could have been Carlos.

Gwen was giving me an impatient look. She didn't seem to think that this part mattered, apparently.

"I think she must have misunderstood," Carlos said. "The bishop would never have done that to her."

"Oh?" I was skeptical. This was the second time someone had suggested that. But Gabriela's English had been good. "He was paying her a regular amount each month, not just reimbursing her for expenses. Why would he do that? That's not standard procedure for the Mormon church at all."

"Well, she needed a lot of financial assistance for her children, with her husband being gone. Bishop Hope knew that," Carlos said. He wouldn't look me in the eye.

"I suspect most of the members in the Spanish ward need a lot of assistance, but Bishop Hope couldn't possibly have given them all that amount of money each month," I pointed out.

Now Carlos just stared. "I'm not a member of the bishopric. I only work for the man. I wouldn't know why he does what he does in church matters."

It was true, and frustrating. I couldn't press him any further on that.

I nodded to Gwen to indicate it was her turn and hoped she'd be gentle.

"What can you tell us about Gabriela? How did you two meet?" Gwen began.

With a look of confusion, Carlos said, "We met last year when she moved in. She was a single mother with three children and we both worked at Celestial Security. We were friends."

"You were more than friends, though, weren't you?" Gwen said in a low voice, as if guaranteeing confidentiality for whatever he told her.

It was enough to change Carlos's attitude from suspicion to guilt. "It wasn't what you think," he said quietly.

"What was it, then?" Gwen asked.

"She was lonely," Carlos said. "She had such an enormous burden of responsibility on her. And she needed someone who understood. That's all I was doing. Listening to her when she needed to talk."

"Until you weren't just friends anymore," Gwen put in.

Carlos sighed. Then he looked up at Gwen. "I didn't kill her," he insisted. "I loved her."

"Did she say she was breaking up with you? Going back to her husband?" Gwen asked, leaning forward with urgency.

Carlos murmured something, possibly in Spanish. I didn't understand it.

Apparently Gwen did, and she followed up with, "Luis wasn't anywhere near here when Gabriela was murdered, but you were. Why should we believe you had nothing to do with it? What about your alibi?"

Carlos cringed. "I was at home. My mother told the police that already, didn't she?"

"Your mother loves you," Gwen said. "She would lie for you in a heartbeat."

My stomach fell at this, but it might well be true. I would probably lie for any one of my sons if he were under investigation for murder.

I saw something change in Carlos's expression. He hardened, and then his defensive stance changed. He looked straight at Gwen, his shoulders straight.

"Did Luis tell you that he physically abused his wife? Did he tell you that Gabriela was terrified of him? That she was relieved when he was deported because it meant she was safe?" he demanded.

"He didn't admit to anything like that," Gwen said, not realizing her mistake until after she'd spoken and glanced at me in regret.

"Of course he wouldn't," Carlos said passionately. "That would make it obvious who killed Gabriela."

Damn. Now Carlos knew we'd interviewed Luis, meaning he was here in town, and it was easy for him to point to the other man for the murder. We were making this too easy for him. Gore would never have let him take control of this interview like that.

Gwen asked, "Do you know this for a fact? Had you ever seen Luis hurt Gabriela?" I could hear her breathing faster. She was too invested in this.

"No, I never saw him in person at all. He was gone by the time I knew Gabriela and it's good for him that he was, because I would have made him sorry for what he'd done to her," Carlos said, and I thought I heard real anger there.

"So she said she was afraid of him hurting her? What else did she tell you?" Gwen asked.

"It wasn't just what she said. It was how she acted all the time. Like a string pulled tight, ready to snap." He put his thumb and forefinger together, then released them with a flick. He went on, "She told me a story once, when it was late and she was vulnerable and upset. She said that on Christmas Day the year before, he had chased her out of their old apartment with the knife he'd been using to cut up the turkey. She had to beg the apartment manager for help."

I thought about the Gabriela I had known, independent and capable. Was it possible she'd made up a story like this just to gain Carlos's sympathy? Or could he have made it up himself? As a salesman, he must be used to saying whatever got him what he wanted from a customer. But I believed him instinctively.

"What happened after that?" I asked as Gwen collected herself. She had a hand over her heart. I was sure the story had hit close to home for her, a domestic abuse victim herself.

Carlos spoke with emotion, a born storyteller. "She had to sneak back into the apartment and get the kids out through the window. Luckily, it was on the ground floor. She was that terrified of Luis." He looked back and forth between me and Gwen.

Luis had clearly been hiding something from us. This could be it.

Carols continued with a dramatic gesture, "She said he was completely unpredictable. Sometimes he would be a loving husband and father. Then suddenly, he would act like a maniac. She didn't know what set him off, but she decided she couldn't take chances anymore. He might hurt or kill her, and then what about their kids?"

I considered Gabriela's position in the United States. Without documentation, she might have felt like she was better off not asking the police for help in case her legal status came up. And the increased raids from ICE in the last couple of years wouldn't have made her feel safer, either. People without citizenship could be treated terribly, and had so much more to fear.

"So, you're saying that Luis made up the story about Gabriela having an affair?" Gwen asked, back in control of her emotions.

Carlos waved dismissively. "Of course he made it up. I'll tell you the same thing I told Detective Gore. He's the one you should be looking at for Gabriela's murder. He wanted his kids back, and Gabriela was standing in his way."

That part I believed, but the rest I didn't know about. Carlos and Luis both seemed like potential suspects, but Gore hadn't arrested either of them so far. I wished I knew what her take on the case was.

We stood up and thanked Carlos for his time, then left.

CHAPTER 24

"**D**o you believe Carlos?" Gwen asked as we sat in the car and stared at the apartment building.

"About Luis abusing Gwen?" I said, trying to sort through my impressions. I knew I'd liked the handsome, well-dressed Carlos immediately, and that I'd seen Luis put his fist through a wall. Was I being led by the nose to certain conclusions? Could Carlos be the murderer here? Could *he* have been the abusive one? Or could it have been both of them, and Carlos just covered his tracks better? "I don't know."

She nodded, then said, "Carlos was a little too slick. But I can't see that he has any potential motive to kill Gabriela."

"I thought Gabriela was killed for something work-related, but I guess it could just as easily be because of something in her personal life," I said, remembering how bright Carlos's eyes had seemed whenever he spoke of Gabriela.

Gwen tapped her fingers on the steering wheel, then changed the subject—or seemed to. "Do you ever wonder what you'd do if your husband was away for a whole year? I mean, how you'd survive?"

"I'm not sure what I'd do without Kurt," I said honestly. He was my rock, my foundation. It would be more devout of me to say that Jesus was my rock, or the church was, or something like that, but it wasn't true. It was Kurt. Which was why I had such a hard time when we were at odds with each other, like we'd been last year. And right now, considering what had gone on last night.

"People always say that. But you'd have no choice but to survive. I mean, you'd figure out some way to get along, wouldn't you? Women whose husbands are in the armed forces run their households alone for years sometimes. And people have to move on after a loved one's death, too," Gwen said.

What was this about? Was she trying to imagine her life without Brad? I wasn't sure I should help her to do that.

"I guess you do what you have to do if there's no other choice," I said lamely, wishing I was able to come up with something more than trite phrases.

"But if it wasn't death, only a long separation, would that make it different?" Gwen said.

"I think it would make a huge difference," I said. "If you knew you were only waiting, you could hold on."

"What if Gabriela had thought she'd never see Luis again? If she had, could you forgive her for having an affair?" Gwen asked, veering back to the case. Or maybe she'd never left it, and it was only me who had.

"It's not really about me forgiving her, is it? It's about understanding what happened," I said.

"But maybe Gabriela didn't see what she had with Carlos as an affair. Maybe she needed him for emotional support, or just . . . physical satisfaction," Gwen said, unconvincingly trying to make casual, adulterous sex sound less crude. "Maybe she would eventually have gone back to Luis. He was her husband, after all. Sealed to her in the temple." Her tone was cold at this.

"Maybe." I shrugged. "You knew her better than I did." I couldn't help but think about the mother I'd gotten to know, hovering over her children, always concerned for them first. It was difficult for me to think of her jumping into bed with a handsome coworker. Then again, I was a mother and also a sexual being. My kids might not be able to imagine my sex life, but I had one.

"If Luis really was abusing Gabriela, why wouldn't I have noticed the signs?" Gwen asked, and I wasn't sure who she was angry at now. Herself? Her father? Luis? Even Gabriela?

"I don't know," I said. "Maybe she was good at hiding it." But I wondered if Gwen had become close with Gabriela because of a subconscious realization that they were vulnerable in the same ways, both abuse victims. It would make sense.

"Luis didn't sound like he felt guilty about anything. He saw Gabriela as the one in the wrong. He was the long-suffering righteous husband and father."

Now I wished I'd taken Luis's letters to Gabriela from the apartment. Gwen's Spanish would have been good enough to read them. But I hadn't thought they were important then.

Gwen pulled out and started driving. I thought she would make another speculation about Gabriela, but instead she asked suddenly, "Do you think my father thought he was right to have done what he did to me? Or do you think he just didn't care what was right?"

Oh, no. This wasn't the time for a conversation of this gravity, but I couldn't evade the question. I wished she hadn't started driving already. "I think your father is an evil man, and I'm not sure why he did what he did, or if that matters," I said.

"Hmm," Gwen said. She was shaking slightly. If I wasn't watching her so closely, I might not have noticed.

"Gwen?" I said. Should I offer to take over the driving? Or just suggest she pull over for a few minutes?

"I'm fine," she insisted, and kept going.

Since distracting her from the road with more talk about Gabriela's situation was probably unwise, I tried to keep quiet and let her focus. I hoped that I'd been right to come with her to see Luis and then Carlos—that I was helping her by being there, not making things worse.

Finally, the shaking was bad enough that she couldn't keep going. She yanked the wheel to the right and lurched to a stop, then leaned over the wheel and started to breathe deeply. I reached over to touch her, but she jumped and glared at me, so I put my hands up and stayed away.

"Gwen? Do you want me to drive?"

She grunted at me and I wished I could do something for her. There were tears on her face, but she wasn't sobbing. They just streamed down until she took a breath and brushed them away. She held her head high and seemed to be trying to come back from wherever she had gone for a while. To the past, to her father, I assumed.

"It feels sometimes like no one cares about us. I mean, women who are trying to recover from abuse. The church doesn't want to see us. Everyone wants us to be healed by the Atonement," Gwen said bitterly, staring out the windshield. "So they can comfortably not have to hear our pain."

I reached over the seats and patted her leg. It was awkward, but I had to do something to show her I was here for her. "I'm sorry," I said softly. It was one thing I'd learned from Georgia's death. People never knew what to say, but it was quite simple. "I'm sorry" was always right.

"I wonder sometimes if I had children if I'd hurt them—not the way my father hurt me, but in some other way," she went on, sagging back in the seat a little. "If I couldn't help it because I'm damaged, not normal." She turned her head and glanced at me for just a moment before settling her gaze on the mountains again.

"You wouldn't do that," I said reassuringly. After what had happened to Gwen, I was sure she was the last person who would hurt a child.

"How can you be so sure, when I'm not?" she asked. She looked at me searchingly now, and I knew it was important for me to give her an answer.

"Because your father made you doubt yourself, and I can see you more clearly," I said, feeling as if the answer hadn't come from me, but from above. I hoped it was what she needed to hear.

She had let go of the steering wheel entirely and her hands were unsettled in her lap.

After a moment, she said, "I look at someone like Gabriela and I think—it's likely she was abused, and yet she was still a good mother. Maybe it even made her a better mother, more likely to listen to and empathize with her children."

"Maybe," I said skeptically, thinking again that Gwen wasn't my daughter, but I wished she was. I wished we had the kind of connection that meant I knew what she needed and could provide it. And, deep down, I also wished that I hadn't lost Georgia and wasn't always trying to find someone to take her place in my heart.

"But I'm not going to be a mother. I'm not going to have children. So what's the point of all my pain?"

I had no answer for her. I didn't know why we suffered. Wasn't

this the great question of theodicy? How could a good and righteous God allow such evil and suffering in the world? I moved
my hand to grasp hers.

I said, "I don't know. I only know that you're good in your own
way, Gwen. Despite everything you've been through, you're still
trying to help other people. That's why you got involved in the
Spanish ward. It's why you became friends with Gabriela and
other people here. And it's why you want to find justice so much
on this case." Even if her prejudices might be getting in the way.

I patted her again. "Gwen, I want you to know that I admire
you enormously for changing your life. You're giving up a lot to
go to the Police Academy. You had a comfortable job, a comfortable life. But that wasn't enough for you. You couldn't just sit and
let your life be easy. You had to do more." If I said it enough times,
would she believe me?

She let out a long sigh and let go of my hand, looking out the
windshield again. "Thank you, Linda," she said after a moment.
She seemed steadier now as she started to drive again, back up
the hill toward our neighborhood.

CHAPTER 25

At home, I thought about Thanksgiving. It was too early to start making pies, but that was what I wanted to soothe myself right now. Flaky, rich pie crust with smooth, creamy pumpkin filling inside. Since it was time to make dinner, I poured my pie craving into a savory recipe: chicken pot pie.

The divine buttery smell soon filled the house. When Kurt got home, the pot pie was just ready to come out of the oven. If I do say so myself, it looked magnificent, the crust a nice golden-brown. The crimping along the edges had stayed intact, and there wasn't a hint of a spill in the oven.

I suppose I could have made a salad to go along with it, but there were peas and corn and potatoes inside, and those counted as vegetables for the meal, right?

"Impressive," Kurt said when he saw my masterpiece emerge.

I bustled around to get plates and silverware on the table, plus glasses and a pitcher of water. By then, the pie had cooled down enough to eat, and I gestured for him to sit.

He seemed nervous, and I was sure he was wondering what revenge might be waiting for him for threatening me with excommunication. I served up the pie and took a few bites to show him there was nothing wrong—with the pie, at least. Then he ate, blowing quickly on each bite before devouring it. About halfway through his first slice, he looked up at me and said in a humble tone, "I'm sorry about what I said before about calling you and Gwen in for a disciplinary council. Forgive me?"

"Forgiven," I said easily. But it wasn't really that easy. It never is.

"Are you going to tell me what you did today?" he asked. He had an uncanny sense of when I was nosing around in a police investigation. I wasn't going to fall for it. But on the other hand, maybe he could help me, even if he didn't know he was.

"Can I ask you about your bishop interviews?" I said. Kurt constantly conducted interviews within the ward—there were the annual youth ones, the ones for a temple recommend, or those for extending a calling. He knew a lot about people lying to try to look better to him.

Kurt's eyes narrowed. "Why?" he said.

"Just curious," I said nonchalantly. "You do them all the time, but we've never really talked about them."

He shrugged. "All right," he said before another mouthful of pot pie.

"Do people lie a lot in official interviews?" I began.

"Well, sometimes, but not too often," he said after a pause.

"But how do you know?" I asked.

"We're not talking about how I know that you're lying to me, are we?" Kurt asked. "Because that's simple. I know your tells after all these years. Like biting your lower lip and looking away from me."

I wasn't biting my lip, though he made me put up a hand to check and see. "We're not talking about me!" I said.

He took another bite of pot pie, then pointed his fork at me.

"All right. Sometimes it's body language. They fidget or tap their feet, or even shake their heads when they speak."

"So what do you do then?" I asked. His interviews were official, but certainly not at the level of a police interrogation. He had to rely on people's desire to tell the truth, to confess. I could learn from his techniques since I wasn't the police, either.

"Well, it depends. I try to get them to understand that I'm there to help them. They usually open up after I assure them that the point isn't punishment, but easing their pain and helping them along the path back to God. My point to them is that God knows the truth, and that lying to me is useless. It just makes it harder for them to move closer to exaltation and the celestial kingdom."

I offered an encouraging hmmm at this.

"But there are some kids who only see the short-term rewards of lying, which is that they don't have to deal with repenting and how difficult that is." He took two more quick bites. I accepted that as a compliment.

"Or the shame of admitting to doing something wrong in the first place," I added.

Kurt nodded at this. "Some of them are afraid I'll tell their parents, and no matter how many times I promise them otherwise, they won't budge."

I raised my eyebrows. "But you do tell their parents, don't you? If you think it's important for them to know."

"Well, with minors, I sometimes feel like I have to call other people in to help. It's my duty," Kurt said. A Mormon bishop didn't have the same rules for confidentiality in confession that a Catholic bishop did, although they were still supposed to keep sins secret. I'd heard about the truth being spilled in meetings with other leaders who could "help" with a problem, but I think Kurt had so far tried very hard not to let this happen.

"Anyway," I said, trying to get him to keep going.

"But adults are different. My responsibility to them and to the church is more straight-forward, so if they lie to me, I can respond directly," Kurt said more carefully. He was only toying with his second serving of pot pie now, which seemed a disservice to my creation, but I could always make more. This conversation was important.

"You mean you call them out on it?" I said.

He tilted his head to the side. "Yes, I do. And I'm not always nice about it. The consequences for certain sins can be more serious for adults than for teens because of the covenants they've made in the temple, so I'm less sympathetic about any lying. I expect adults to have learned to admit wrongs a little more easily and to be willing to accept a little pain to deal with a long-term fix."

I wondered if that was fair. Were adults really better able to deal with guilt and pain than children and adolescents? "Is it harder to catch adults lying?" I asked.

He thought for a moment, putting down his fork at last. "I think so. Most who would bother lying are very practiced at it. They've chosen it as a way of life, and they rarely have the same kinds of tells."

A reminder that I wasn't good at lying. "Is that a compliment?" I asked.

He laughed, then went on, "Or they've been lying to themselves for so long they don't know the difference between truth and lies anymore."

"Then what do you do?"

He sighed and ran a hand through his hair. "It's tricky. For one, when I'm in a situation like that, I generally have other incriminating information. From another family member, for instance."

I imagined the situations Kurt was talking about and began to feel sick. Spousal abuse, child abuse, affairs, embezzling money . . . and if Kurt had seen these sins, it meant people in our ward were guilty of them. Some really were crimes, not just sins. I went cold, wondering if Kurt had ever had to call the hotline the church advertised to help bishops deal with criminal situations in their wards.

He leaned back in his chair, tone distant. "If I'm getting contradicting information, I press them on the details, and there's usually a tipoff that they're holding back something I know about from other sources. When I point it out, they try to talk around it, but their story unravels quickly."

I was silent. I hadn't realized Kurt regularly confronted this kind of thing—we'd really never talked about it.

"But those are all situations when I'm using something other than the Holy Spirit to find out the truth. There are definitely occasions when the Spirit will tell me what I'm hearing is a lie without me having any other information, because of my mantle of bishop," Kurt said.

I understood that spiritual mantle. I'd felt the weight of it descend upon him when he'd been set apart as bishop, and I'd seen it on his face every day since then. I also knew when he was acting as a husband or a father instead. Now that I thought about it, that threat of excommunication had been from my husband, not my bishop. There had been no sense of spiritual stewardship there, just anger and frustration. But why had he done it? He'd apologized without explaining that part.

He glanced down at his plate, then pushed it away, only half finished. After a moment, he said, as if trying to make sure he omitted certain details, "I can't tell you any specifics, but there was a woman who came in. I asked her all the regular temple recommend questions, and at the end, I just knew something was wrong. I didn't know what it was, so I told her I needed to ask the questions again. She gave the same pat answers, but I still felt something was wrong."

"Nothing specific?" I asked. The temple recommend interview was a list of fourteen set questions, from whether we sustained the current prophet and leaders of the church to the Word of Wisdom and general questions about integrity. While anyone could go to a Mormon church, the temple was reserved only for the most worthy, and the ordinances done there included temple marriages sealed forever, baptisms for the dead, and endowments with the highest level of covenants that a Mormon could offer to God.

Kurt shook his head. "I only had this impression of a dark veil over her, and I could see her struggling beneath it. It wasn't one answer to one question. It was all of them, I think." He paused a moment. "Finally, I told her I knew she was lying, and that we were both going to sit there until she told me the truth because I couldn't in good conscience give her a temple recommend."

I leaned in toward him, quite curious now. "What happened?"

"She got up and hurried out of the interview room without another word," Kurt said. He stood up, took both of our plates to the dishwasher, and rinsed them off. I let him go, even though I'd been considering a second piece of pot pie for myself. Apparently, his appetite was gone.

I pressed my napkin to my lip and stood up, following him a few steps to make sure the conversation didn't end. "Really? And you let her go?"

He finished with the plates, then turned around and frowned in thought. "I didn't know what else I could do at that point. I had other appointments, and even if I hadn't, I'm not a detective." He let me see a faint grin. "I can't legally force people to talk to me. They have to do it of their own free will and choice."

"You never found out what was wrong?" I asked, that old curiosity of mine itching at me.

"No, I never did." He stood there, hands searching for his pockets.

"Do you think it was something that had been done to her, or something she'd done to someone else?" I asked.

Kurt shook his head. "I have no idea. She moved away from the ward shortly afterward, maybe in part to avoid talking to me again."

That was a big step to take just to get away from a bishop's questions in a temple recommend interview. I tried not to think of who had moved out of our neighborhood since Kurt had become bishop. He'd been trying so hard not to give me any identifying information.

"Anyway," he said, moving back out of the kitchen and toward the living room where we so often watched television at nights when he wasn't at the church. "That's one of those questions I think I'm going to have to wait to find the answer to until I'm in heaven and I meet with Christ to review my life."

I sat down next to him on the couch, staring at the blank screen before us. I thought about Gabriela and Carlos again and let out a long breath. "What would you do if you weren't sure someone had lied to you, so you'd let it go, but realized later that a sin had been committed you could have prevented?"

Kurt held my gaze, as if to emphasize that this was important and he wanted to make sure I absorbed every word. "I'm not sure I believe that could happen. Linda, I've been called to be the bishop of this ward. That means that unless I close myself off to the Spirit by sin, I'm the designated mouthpiece of the Lord. I believe that He will give me inspiration when it needs to be given. Sometimes hitting me over the head, if He has to."

Wow. I wished God would hit me over the head sometimes. It was what I needed with Gabriela's murder. It felt like Gwen and I were just guessing, wandering around in the dark. Maybe I would be called and set apart one day as official nosy neighbor of the ward so I could get the kind of revelation Kurt seemed to expect.

"You think that works one hundred percent of the time?" I asked.

"Yes, I do," Kurt said solemnly. "That's what it means to be bishop. You have to show up for a lot of boring meetings"—he let out a short laugh—"but the reward is knowing that God has your back and will make sure that you never make a mistake so terrible that other people will hurt for it."

I really wished I believed in God the way Kurt did. But I knew I'd never come back to the same kind of confidence in Him I'd had before my faith crisis in my twenties. I still believed in a beneficent God who loved all of His children and wanted what was best for them. I believed in a God who whispered what was good to us. But I didn't believe in a God who made things happen the "right" way all the time. Surely the world wouldn't look like it did if God was like that.

But Kurt didn't seem to be bothered by that. For him, the world wasn't full of suffering, at least not in the long term. The gospel promised blessings, and he seemed to see them. Was his view wrong? I guess if you put in that many hours a week doing the work, you'd want some kind of guarantee it was worth it, at least for the people around you.

On the one hand, I was jealous of Kurt's worldview. On the other, it seemed naïve and self-centered. As long as men had the true priesthood, God would protect them from terrible things? So if there were mass killings and famines and rapes happening in other parts of the world, it was because the gospel hadn't been preached there yet, so the people had no protections? And that was why it was so important for missions to be opened everywhere, for missionaries to spread the truth of the church and to baptize and ordain men to the priesthood?

I didn't believe in that. No wonder Kurt and I had fought so much over the new policy excluding same-sex married members and their children. If he believed the leaders of the church got their revelations right one hundred percent of the time, then saying the new policy was wrong was akin to saying that they were deliberately going against God. Or even worse, that there were no promises that came with having the priesthood—only regular everyday protections based on fallible common sense and the limits of human knowledge.

I thought about asking Kurt to explain all the news stories about corrupt bishops—ones who stole tithing money, slept with other men's wives, abused teens who came in for interviews, used camping trips as an excuse to molest young boys, and so on. What about their mantles? If the priesthood worked so well, why had we ever made mistakes like denying black people temple ordinances?

Because we didn't understand all things. God would explain it all in the afterlife and we'd see how every part of it was necessary, I guessed Kurt would say.

In a way, I wished I could believe all that. It would be easier to live in Kurt's world. But since I didn't have Kurt's absolute faith, I couldn't be allowed in. I had to stand on the outside, looking in from the cold.

"Linda, you might as well tell me what's going on. I know this has to do with Gabriela Suarez, and it probably has to do with you and Gwen Ferris meddling in things you should be leaving to the police, despite my warnings last night that you should stay out of it and look out for your own safety. So are you going to tell me the truth or not?" His arms were folded across his chest. I supposed he was interviewing me now.

Fine. I didn't like keeping things from Kurt. "Gwen and I went to talk to Luis, Gabriela's husband, and Carlos, a . . . friend of hers."

"And?" Kurt said. I could almost see him putting aside what he really wanted to say and focusing on remaining calm.

"Luis says Gabriela was having an affair with Carlos. But Carlos says that Luis is the liar, and that he abused Gabriela, which made her terrified of him."

"Ah," Kurt said, and took a long drink of water.

"What's that supposed to mean? Aren't you going to help me figure this out?" I was peeved. "You just told me you got answers from the Holy Spirit that were always accurate."

"But Linda, I wasn't there to hear either of these men you interviewed without permission from the police." He implied the criticism rather than stating it out right. "And even if I had been there, the spiritual promise to me as bishop only works for those who are directly in my care. Ward members, that's it. Gabriela wasn't in my ward, nor were these men. I could only make a guess, and there's no reason my guess would be any better than yours."

And this brought us back to church authority and the priest-hood and why men were in charge of everything and women were just supposed to do as they were told.

"I think the church is missing out on half the population who could do wonderful things," I said. Kurt knew I meant women and the reality that they weren't allowed to hold the same priest-hood office as men.

Kurt patted my hand gently. "Women are perfectly capable of listening to God and doing good in their own spheres," he said. Classic church line.

I tried not to be insulted by it and said calmly, "But our callings are so limited. And you know as well as I do that even those callings tend to go to women whose lives fit with the photos in church magazines." Stay-at-home mothers in particular. Gwen Ferris wasn't among them, which meant we could lose her, and I hated that thought, even with her flaws, her lying, her preju-dices and her anger. She had the potential for incredible good, even if she felt forced to take those abilities outside of Mor-monism.

"The church doesn't change to suit individuals who don't fit the mold," Kurt said, seeming perfectly content with that answer.

"Well, maybe it should try. It seems like we're alienating and excommunicating the women who are the strongest and most capable."

I thought of Kate Kelly and Sonia Johnson before her, and Maxine Hanks and Lavina Fielding Anderson and Margaret Toscano and all the feminist Mormon women who had been excommunicated in the past and would probably continue to be excommunicated in the future because they drew outside the lines of an orthodox Mormon woman.

Kurt lifted the remote and turned on the TV. As it booted up, he said, "You should trust the police to find the culprit in this case, Linda. I'm sure they're doing a lot more behind the scenes than you think."

I fumed as Kurt flipped through channels. Of course he would say that. He trusted authority figures all around; he was an authority figure himself. But no matter how good a system was, there were always holes in it, cracks people fell through. And right now, I worried that Gabriela Suarez had fallen through one hole, whether through her husband's abuse or the immigration system, and that Gwen was falling through another. How could anyone blame me for trying to stop that?

Kurt could—and did, I supposed. Even if he apologized, he still thought that he had authority over me. Not just as my bishop, but as my husband. He could receive revelation about me, but it didn't work the other way around.

CHAPTER 26

Saturday night, Kurt and I were watching the news again and saw that a man had been arrested in the death of the local woman whose body had been found behind the Pro-Stop dumpster.

I sat up straight and turned up the volume. "That's Gabriela's case," I said.

There were some photos of the gas station from two weeks ago with police cordoning it off, which we'd already seen. But this was followed by footage of the outside of Gabriela's apartment building.

"Sources say the suspect's name is Carlos Santos, and he is believed to have been in a romantic relationship with the victim," said the red-cheeked, besweatered male reporter. "More details should be forthcoming as the investigation continues."

I was already up and walking toward the front door.

"Linda, there's nothing you can do about this," Kurt said.

My phone buzzed as I debated what to say to Kurt. I pulled it from my pocket and saw it was Gwen.

Before I had a chance to say hello, she immediately started with, "We can't let them do this to him. They're taking the easy way out. Someone should call the news station and demand that the whole situation be looked into more carefully. This is all so . . . so racist."

Her tone was near hysterical. But hadn't she been the one to press Carlos about his relationship with Gabriela? She'd suspected him of the murder, as well as Luis. She should have been celebrating the fact that the police had been working the case in the same direction we had gone all along, but her personal history made her convinced that the police would never do what was right in the end.

"Gwen, calm down," I said, glancing at Kurt since I'd said her name for his benefit. "Why don't you come over and we'll talk about what to do next?"

"I already know what to do. I'm going to talk to Detective Gore." I heard a car door close and an engine start in the background. She was on the move less than a minute after the news had broken, which seemed like a really bad idea to me.

"Gwen, this is an official police investigation. Please don't jeopardize your future at the Police Academy." I had to remind her of the future that mattered so much to her, a future that would help other Gabrielas and other versions of her past self. But it was too late—she had already hung up.

I put down the phone and cursed.

Kurt looked up, concerned, and said, "Should I call Brad?"

I shook my head. I didn't want to make things even worse between them. "Do you mind if I go to the police station and try to talk her out of this? Or at least stay with her while she says her piece?" I assumed that was where she was headed.

"Go," Kurt said with a sigh. I think he was just glad to know where I was going this time.

I also hoped Detective Gore would understand the situation and be willing to help.

I DID MY best to obey traffic laws as I rushed to the station. When I got there, the woman at the front desk recognized me and said, "Are you here to see Detective Gore, as well?"

"Yes," I said, feeling relief that I must have guessed right. "Is my friend already here?"

She nodded and led me to the same room we'd been in before, where the theatrics had been so spectacular. I hoped the conversation wouldn't get as loud this time.

"You didn't have to come after me. I don't need rescuing," Gwen said when the door closed and we were alone. But she already looked like she regretted her decision to come here.

"I just thought I'd lend some support. As a friend," I said gently.

Gwen brushed her hair back, and I realized she'd gotten it cut since I last saw her. It was much shorter than before, almost a bob. Did she think this would suit her better for the Police Academy, or was it an act of rebellion against the more traditional long, feminine hairstyles of the church?

"Gore is a good police officer," I tried to remind her.

"I know you think so," she said, and I didn't know what else to say.

Sooner than I expected, the door opened and Detective Gore walked in. "Ladies," she said curtly. "What can I do for you?"

"I want to know what your evidence against Carlos Santos looks like," Gwen said in a hard tone that implied she had the right to demand it. But she wasn't his lawyer or family member or even his friend. We'd met the man once and spoken to him for only a few minutes.

"I'm afraid I can't give you that information, as it's part of an ongoing investigation," Gore said with a hard, tight smile.

"He didn't kill Gabriela!" Gwen burst out. "He loved her. He had no reason to want her dead. She wasn't going back to Luis. Her husband was abusing her!"

Gore glanced at me, and I struggled not to remind Gwen that Carlos might have been lying. But the truth was, I didn't want to tell Gore that we'd been out interviewing anyone. In particular, I didn't want her finding out Gwen had claimed to be a police officer.

"I would think you, as an aspiring police officer, might trust us to have done enough research and field work to be able to understand this case more clearly than you do from the outside," Gore said sharply, her eyes pinning Gwen to her seat.

I could feel the last meeting's tension rising between them again. Why couldn't these two women I liked and admired so much get along with each other?

"Detective Gore, Gwen knew Gabriela personally. And she has her own history with the law not serving her." I wished I could offer more, but it wasn't my place.

"Knowing the victim personally is precisely why she should stay out of this," Gore said.

"But the past—" I tried.

"I don't know what she went through, but she can't use the past as an excuse to make stupid mistakes," Gore cut me off harshly, staring straight at Gwen.

I winced on Gwen's behalf. I didn't think Gwen was doing that, and it seemed unfair of Gore to refuse to sympathize when she'd had her past determine her career. Things had started off wrong between these two, and I wasn't sure I was in a position to fix them.

"Please, just . . ." I began, but trailed off, not knowing how to finish.

"What do you want to tell me?" Gore said, turning to Gwen.

An attempt at reconciliation, maybe? Though I wasn't sure Gwen could see it that way.

She gritted her teeth and argued, "Carlos's story makes a lot more sense than Gabriela's husband's. Luis should be your suspect. He physically abused Gabriela for years before she got away from him. Once he was back in town, he had every reason to want her dead so he'd get custody of their three children."

Gore's carefully sculpted eyebrows went up. "And you think that I don't already know this information?" she asked. "We're going on evidence here, not who we like best, you know."

Gwen flushed and glanced at me.

I intervened. Maybe Gore would give my opinion more weight? "Everything points to Gabriela being afraid of her husband. Luis has been back in the country for months, and Gabriela chose not to live with him and she kept him from the children. Given that, it seems more likely Carlos is telling the truth, that she didn't want anything to do with her husband because she was afraid of him." Did Gore already know Luis's alibi had been faked, as he'd admitted to us?

"What if I told you—and this is strictly hypothetical, mind you—that Gabriela's relationship with Carlos was more than just a romantic one? And that those complications led to the murder?" Gore said with a sigh. She sounded almost sympathetic, and she looked for a moment at me.

"What kind of complications? What do you mean, more than romantic?" Gwen said immediately.

Gore shook her head. "I can't tell you any more than that.

You'll have to trust me when I say Gabriela and Carlos had many reasons to argue, and that their romantic relationship was only one of them."

"Are you going to try to convince me that Luis didn't abuse Gabriela?" Gwen asked. "I know the man is violent. I—" She cut herself off before mentioning she'd been at his trailer impersonating a police officer, thankfully.

Gore shook her head and then seemed to shut off. There was no more sympathy for Gwen in her tone. "There is no proof of Luis ever having abused Gabriela. No witnesses, no hospital records, no photographs."

"And so he gets off scot-free?" Gwen asked. "Because he scared her so much she never dared to ask for help? That's a very neat arrangement for you. You don't have to do any paperwork on him. You can just turn a blind eye and go on with your day."

Why did she have to antagonize Gore? "Gwen, I think it's time—" I tried to say.

But Gore stood up and said in a tone that brooked no more argument, "I'm going to remind you again that this is about proof. That's how being a police officer works. You have to be able to bring evidence to a court of law and that's what we're doing. What I have proof of is that Luis wasn't at the Pro-Stop the night that Gabriela was killed, and Carlos was. We have a videotape that puts him there within fifteen minutes of the time Gabriela died."

I was stunned that Gore had shared this with us. Maybe she didn't think as badly of us as I'd feared, but Gwen didn't seem to understand the implication of the reveal.

"But Luis could—" Gwen spluttered and then stopped. Her head dropped.

Good, I thought. Maybe she was finally being rational about this and realizing that Gore was on our side.

"Sometimes the simplest solution is the right one," Gore said. She glanced at me again. I really wished that I understood why she'd come by the house before. It felt like there was another conversation going on here that she was trying to explain to me without words.

I put a hand on Gwen's shoulder and felt defeat in her lack of response. "Let's go," I said softly.

She twitched, and there was a brief moment of defiance in her stance as she rose. "Yes, let's go. I'm sure we don't want to waste any more of Detective Gore's time," she said.

"Thank you," Gore said, standing up as well. "There's a lot still to be done to make sure this is properly prosecuted in court. I've got a long night ahead of me—a long series of nights, in fact. All that paperwork," she threw at Gwen.

Gwen didn't respond, though. She was finished.

I walked her out to the car, feeling her weight sag against me as we got closer to it. I had to help her into the driver's seat before getting in on the other side, even though I had to drive my own car back. First, I had to make sure she was okay.

"Do you think she's right? That Carlos really killed Gabriela?" she said.

I didn't know, but said, "He could have, I think."

She let out a sigh. "I guess you're right. But I really liked Carlos, didn't you? I wanted so much to believe in him. And Luis creeped me out." Gwen said. She shivered in her coat and pulled the hood over her head, despite the fact that we were already in the car. She neglected to start it and turned on the heat instead.

I was sure that Luis had reminded Gwen of her own father,

but I didn't draw her attention to it. I thought it might make things worse.

"Maybe we misread them both," I said. It wouldn't be the first time that had happened to me, unfortunately.

We sat there for a long moment.

"What about the kids? Do you think they should go to Luis?" Gwen asked.

I didn't know what to say. I hadn't liked the man, but I really didn't know anything about him, and even if we'd seen him punch a wall, that didn't necessarily mean he'd ever hit his wife or children.

"For now, I imagine they'll stay in foster care," I said. "He's not in the country legally, so I doubt he can prove his parental rights. I hope not, anyway."

Gwen looked up at me. "So you don't think they should be with him, either."

She was right, and that made me uncomfortable.

After a few minutes, she started the car and nodded to the door. I took her meaning and got out. I watched her drive off before getting into my car and doing the same. I hoped she would be all right, but wasn't sure what "all right" looked like for her anymore.

CHAPTER 27

Kurt came home from church earlier than usual and we watched the news again, though I tried to avoid doing that on the Sabbath since it often disrupted the Spirit. I just needed to see if there were any updates on Gabriela's case. The breaking story was that Carlos Santos had confessed to the murder.

"Texts between the victim and Mr. Santos made it clear that they had a romantic relationship, which she had recently broken off to return to her husband and the father of her three children. In addition, video footage of Mr. Santos arguing with the victim at the gas station where her body was found, just minutes before the estimated time of the murder, has been released. Though murder investigations can sometimes take years to solve, it appears that this time, justice has been swift," said the reporter.

This was only part of what Gore had told us yesterday. She'd given more to us than the press, which I reminded myself meant something. She trusted us, or at least me.

"Well, I suppose this will be the end of you and Gwen running around playing detective," Kurt said so smugly that I remained silent.

I looked at my phone, but had received no texts from Gwen since yesterday's debacle at the police station.

"Linda, I want to talk to you about something serious. Are you up for that now that Gabriela's murder has been resolved?" Kurt asked. He'd muted the television and was looking at me with concern.

I paused, nervous that we were going to revisit the absurd conversation about a church disciplinary council for me and Gwen.

But instead he said, "I'm wondering if you'd like to have a calling of some sort in the ward."

"A calling?" I echoed.

"I know that bishop's wives don't traditionally have callings because they're busy picking up the slack their husband's absence leaves behind, but our children have all left home, and I wondered if you wanted the chance to connect more within the ward. It seems like you've felt like an outsider lately, which could be the cause of some of the problems you've been experiencing." He was looking at me earnestly, his arms outspread in an open gesture.

But I shook my head. "We might not have children at home anymore, but there are plenty of family things I need to be able to focus on when you're not around," I said, thinking of Samuel and the phone calls I'd dealt with in just the last couple of weeks. Not to mention organizing the family gatherings in the upcoming holiday season.

"It wouldn't have to be a time-consuming calling. I'm not talking about a presidency or anything like that, but I think you'd be happier if you felt needed," Kurt tried again, still earnest and open.

What was going on here? Had President Frost told Kurt to do something to rein me in? Give the little woman something to do with her time so she stopped asking so many questions and making so much trouble?

"Kurt, I'm not interested in being given a calling where I have to answer to a bunch of other people." Especially men. Especially him.

"In what sense does a Primary teacher have to answer to other people?" Kurt asked.

So that was the calling he was thinking of giving me. I wondered if Shannon Carpenter had suggested this or if it was all Kurt's idea. In any case, I didn't think keeping me out of Relief Society and Sunday School was the best choice for him as bishop. Primary took two hours and would mean I was only in the regular meetings for Sacrament, where I would have no chance to talk to anyone.

I thought I'd been useful to Kurt in helping him understand the heartbeat of the ward. There had been numerous circumstances in the last couple of years where Kurt hadn't known about ward problems: friction in the Relief Society Presidency, financial problems with the Jones family, the near-divorce with the Tates I'd seen coming. If I took a calling in Primary, I'd be out of the loop completely.

"You'd get to teach the lessons the way you want. I thought you'd like this." Kurt said when I didn't answer. He sounded so sincere. He had really convinced himself I'd be happy to say yes, like I might have ten years ago? Or even two years ago? But so much had changed since he'd become bishop.

"I don't want to teach in the Primary, Kurt. I've spent thirty years with children, and I'd like to spend some time with women my own age. Is that too much to ask?" I said, cutting him off.

He took a breath and held it, his arms falling inward as his pose tightened. "All right," he said finally. "If that's what you think is best."

I hadn't realized it until Kurt started talking about Primary, but it seemed the niggling sense of unease I felt about the Gabriela Suarez case was a reminder that I wasn't finished with it yet. I wasn't at peace with Carlos Santos's confession, even with the evidence cited by the news report we'd seen. I just didn't know what to do yet.

CHAPTER 28

I called Gwen the next day and asked her what she thought about Carlos's confession. I worried bringing it up again was a mistake if she'd decided to let it go, but her tone when she answered made it clear she was still upset.

"I've thought about it over and over, and I can't believe it. They must've pressured him into a false confession. When we talked to him just the day before, he insisted he had nothing to do with it. That he was just worried about her."

"Do you think the affair was a lie?" I asked. "Or the abuse story?"

"I don't know," she admitted. "But I think we're going to have to look into it some more."

I was relieved that I wasn't alone in that thought, though I felt guilty.

"We should go back to talk to Luis," I said, wondering if I'd been as prejudiced in my assumptions about him as Gwen had been in hers.

"Exactly what I was thinking, Linda. If we can get him to confess, do you think Detective Gore would change her mind?" Gwen said eagerly.

That wasn't what I'd been thinking, but it worked. "I don't

think she can use anything we find in court," I said. "Even if we record it. But that doesn't mean it won't be useful." If we at least knew the truth, we could start to hunt down the right evidence. That could set not only Carlos free, but Gwen, as well.

A few minutes later, I picked up Gwen. She seemed jittery, full of energy, but she wasn't speaking.

We drove back down to Rose Park, and once there, I had to work hard to keep up with Gwen's quick footsteps as she sped ahead of me. But no one answered the door of Luis's mobile home. I was disappointed, but reminded myself that as a trucker, he was probably gone for days on end.

"I bet I could jimmy the door open," Gwen said, fiddling with the lock.

The mobile home park was eerily quiet, making every sound we made louder in comparison. "Gwen, we came to *talk* to Luis," I said. I didn't want either of us arrested for breaking and entering.

"Maybe we'll find out more without him here. We can look around and see what he's left behind. This way, he can't hide anything."

"I don't know. It seems like a bad idea," I said.

Then the door clicked open, and Gwen nearly fell into the mobile home.

So here we were, trespassing. Again.

Somehow, I had to get Gwen to make it out of this without sabotaging her future career. Maybe once this case was finally over with, she'd be able to go on and finish the Police Academy with a clearer head. She was just too personally involved with this case.

"Are you coming?" Gwen asked.

Well, standing alone out here wasn't going to help. So I went in, trying to suppress an adrenaline rush that betrayed my better judgment.

Inside, Gwen pointed me toward the bedroom area and started looking through the kitchen herself.

The whole place smelled terrible, and I finally found the source of the stench in the back of the trailer. There were old food cartons in grocery bags that hadn't been disposed of, and I saw signs of mice in the chewed-on carpet and bedding, as well as tiny droppings. If I'd needed any further reason to hurry out of here, this was it. I had a phobia of mice and instantly made a full turn to check for one nearby. I couldn't see any, but that didn't mean they weren't there, lurking.

The bedroom had a single mattress on the floor, covered by a handmade quilt. It had once been white and had a faded image of the Salt Lake temple on it. Gabriel and Luis's wedding quilt? It wasn't in good shape now, but the fact that he'd kept it on his bed indicated that even after her death, Luis hadn't forgotten about their marriage. I wondered if this made it more or less likely that he'd killed Gabriela.

I turned and saw a small plastic chest of drawers with only a few items in it. I recognized a set of worn and graying temple garments and averted my eyes, feeling that I'd taken a step too far in invading the man's privacy.

The bathroom had a fairly standard set of over-the-counter medications—cold medicine, cough syrup, and some Advil. A toothbrush and gum-sensitive toothpaste.

I remembered Gabriela's bathroom, without any adult medications, and contrasted it to this one. Despite the fact that there wasn't much in this room either, I still thought Luis

was selfish for not sacrificing everything for his children the
way that Gabriela had.

I looked under the sink and then peeked under the top of the
toilet, just for good measure. Nothing. What had I expected to
find? I cringed at the unconscious assumption I'd just made that
an undocumented immigrant's presence was likely connected
to drugs. Gwen and I were doing the same things she'd accused
Gore of doing from the first.

"I don't think there's anything here," I said, coming out of the
bathroom.

Gwen was on the floor in the living room, looking under the
couch. She was still making quick, jerky motions that seemed
to indicate a disquieted state of mind. "Hey, can you take a look
at the card over there?" she said, pointing to the kitchen
counter.

It was an anniversary card. My heart felt a pang when I
opened it. It was addressed to Gabriela and written in Spanish,
so I couldn't read it.

"Bring it over here," Gwen said. She straightened up a bit and
looked at it as she translated it aloud:

> *Gabriela, I know we have had hard times and I have not
> always treated you as I should have. But I love you eter-
> nally, and I want our family to be together again.*
>
> *Love, Luis.*

"So he admits to abusing her," Gwen said. She stood up and
brushed off her pants.

"I'm not sure that's true." The wording was pretty vague, at
least in translation. I doubted Detective Gore could use that card

alone as proof of abuse in court. Not to mention the fact that we'd contaminated evidence again.

Just then, the door opened, and suddenly Luis was standing in front of us. "You!" he said, eyes wide. He dropped his hands, which had previously been gathered into fists in a defensive stance. "You have no right to be here! You lied to me."

He must have talked to the police after we'd visited and realized that Gwen and I weren't affiliated with them. Had Gore found out what we'd done? If so, what would happen now? She didn't seem likely to take pity on Gwen's inexperience, given how far we'd stretched her sympathies.

"You didn't tell us that you hit Gabriela. Did you hit the children, too?" Gwen asked, her tone hostile.

What was she doing, trying to set him off? We both knew he could be violent.

"I would never hurt my children," Luis said. His hands were in fists again at his sides. I kept staring at them, trying to position myself between him and Gwen.

"You're a liar, too, aren't you? A wife-beater and a liar. Does it make you feel manly to hit a woman who's so much smaller than you? To make your children cringe in fear?" Gwen said, her tone vicious. She was on the balls of her feet, too, ready to move.

It was as if she was confronting her father. This wasn't what I'd hoped in terms of the case setting her free from her old demons.

"Gwen, let's get out of here," I tried to tell her, putting my face close to hers.

She put out a hand and pushed me away, stepping closer to Luis, her body thrumming with energy. "You killed her, didn't you? You never wanted anything else from her. You came back to this country with one sole intent, to take revenge against the woman who had escaped you, embarrassed you, made you feel less like a man."

"No! I wanted to be with her again. I loved her. She was my wife. We were sealed for eternity." Luis's voice was choked. His face was completely red, and I could hear his accent thicken.

"Gwen, let me do this," I said, stepping in because it seemed the only way to get her to calm down. I turned to Luis and said calmly, "You said she was having an affair. But not that she'd agreed to come back to you."

"We were . . . discussing it," Luis said.

Had Gabriela told Carlos she was going back when she wasn't sure? Or had Gore lied to the press? More likely, Carlos was the one prevaricating here.

Gwen stepped around me, impatient with my level tone. She seemed to want another violent reaction from him. "Just admit it! You didn't love Gabriela. You just wanted to keep her under your control. You wanted to make her feel smaller than you, like she needed you and couldn't survive without you. What kind of man are you, Luis? Huh?" She said this last as she took one more step closer to him, her chest colliding with his.

I saw his fist begin to swing, but it moved too quickly for me to stop him. Gwen only had time to let out a cry as it crashed into her face and she was thrown to the ground.

I thought the force of the blow would keep her down there. I scrambled to reach her, but she stood up quickly. She looked triumphant, like she'd proven her accusations.

"I think we all know what kind of man you are now," Gwen said flatly.

I moved toward her then, grabbing her by the elbow to pull her away.

Luis began to sob. "She's gone now—gone. The only woman I ever loved. The mother of my children, my wife." Then he transitioned into Spanish, which I didn't understand but assumed was more of the same regrets.

"Let's go," I urged Gwen, trying to push her to the door. She yelped in pain at my touch, so I dropped my hands.

She glanced at the door, then tightened her jaw and looked back at Luis. "You abused Gabriela, didn't you?" she asked.

He nodded slightly. Well, there it was—the admission we'd wanted. Nothing the police could use, but at least we knew for our own sakes. Unfortunately, it didn't definitively mean anything—not that he'd killed her, or that Carlos was innocent. We were stuck.

"I loved her. I didn't know how to forgive her, but I loved her," Luis cried .

I felt terrible for him, but it was Gwen I was responsible for. "Come on," I said again, trying to block her view of Luis and nudge her toward the door.

Once we were back in the car, I leaned forward and let myself take a breath of relief. We'd both survived that. And this time, I couldn't pretend to Kurt there'd been no danger. Why did I keep doing these things? I'd known Gwen was in a belligerent mood, and I'd come with her anyway.

"I knew it," she said, entirely unrepentant. "I knew he was lying about the abuse."

"But Carlos could still have killed her," I said, taking the wheel. She was in no shape to drive.

She turned away in silence, and I realized she'd fallen asleep against the passenger-side window as I drove us home.

CHAPTER 29

Wednesday night, I went to the church for our weekday Relief Society meeting and was surprised to see Gwen there. Our night was dedicated to a service project for refugees. There were tied quilts to work on and a live auction happening, along with the assembly of hygiene kits for newly arrived refugees and a video playing on repeat in the background about who we were helping and the political, economic, and environmental horrors they had escaped from.

I hurried over to Gwen when I saw that she and Shannon Carpenter were working on the same quilt, which had already been set up on a frame. Three layers of fabric, batting, and more fabric, taut and ready to go. The top was a floral design in dull greens and tans, and I really wished whoever had started it hadn't decided to place the ties in strict lines. If they'd just asked me, I could have shown them how to place the ties in the middle of each flower so they were integrated into the printed pattern. But people didn't think of tied quilts as art. They were functional and only had to be good enough. It's not like anyone would end up displaying these on the wall.

"Gwen, how are things looking for the holidays at your house?" I asked, trying to make casual conversation that would fit better at church than the murder investigation we'd inserted ourselves into. As I spoke, I pulled out a long strand of green yarn from the skein on top of the quilt and threaded a big yarn needle with it.

"Fine," Gwen said, working hard to pull her own thread through the layers of fabric and batting neatly. "Though I don't think we're doing much this year. Brad and I are both just too busy."

"That sounds terrible!" said Shannon Carpenter. "Would you like some help with Christmas decorations?" Her tone was overly eager.

"Um, no, thank you," Gwen said.

"Oh, well, I'm starting a home decorating business for the holidays to help people who don't have the time to decorate," Shannon went on, trying to thread the yarn into the needle without much success. "It's just a part-time thing, so I still have time for my own family, but I thought I'd offer."

"I think it's a great idea that you've decided to start a business, Shannon," I said before Gwen could respond. Considering their last encounter in this room, I figured it was politic. "What gave you the inspiration?"

Shannon paused her quilting, apparently unable to tie a quilt and talk at the same time. "I think it was when I got so many compliments on our house last year. I realized not everyone has my artistic gift."

Well, that was a bold statement. I knew I shouldn't be bothered by it, though. Most Mormon women were all too modest.

"How wonderful for you, making the most of your gifts," Gwen said sarcastically, putting another stitch in.

"Well, people don't value what they get for free, do they?" said Shannon in a clipped tone.

I paused, nervous that we were heading toward a repeat of the ward Trunk or Treat situation, especially if Gwen brought up her work in the Spanish ward that was keeping her too busy for Christmas decorations.

"I just think it's interesting that you think women should stay home and take care of their children, and yet here you are, going out to work," Gwen said, glancing up at Shannon.

Gwen was being so rude to Shannon, but I had the sense it was a defense mechanism. Shannon was the one who'd emphasized her role as the perfect mother in their last encounter, unconsciously digging at Gwen's sorest spot—infertility. Mormon women could be so passive-aggressive when they were crossed.

"I'm still at home with the children," Shannon said, her voice even. "Except for a few days when my husband can babysit them, since he has time off work."

I'd stayed home with my children, but had I been so sanctimonious about my choice? Maybe I had once.

"Too bad not every woman has the same choice," Gwen said. "Like so many of the refugee women who have to work to feed their families and keep a roof over their heads."

Shannon tensed, and for a moment I felt sorry for her. "I'm just earning extra money for Christmas presents," she said. "I don't see anything wrong with that."

"Of course not, since your family would have nothing without that," Gwen said acidly.

"I don't think—" I started.

But Shannon interrupted me, bursting out, "Why are you

constantly trying to put me down? I thought we'd be on the same team, women who are underestimated because we're small."

I stared at her, shocked. It had never occurred to me that she had been looking for validation from Gwen because she saw a physical similarity between them. I suddenly felt ashamed that I'd only ever seen Shannon as a stereotype.

"You and I have nothing in common," Gwen said flatly. It was clear she wasn't ready to forgive Shannon after their feud, despite the indirect olive branch.

"Shannon, why don't you start a new quilt? We're almost finished with this one," I said pointedly, hoping to defuse this situation.

"You don't think you need to turn it again? I don't know if I can reach those last spots in the middle," said Shannon, gesturing at the center of the quilt. "My arms are so short."

I felt that pang of pity again. But Gwen never made me feel sorry for her, and she was nearly the same size.

"I've got this, if you give me a little space." As I spoke, I ducked under Shannon's arm and gently pushed her aside as I did a set of six ties precisely in the center of the quilt.

"All right," said Shannon, stepping back and evaluating our work.

She stared at the folded pile of fabric and batting for the next quilt, and I realized she had no idea what to do with it. She could tie, but she didn't know how to set it all up.

I hurriedly finished the last row of ties between my row and Gwen's and waited impatiently while she finished the last two ties in hers. Then it was time to unpin the ends and unroll the whole thing.

There was a sacredness to this that I could only compare to

the feeling I got at the temple, after taking a family name through from beginning to end: baptism, confirmation, endowment, and sealing.

I could hear Gwen let out a small gasp as she saw the completed quilt, and Shannon didn't say anything at all—she just backed up so she could see the whole effect. Quilting was a dying art. I wondered how many of the women in our ward ever quilted outside of Relief Society meetings. Did even one of them own her own quilting stands? My son Joseph had made a set for me in his metalworking shop at school his senior year. It was possibly the best Christmas present I'd received from one of my sons. I still used them, and it had been a relief to get rid of the old wooden stands I'd had since the boys were babies.

I had good memories of those quilt-making days. My sons had played happily under the quilts for hours as I worked above. Sometimes they'd wanted to sit in my lap, but I'd often managed to quilt while they occupied themselves. I quilted while they played cowboy and Indian, or pioneer, or space army. The quilt above functioned as a fort, a tent, or an oxygen dome. Occasionally, I'd tried to teach them to quilt, since I didn't have a daughter to pass the skill along to, but none of them had been interested beyond basic curiosity.

With Gwen's help, I folded the finished quilt.

"I feel so good inside, thinking about the refugees receiving this," said Shannon cheerfully. "They're going to feel so blessed because of our hard work."

Gwen said, "I'm glad we're doing something to help people in the here and now." It could have sounded critical, but I think she was truly pleased. Sometimes the Mormon church focused so much on afterlife issues, getting names to the temple and making sure people's "work" was done so they didn't roam as solitary souls in spirit prison. But here, we'd all teamed up for a worthwhile charitable project. This was the best part of Mormon sisterhood, bringing together women as different as Shannon and Gwen.

"How did it go?" Kurt asked when I got home sometime later.

"Well, I think there was actually a moment that Shannon and Gwen didn't hate each other."

Kurt rubbed at my shoulders. "I'm glad," he said. "You're too hard on yourself sometimes, you know. You think you should be able to change the world. I actually love that about you."

Did he? I turned around. "I thought you were mad at me about the case." I hadn't even admitted all the latest interference I'd gotten into, but I think he suspected.

"I'm really worried about you sometimes, but could never stay mad, Linda. I admire you too much." He kissed my neck and suggested heading to bed, though it wasn't quite 10 P.M. I didn't think I could sleep, but I wanted nothing more than to be in my own bed with Kurt beside me.

CHAPTER 30

*D*o I need to apologize about Relief Society last night? Gwen texted me the next day.

I think it went all right in the end, I texted back, wondering if this was really all Gwen wanted from me. And then Gwen got to the real point.

I've been thinking about why Gabriela was at the Pro-Stop with Carlos. It makes no sense. Why wouldn't they just have met at one of their apartments? I think they must have gone together to meet someone else.

Damn! I realized we'd forgotten to mention the voice mail message when we took Gabriela's phone over to Gore at the station? Probably because Gore had been so angry with us.

And then another message from Gwen: *I think this has something to do with Celestial Security. She and Carlos were both working there, and that could be what they were arguing about. Gore might not realize how involved Bishop Hope is.*

Gwen was making some serious leaps, but I did believe there was something very wrong at Celestial Security, past what we'd seen there ourselves. They'd ushered us out immediately after Gwen had mentioned Gabriela, and Bishop Hope had even taken the time to call my husband. I texted, *We can't go back there.*

We have to. I'll demand to talk to Bishop Hope and hint that I know something. I can remind him I've seen him at church talking to Gabriela and Carlos.

Would that work? I worried that her pressuring him could be dangerous. Kurt had already hinted that he didn't think it was safe for us to go there in the first place. He hadn't said why, but he'd definitely feared something serious.

Maybe we should talk to Gore about Hope. She might know what's going on, I suggested.

There's no way she would listen to us at this point, Gwen responded. *Or give us any more information.*

With a sigh, I acknowledged she was probably right on that point.

I can go alone. I'll talk to you about it later, she texted.

And I knew then that there was no way I was going to let her go by herself. It was partly me wanting to keep her safe, but also partly a burning curiosity, wanting to see more of Celestial Security firsthand, to understand what Gabriela's role had been there.

Gwen drove over and picked me up. On the ride north, she was absorbed in her own thoughts. Still silent, she parked and put her hands on the steering wheel. They were shaking again, but not as badly as last time. "Ready?" she asked.

I nodded.

We walked in together. I sat down in one of the chairs in the reception area while Gwen went up to the front desk to speak to Debbie, the current receptionist. To my surprise, I heard no argument. After a few minutes, Gwen came and sat down next to me.

We sat there for about thirty minutes without anyone speaking to us. I was trying to make a list of Christmas gifts on my phone, but Gwen was fidgety and went up every few minutes to nudge Debbie.

Debbie seemed unfazed, telling Gwen each time that someone was coming to answer her questions, then asking her to sit and wait again. Finally, a tall blond man in a dark suit, white shirt, and red tie came out, spoke briefly to Debbie, and looked toward us. Of course, I knew immediately who he was. He looked exactly as he had in the heavily posed photos on the Celestial Security website. It hadn't occurred to me I'd never met him before, despite the fact that he seemed to be the key figure in this whole case.

"Sister Ferris, how are you?" he said to Gwen. Then he turned to me. "And you must be Sister Wallheim. So good to meet you," he said, smiling. "I'm Greg Hope." He held out his hand. He was handsome and gracious and said nothing about the last time we'd been here.

Gwen stood as I returned his handshake. I could smell a faint musky cologne on him, but it wasn't overpowering. He stood at least a few inches above six feet, with broad shoulders, but wasn't so muscular that it interfered with the fine lines of his suit, which had to be more expensive than anything Kurt had ever tried on, let alone purchased.

But it was his relaxed manner of speaking and extreme attentiveness that impressed me. I had been determined not to like him from the moment he walked toward us, but even so, I felt unable to turn away from his attention. When his eyes met mine, I couldn't detect a note of falseness.

"I understand you have some questions about poor Gabriela," he said, spreading his hands in a welcoming gesture. "You must know I was devastated to hear about her passing. We at Celestial

Security will truly miss her impeccable work ethic and sunny nature. I can only take solace at the thought that our justice system has found the criminal responsible for the gap left in the world by her absence."

It was a pretty speech, and one that seemed to flow so genuinely from his lips. I glanced at Gwen and saw that while her own lips were pursed, she wasn't reacting negatively to this. Good.

"We want to know what her role was here on your workforce," I said bluntly.

Hope added, "Ah. I have nothing to hide, here or anywhere else."

Gwen rolled her eyes at me, but there were no signs she was about to retort.

"I'll show you around. Come, walk with me," Hope continued. He waved a hand at Debbie, who pushed a button beneath her desk to open the glass doors behind her.

He led us through them, narrating as he went. "This is the call center. We have people here twenty-four hours a day, every day of the year, to make sure that any breaches in security are dealt with." There were some twenty desks here, all close together with cubicle walls between them. Two or three women were on calls, but the rest were typing or simply waiting. All of the women there were Hispanic.

"Did Gabriela work here?" Gwen asked.

"No, but as I said, I wanted to show you everything."

Gwen looked at me and made a face. I couldn't argue with her. This felt like no more than a distraction.

"And back here," said Greg Hope as he kept walking through another set of doors, "is our packaging center."

This looked far more industrial. The lighting was bright, and there were massive long tables lined with men and a few women—again, all Hispanic—dressed in white jumpsuits and sporting huge goggles that covered their faces.

"Gabriela worked here in the packaging center twenty hours a week—or as many as she could manage with her daycare schedule. Of course, sometimes she had to stay home with sick children, but we understand that here. The pay is the same, no matter how many hours you work. As long as you're making the effort, we reward you for it," said Bishop Hope warmly.

So that answered our questions about why Gabriela had the same salary every month, $1,000. Or did it? I did a quick math calculation in my head. If she worked twenty hours a week, she was getting decidedly more than minimum wage in Utah. Those terms were very generous—suspiciously generous, in fact, if she often worked fewer than twenty hours. What was going on here?

"You can really afford to pay people who don't work?" Gwen asked.

I tensed, but Hope didn't seem offended.

"I like to think of it as paying for them holding a space for work in their lives," said Hope easily.

Gwen looked at me, and I could see her jawline tighten at his tone. Uh oh. Now was the time to watch her more carefully, in case I had to stop her from saying something that would get us kicked out again.

"How many hours a week did Gabriela work here, on average?" Gwen asked.

"Well, I'd have to look that up, but I'm sure she did what she could, when she could," said Hope.

Gwen looked at me again, murmuring sourly, "Yes, I'm sure."

I wondered if we'd have found out more about the business

if we'd simply gone around Gabriela and Carlos's apartment building and asked Hope's employees about their work. Or were they all too loyal to him? Maybe too afraid of losing their jobs?

"There is one thing that I feel bad about with regard to Gabriela," said Hope as he walked us back through the building to the front.

"What's that?" Gwen said, her tone disbelieving.

"I introduced her to Carlos Santos. I never thought that they would begin a relationship. When I realized that they'd begun to see each other socially, I should have done something. I knew Gabriela was married. It was part of her church membership record, and I should have called her in to talk to her. But I felt sorry for her as a lonely single mother with three young children."

He gave a look of sympathy so perfect I couldn't believe it.

"Did you try to stop them?" Gwen asked.

She seemed to be keeping it just under control. I hoped we'd end this tour soon, but didn't know how to hurry it along. Hope seemed happy to keep drawing it out at this point, loving the spotlight.

We took a detour from the call center and ended up in a small room with a single desk off to the side of the building. Why had he brought us here? "I also wanted to show you the space where we offer help with the paperwork for our workers to get proper citizenship in the United States. Or the necessary visa, if they prefer."

Had he just admitted he knew that most of his workers were undocumented immigrants? Didn't that have serious legal consequences? There had to be hefty fines, at the very least. I wondered why was he telling us this when we could so easily report him.

But he probably had people so high up politically on his side that he felt he had nothing to worry about. I felt a banked fury at this. I'd seen the same thing too many times before—favors or offers to look the other way because someone was a "good Mormon."

I reminded myself that I was here for Gwen, and I couldn't get pulled into her anger at Hope right now. I needed to keep her out of trouble.

"If you were helping Gabriela with her citizenship papers, why did she come to the class I offered at the church?" Gwen asked.

More to the point, why hadn't Bishop Hope simply told Gwen why the class was unnecessary instead of letting her go ahead, when he'd known few people would come? It seemed cruel in retrospect.

"I could tell you needed to feel useful," said Hope. He didn't pat Gwen patronizingly on the head, but the effect of his words was exactly the same. He was done telling his seamless story. We were supposed to believe it and walk away.

I wondered briefly what Detective Gore had thought of the man. I didn't believe she'd have bought into any of this.

To my relief, Hope then escorted us to a side door that led to the outside. "Anything else I can answer for you?" he asked as he opened the door for us.

I realized that now was my chance to ask about the embezzlement accusation. Maybe it wasn't related to the murder case, but I wanted to see how Hope would react. "If you don't mind, I do have a question," I said.

Gwen glared at me. She had her own questions, I knew.

"Gabriela told us that you were going to call the police about money from the church that you'd given her. She said you were accusing her of embezzling the funds—that you were asking for receipts she didn't have?" I asked.

For the first time since we arrived, Hope seemed caught off guard. It was just a fraction of a second of real surprise and anger, which he quickly covered with bland neutrality, but I'd seen it even so. "I don't know why she would have said that. I've never accused her of anything like that."

"No? We noticed that you gave her a monthly sum that was quite substantial from the ward, in addition to her income from your business," I said, still watching him closely.

But he didn't show any sign of discomfort this time. "She was struggling to pay bills. Of course I was helping. Temporarily, as any sympathetic bishop would."

"You never threatened to call the police?" I pressed again.

He shook his head emphatically. "Why would I do that? It was a church matter. She didn't have access to funds other than the ones I'd given her. If I'd been upset with the way she was using that, I'd simply have refused to give her the next month's payment."

This actually made a good deal of sense to me, but there was no way Gabriela had misinterpreted to the point that the accusation had been made up. "Did President Frost call you about it?" I asked, because Kurt had gotten involved in that, even though I hadn't expected him to, and I'd never heard about what happened next.

Now Hope twitched, then went very, very still. "I don't recall if he did or didn't," he said.

"But you must remember," I said before I realized what this meant. This was important. He was denying that anything had happened. Which made no sense if he had really been unafraid of what Gabriela had said about him calling the police.

A realization struck me. Gabriela had wanted this to get back to him. She'd involved me and Gwen not because she'd wanted us to help her, but because she'd been threatening Hope in some way I didn't yet understand. She'd been saying to him that she could get the police involved, and that wasn't what he wanted.

Had this been what had gotten her killed?

My mind whirled, unable to put all the pieces together. The only thing I knew was that I wanted to get out of here. I could hear Kurt's voice in my mind, telling me that coming to Celestial Security had been dangerous. There was a rush of sound around me, and I felt cold, unable to move. This had not been a smart thing to do.

I glanced at Greg Hope's face, glittering with malice that he was no longer trying to disguise. I wanted Kurt to come save me, but I couldn't call him. He'd told me not to do this. He'd warned me more than once, and I'd ignored him. I moved to leave.

"You ladies should really get back to your homes. I'm sure your husbands are waiting for you," Hope said.

It was exactly the wrong thing to say. Gwen bristled. "Gabriela called me the night she died. She told me that she was meeting you at the Pro-Stop, and that she was afraid for her life."

But she hadn't said that. "Gwen, I don't think—" I tried to say. I hadn't liked the way he'd dismissed us, but we had the information now that he hadn't wanted to give us. Surely it was time for us to take the win and leave.

"Be quiet, Linda," Gwen said sharply. "Let's give Bishop Hope a chance to respond. He said we could ask any questions we wanted and he'd answer them."

Hope looked angry, but more sure of himself now. "I don't meet with employees outside of work hours," he said firmly. "And I was at a late business meeting that night. The police have already checked my alibi, I assure you. A dozen witnesses could place me miles away from where Gabriela was killed."

His voice was smooth, but all I could hear was his own sense of importance. I tried to comfort myself with the thought that if he'd had to give an alibi, Gore must have thought of him as a suspect, at least at some point. But if she'd arrested Carlos, she must have cleared Hope.

"Then why did Gabriela think you were going to meet her?" Gwen pressed. She seemed inclined to push angry men to a breaking point lately.

"I think you must have misunderstood the message she left you that night," he said. Then he looked at me and added, "Maybe you misunderstood her about the accusation of embezzling, as well."

Gwen gritted her teeth. "I don't think she misunderstood at all. Gabriela knew something incriminating about you or your business. Didn't she?"

At last, Hope seemed to realize he shouldn't give us any more information to work with. Without looking at me, he turned back to the building and said, "Please tell your husband I said hello, Sister Wallheim. And excuse me. I need to finish a few things up before I head home." And he closed the door on us.

I kept quiet as we walked back to her car.

Gwen yanked her own door closed, frowning in frustration. "If only I'd called her back that night, I could have asked her what was wrong. She might have told me what—who—she was so afraid of. She might still be alive."

"We should go home," I said. And call Gore, I thought, but I didn't say that to Gwen. I wasn't sure how she'd react.

Gwen shook her head. "I still don't believe Carlos killed Gabriela. He had no reason to hurt her. There has to be more to this. Something bigger is at stake than a love triangle."

"Maybe you should let this go, Gwen. Focus on getting through the holidays and starting the Police Academy," I said.

"Maybe," she said.

When we got home, I sent a quick text to Gore about the phone message Gwen had from the night Gabriela was murdered. I expected to hear back from her immediately, but there was nothing that evening, or during the night. Maybe it didn't matter as much as I thought it had? I tried to let it go, just like I'd told Gwen to.

CHAPTER 31

The next day I was working through my frustrations via pie crust dough when I got a text from Gwen. She wanted me to come with her to visit Carlos in jail.

I want to ask him point-blank if he did it. If he says yes, then I'll let this go. If he doesn't, we have to find out who did and get the police to listen to us.

At least she wasn't talking about confronting Greg Hope again. Even if I'd promised Kurt I'd stay away, a prison seemed like a relatively safe place to meet one of the murder suspects. Maybe this would give me some closure, too, since Gore still hadn't gotten back to me.

I cleaned up the counter and put the rest of the crust dough in the fridge, covered. Then Gwen arrived and I hopped into her car. The central county jail was a twenty-minute drive from Draper. On the way over, I asked Gwen how things were with Brad.

"He's still putting up with me," she said. Brutal honesty.

"That seems good," I said tentatively.

"Does it? I don't know if it's enough." She sounded breathless, almost like a parody of someone who'd just fallen deeply in love, since it seemed the opposite here. "I want him to admire me, not just tolerate me. I want him to think about getting home to me every minute of the day that we're apart. It was the way things were between us when we were first married. But maybe I'm just stupid to think it will ever be that way again."

Her words shamed me. I'd been accepting a lot less than this from my marriage, too. But I wanted all the things she'd said from Kurt. I didn't want to be the reason he made excuses at church, or for him to shake his head when he thought of me.

"It's not stupid," I said softly. I'd been thinking about her situation as a church problem, not a marriage problem, but maybe I'd confused things.

"I used to spend time trying to figure out what Heavenly Father's marriage to Heavenly Mother was like, and how I could make my marriage like that. It's so messed up, though, because we never talk about her, and we accept that it's because Heavenly Father is protecting her. She's basically invisible. As far as we know, she does nothing that's divine except herd all those spirit children around somehow. We don't pray to her or ask her to do anything, because she's not the one with power."

I felt sick at this. I was always telling people that I loved the doctrine of Heavenly Mother, that it was one of the reasons I stayed in the church, but now I wasn't so sure. Gwen was right. It didn't make things any better for women to talk about a divine mother who was voiceless and powerless.

"I guess I keep waiting to hear more about her. Further light and knowledge," I said.

Gwen let out her raspberry sound again. "It doesn't seem to me like the men in charge have any interest in further light and knowledge about her. Anyone who asks is told they need to settle down and stay in their place."

I couldn't argue with her point. Since Ordain Women had begun agitating for change, women had more visibility in the church now, allowed to say prayers in General Conference and speaking more often in church, but that was as far as it went. They could be on committees, but not in charge of them. They could speak in meetings, but not preside. The church talked a lot about marriage as a partnership, but they also maintained the idea that men had a special role as leaders in their homes.

Gwen's whole body seemed tense. "Then I decided I could throw it all away. Stop thinking about God as male to begin with. She doesn't need Him. Maybe I don't, either."

A sharp pain cut through my heart. Was this the inevitable answer for women asking for more power within the church?

"If I invented a god of my own, I wouldn't need to keep any of the parts of my father. Or my mother. Why should I hold on to any of the old traditions of godhood if they hurt me? I've spent so much time and energy working around them. I'm done, Linda. I'm finally done." Her breathless tone had verged toward manic, but she sounded pretty lucid otherwise.

"I'm not going to try to get you to reconsider," I said sadly. "Maybe this is where you need to be, Gwen. I respect that, and I'll honor it. I know good people who have left Mormonism and taught me a lot about living well in the world without it." I thought of my son Kenneth. It was somehow harder to let go of Gwen than it had been with him. Because she was a woman? Or because she felt like the daughter I'd already lost?

She drove in silence the rest of the way, as if she'd used up all her energy at last.

"Ready?" she asked, when we got to the parking lot.

I croaked out an affirmative and we walked in.

We had to wait for a few minutes to see Carlos, but apparently Gwen had already set up a visit for both of us in advance, since we were both on the list.

We signed in, then passed through a metal detector. We gave up our phones and purses and were then sat in a small room to wait for Carlos.

"I arranged to put a little money in his commissary account," Gwen explained. "So he has a reason to show up to the visit."

Was that the way it worked? It would never have occurred to me, but us buying this meeting made me feel a little sick. What bribe would matter to someone who was imprisoned and facing a murder trial?

I was shocked at the marked change in Carlos's appearance when he arrived. He seemed shrunken compared to when we'd spoken to him at his own apartment, his head and shoulders slumped, his good looks faded. There was sweat along his forehead and above his lip, and he was breathing heavily as he settled into his chair.

"Carlos, Linda and I came here today because neither of us think you're guilty of killing Gabriela," Gwen began.

He shifted, and I felt uncomfortable with the weight of his gaze on me.

"Tell us your story. We believe you," I said. Maybe I was being fooled, but it didn't feel like it as I gazed into his eyes.

He teared up and bowed his head for a moment. "Thank you," he muttered.

Gwen spoke up. "We don't know why you confessed to killing Gabriela, but if you want to take back the confession, you can do that. You know that, don't you?"

He gave me a pained look, then turned to Gwen. "I didn't kill Gabriela," he said. "I could never have done that to her."

But if he hadn't killed her, why had he confessed to it? I didn't believe Gore would have had anything to do with forcing a statement out of him, even if I couldn't convince Gwen of that.

Gwen bounced with excitement. "Then you must have been under duress. Did someone threaten you to make you confess?"

Carlos shook his head. "No."

"Well, do you have a lawyer? We can help get you a good one, not just a public defender. You can tell them the truth, all right?" Gwen glanced at me as if expecting me to give them a name.

There were a couple of lawyers in the ward, but neither of them handled criminal cases, and even if they had, I couldn't promise they'd represent Carlos. He'd already confessed, and while he'd been better off financially than Gabriela, that didn't mean he'd have the money for hefty legal fees. I was pretty sure the church wouldn't pay them in this case.

"I already have a lawyer," he said. "Bishop Hope got me one."

I stared at Gwen. If Bishop Hope was paying for his attorney, what was he getting in return? Was that why Carlos had confessed to the murder?

"You don't have to use his lawyer if you want someone else. Did they encourage you to confess?" Gwen asked.

Carlos was looking at his hands. "I loved her. And her children, too. We were going to be a family."

"You were at the Pro-Stop with her just before she was killed, right? The police have you on tape, arguing with her. What were you fighting about?" Gwen said.

Carlos shook his head slowly. "I should never have fought with her. I should have taken her home. Kept her safe."

He sounded guilty, but of what? I tried to read his expression, but he just stared at his hands.

"Are you saying you should have taken her home because you knew she was going to do something dangerous? What did she say to you, Carlos? What was her plan?" Gwen peppered him with questions, but he didn't seem to hear them. His head was down now, his elbows on his knees.

I put out a hand to Gwen to get her to give me a chance. "Carlos. What did you argue with Gabriela about? The argument that was caught on video at the gas station?" I asked in a soothing tone, the one I used when the boys broke something and didn't want to admit to it.

"Luis. He wanted to be back in the children's lives. He said he had changed. He wanted another chance." Carlos sounded distant from all this information, neither angry nor sad. I thought of Kurt's story about the woman whom he'd known was lying because she'd given him pat answers, even if he hadn't known what she was omitting, and I felt the same phenomenon here. Carlos wasn't telling us the whole story.

"She said she was going back to her husband, is that right?" I asked. Gwen turned in her chair and was about to say something, but I signaled for her to wait and give my strategy a chance.

"Yes, back to Luis," Carlos said.

"And you were angry? Did you try to talk her out of it?" This didn't mean it was the only argument they'd had that night. I was just trying to make Carlos feel comfortable enough to tell us more.

"I tried, but she wouldn't listen," Carlos said.

"Were you physical at all with her?" Maybe that was what had been caught on tape and led to Gore arresting Carlos.

Carlos shook his head. "No, no," he said.

"Did she try to get away? Maybe you hurt her then, by accident." The police had to have a good reason for arresting him, not just his confession. Gore would want plenty of evidence to take to court. I knew her too well to imagine she'd be any sloppier.

"I didn't hurt her. I could never have hurt her." Carlos started to sob, his shoulders shuddering with each intake of breath.

I felt terrible that I'd pushed him so far, but I should have been focusing on Gwen instead of Carlos, because my pause allowed her to take charge of the conversation.

"You said you should have kept her safe, Carlos. Who were you keeping her safe from?" Gwen asked.

Carlos kept sobbing.

"Carlos, if you didn't kill her, who did? You must have some idea. You knew Gabriela as well as anyone. You knew who she was afraid of. Give us a name, anything that can help. We can't get you out of here otherwise."

But she'd pushed him too far. We both had. Carlos stood up, still shaking with sobs, and went to the door to call for a guard to take him back.

"Wait, come back! You haven't finished answering our questions!" Gwen called after him.

But we had no way to make him keep talking to us.

The guards came and ushered us out of the room, so the rest of our conversation was as we left. Gwen wasn't crying, but she looked distraught, pale and unsteady on her feet.

"He loved her, Linda. How could he have killed her?" she whispered.

"I don't know. People get confused in their thinking," I said.

I'd seen far too many cases where men had killed or abused the women they thought they loved.

"You know this has to do with Bishop Hope and Celestial Security. Linda, you had the same bad feeling about him when you met him, right? I've felt this way for weeks now."

"A feeling isn't evidence, Gwen," I said morosely.

We stepped out of the jail into the pale November sun. "Linda, do you really think Greg Hope hired an attorney for Carlos out of the goodness of his heart?"

She was right on that point. "Maybe he just thought it would make him look good," I said.

"That's not enough. He'd want more than that for his investment. Linda, this stinks to high heaven."

"Let's just go home," I said, reaching for the car door. When I got home, I texted Gore again. But I got the same response. Nothing.

CHAPTER 32

We sang the usual handful of Thanksgiving-themed hymns at church on Sunday. "Now Thank We All Our God," "Come Ye Thankful People" and my favorite, the more traditional "Praise to the Lord, the Almighty."

The Primary children wandered the halls after church with paper pilgrim hats or bonnets on their heads and paper buckles on their feet. They'd drawn cornucopias to show off and had made fresh butter in baby food jars they'd rolled around during Singing Time.

Shannon Carpenter might be twenty years younger than I was, but she'd recreated the Sundays before Thanksgiving of my childhood nearly perfectly. I wasn't sure if that was good or bad, that nothing ever changed in Mormonism.

I saw Brad Ferris in the foyer on my way from Relief Society to Sunday School. He waved and I waved back, but by the look on his face, I could tell he wanted to talk. Frankly, Sunday School wasn't my favorite part of the three-hour church block, so I figured it was as good a time as any to linger in the hall and chat.

"How are you doing?" I asked, pulling him into a corner away from the front doors. I worried about how that might look, but it wasn't as if I was in a dark room alone with him.

"Fine, fine. How are you?" he asked.

Typical Mormon insistence on everything being happy. If you had the gospel, you weren't faithful if you didn't feel glad all the time.

"How are you really?" I pressed. "You and Gwen?" I'd heard her side of the story, but he must have his own.

He paused for a long moment, then spoke slowly, carefully. "I'm not sure how we are, honestly. We don't talk much anymore. It feels like the house is a battlefield and we're both just waiting to take up our weapons at the slightest provocation. So I try to make sure there's nothing to set either of us off."

I suspected he wouldn't have been this honest with anyone else, maybe not even to Kurt. Especially not to Kurt, whose opinion he valued so highly.

I neglected to mention she'd told me she was leaving Mormonism yesterday. I couldn't bear to tell him. "I know you see things differently when it comes to the church."

He let out a half-laugh, half-sob. "You could say that. She's just so angry about everything, it's hard to tell if there's anything that can make her happy anymore."

I knew she hadn't meant for things to come across that way to Brad, but I thought he was right. She was generally unhappy nowadays. "I'm so sorry," I said.

The words seemed to strengthen his resolve. I saw his shoulders rise. "She still loves me, I think. I know I love her. I always believed that would be enough, but I'm not so sure anymore."

"I think this is a lot of delayed processing," I said. "It may not be fair, but if she's directing her anger at you, it's because it's safer that way." She knew with certainty that Brad would never raise a hand against her. Not like her father. Or Luis.

"It feels like she hates all men, in the church and out," he said, shaking his head slowly as if it were weighted down. "I understand that she's trying to carve out a new space for herself, to figure out who she is after everything her father did to her is scraped away. But I'm not her father. I thought when she married me, it was because she knew that."

It was one of the most heartbreaking things I'd ever heard a man say. I reached out to give him a hug, then realized it might not be appropriate and pulled back, patting him awkwardly on the shoulder instead.

"Just keep loving her," I said. "That has to be enough."

"I'm trying, but if she leaves the church, everything will change. Prayers and scriptures and church together. Christmas and Thanksgiving and every other holiday. I don't know who we are together without all of that."

Brad had only spoken to me this way once before, and I knew it was unusual for him to be so vulnerable. I tried to honor the gift with my best advice. "Gwen is changing, but that doesn't mean things have to be worse between you. You can still find things to do together. New things. New traditions." I loved the holidays, but they weren't the heart of my family. "You have to remember not to make her feel like she isn't enough. You can't keep praying for her to come back. Or pitying her, either." That might be worse.

"How can I not want her to be happy again?" he asked, his voice breaking on the penultimate word.

"Happy, yes. But maybe not in the same way," I thought about Kurt and how he'd thought I would be happy if I just let my questions about the church go, but that wasn't how life worked. You couldn't go backwards like that, and happiness wasn't always what it looked like. Sometimes you could be happy and angry, happy and tired, even happy and sad. "Let her know she can talk to you about anything," I added.

"She doesn't want to talk to me. Any time I try to get her to open up, she pushes me away," he said, rubbing at his eyes to staunch the tears.

"Maybe you have to start with something that's scary for you to admit. You could tell her about all of this, right now."

He thought about this for a long moment. "All right. I'll try," he said finally.

"Don't just try, *do*," I said, echoing Kurt's revision of Yoda that I'd heard him repeat so often with our sons. Then I patted his shoulder one more time. "And make sure she knows where you are. Right at her side, every step of the way."

At home after church, Kurt asked me what I'd talked to Brad about.

"Are you stalking me?" I teased. Wasn't he too busy to hunt me down during church hours if I wasn't in my meetings?

"I heard from at least three different sources that you and Brad had a very intimate conversation during Sunday School," Kurt said.

Oh. I blushed. "It wasn't that intimate," I said defensively.

"Then why don't you tell me what it was about?" he asked.

"It was about Gwen. And how to stay married now that she— if she leaves the church." I said, rephrasing at the last minute in an attempt to maintain her privacy.

"And what advice did you have about that?" Kurt asked, his look intent.

"I told Brad that he needs to make sure he can love her without judgment," I said. "And to be honest and vulnerable with her, even if he's afraid she might hurt him."

Kurt nodded at that and seemed to let go of the breath he'd been holding. "Good advice," he said.

And that seemed like the end of it, except that I asked him just before he went into his office, "Was Brad one of the people who told you about our talk?"

"Actually, he was," Kurt said with a faint smile.

If I'd known, I'd have been less worried about explaining everything. But Kurt had known that very well and used it against me.

We went over our schedules for the week, as we usually did.

"Greg Hope called me this morning," he said.

I tensed in anticipation of Kurt upbraiding me for going back to Celestial Security with Gwen two days ago.

But to my surprise, Kurt said, "He wants us to come over for dinner with his family Tuesday night. What do you think?"

It was hard for me to not answer this immediately with, "I think that's a really bad idea." I hadn't liked the man beneath the mask that I'd seen, but the fear I'd felt at Celestial Security had faded enough that I was curious. What kind of a woman had Bishop Hope brought back from Mexico and married? What were his children like? Could someone who seemed so shallow and cor- rupt still have a decent home life?

"Linda?" Kurt asked again, anxious.

"You already told him yes, didn't you?" I guessed. Of course he had. Kurt was the man of the house and the priesthood holder. He made the decisions for the family. It was his duty and his prerogative.

"Don't you want to see him in his own habitat?" Kurt asked. Was he actually encouraging me to snoop around?

"So you're saying you don't mind if I disappear in the middle of dinner on the pretext of going to the bathroom and look through his medicine cabinet, plus any papers he's left out in the open?" I said.

Kurt rubbed his eyes and said, "Linda, please tell me you're not going to do that while we're there."

I sighed. I considered telling him about the terror I'd felt when Greg Hope had talked about Gabriela Suarez and the supposed embezzlement charge, but then I'd have to admit to doing what Kurt had told me not to, and I didn't want to get into that.

"What is this really about?" I asked instead. It was right before Thanksgiving. What woman wanted to have guests over then? A woman whose husband demanded it, I supposed.

"I just want to get to know him a little better," Kurt said.

I was pretty sure there was more than that, but Kurt wasn't offering anything else, and I found I was too tired to press him. Fine, I'd play the good wife, and if there was a chance to find out what I wanted to know, I'd do that, too.

CHAPTER 33

In the morning, I went back to pie-making. Pecan and pumpkin first, because they kept the best. Apple and mincemeat next. And finally, the cream pies. There were always at least ten pies at a Wallheim Thanksgiving, and I was going to enjoy making every single one.

I spent hours dripping sweat in a hot kitchen and tasting melt-in-your-mouth crust and fillings so I didn't need to worry about lunch.

I started to think about what to bring as a gift to the Hopes' dinner. Outside of Mormondom, the proper thing for a dinner guest to do was to bring a bottle of wine. Obviously, that didn't work when you had the Word of Wisdom to follow. Nonetheless, I wanted to be gracious to our hosts. What would be right? Maybe a bottle of sparkling cider? Some Mormons had rules about soda, and others just didn't like the idea of soda served out of a bottle that looked like it held wine, but those lines didn't make sense to me.

I finally settled on a fancy box of roasted nuts that cost so much I grumbled out loud at the store.

When Kurt came home that evening, he showered again and put on a tie and jacket. He sat there and stared at me until it was clear he expected me to change out of the sweatpants and T-shirt I'd worn all day. So I threw on a skirt and the most obnoxious Christmas sweater I owned, with red satin reindeer and real clinking jingle bells. We'd bought it last year for the bishopric's ugly holiday sweater contest, which I'd won. It might be a little early, but these days, the holidays kept moving up, and I figured I'd just be seen as excited to celebrate the birth of Jesus.

When Kurt saw it, I swore I could see a smile twitch across his lips. "Ready, then?" he said.

We drove over in his truck, and he knocked on the door.

The house was already bright with Christmas lights; traditional white twinklers lined the rooftop and swirled around the trees in the yard. There was no snow yet, but it would only make the lights sparkle more charmingly when it came. The house was large, as many of the houses on our side of the mountain were, but it wasn't much bigger than ours. It certainly wasn't as big as some of the other houses with Celestial Security systems.

Bishop Hope answered the door in a light-gray suit and pastel-blue tie. I tried not to react to my memory of his glittering, malicious stare the last time we'd met. He seemed effusive and welcoming again, the perfect host.

Once we came inside, he introduced his wife, Maria, who was waiting in the entryway. She was a petite woman with long dark hair that seemed to overwhelm her with its thick waves. She wore a skirt and Christmas sweater under her apron. It wasn't until she took off the apron at her husband's urging that she and I realized we were wearing the same sweater.

We both laughed, though I was pretty sure she was wearing hers unironically. It suited her earnest air.

"It is the best way to celebrate Christmas, don't you think?" she said with a slight accent.

"Of course," I said, feeling a little bad that I'd worn mine with such ill intent.

The front room was small, with a glossy black baby grand taking up almost the entire space. I was a little jealous, comparing it to my own pedestrian instrument. But I reminded myself that I was perfectly happy with my house and my piano, especially considering what else went along with this house.

Kurt and I sat on a microfiber sofa of a rust color that fit with the overall décor. The carpet was tan, but there was the same burnt orange-brown in the floral curtains and on the border of the wallpaper surrounding us. I thought it looked odd. Not old, but like maybe someone had talked them into taking the least popular style by claiming it was "up and coming."

We chatted a little, and I became more and more conscious that English was the only language spoken here. There were no asides in Spanish, even if Hope spoke it fluently. It seemed an odd measure of control, but not out of the character I'd seen so far in him.

"Young men!" called Hope as he looked at his watch. His voice was booming as he stood and moved to the stairs.

Young men?

Seconds later, I heard small feet hurry down the stairs and collect in a line at the threshold of the room. I couldn't help but be reminded of Captain von Trapp in *The Sound of Music*, introducing his children to the other Maria. These three little dark-haired boys seemed as well behaved, and as in need of some fun. They stood at attention, stiff, with their arms behind their backs.

"Connor, Jason, and Lee," Hope said, sweeping his hand toward them. The names were very Anglo, with no hint to their Latino heritage. They seemed close in age, and definitely under eight years old—maybe four, five, and six? "This is Bishop Wallheim, and Sister Wallheim."

The children echoed our names in unison. It felt far too formal, and some part of me wondered what Bishop Hope would have done with a daughter. All three boys seemed much more like their mother than like him, with dark eyes and olive skin, though there was something of their father in the sharpness of their jaws.

Once they'd been introduced, they were commanded to "go wash up for dinner," which they hurried off to do without a word of complaint.

I presented my box of nuts to Bishop Hope. He took them with a nod and handed them to Maria, who whisked them away to an undisclosed location.

Then we were called for dinner, and I got to see the open kitchen and dining area, with vaulted ceilings that again recalled the ones in most celestial rooms in temples. I felt a twinge of unease and hoped that I wouldn't get the same sense as I had at Celestial Security that we were being sold something.

Dinner was spaghetti and meatballs with salad and garlic bread. It was one of the most common meals I'd eaten at church dinners, and it wasn't badly made, though I found myself comparing the blandness of the sauce to my own homemade tomato sauce's more robust flavor. I wondered if Maria had felt obliged to cook something that wasn't Mexican to show how "American" she was. Maybe she always cooked like this for her husband.

Maria came and sat down next to me, and she seemed anxious

for my approval, so I said, "Thank you so much for inviting us. The food is delicious."

I tried to remember the last time I'd been to anyone's house for a social occasion unrelated to church. When Mormons got together, it was usually in big groups that could only be accommodated at the church building. Kurt and I used to invite other young couples over for dinner in the early days of our marriage, but it had to have been at least twenty years since we'd either gone to someone else's house for a meal or invited them to ours.

Kurt and Greg Hope moved to the living room and were involved in their own conversation, so Maria and I sat on the opposite side of the room and talked privately.

"I hope the children aren't too loud," Maria said, glancing over at her boys, who were clearing the table with no horseplay, virtually silent.

Was she joking? No, she seemed serious. "I remember when I had five boys at home. I assure you, mine were much louder than yours," I said

"Oh?" She brightened and sat up a little straighter. "My husband complains they're disrespectful and says I should discipline them more, but I love them so much, I don't really care."

"You shouldn't! This is the most wonderful age for boys. They're not babies anymore, but not teenagers yet." I said, feeling a wave of nostalgia for when my boys were this age.

In a whisper, she confided, "I don't want my sons to think of me as a doormat, like Greg says I can be. But isn't doing what *he* says as much being a doormat as doing what they say?" she asked.

I felt unexpected empathy for her. I'd expected to find her

false and saccharine, like Serena at Celestial Security. Instead, she seemed vulnerable and painfully honest.

I noticed that Kurt had taken out a business card and given it to Greg. What were they doing? I thought this was just a chance to share bishoping war stories.

I turned my attention back to Maria. "They say that boys who love their mothers never outgrow it. They'll be easy as teenagers," I said reassuringly.

Maria smiled warmly. "That is very kind of you to say. I hope it is so. You have grandchildren, then?"

"Two," I admitted. "And they are just as wonderful as they say. But that's a long way away for you. I won't pretend that I didn't wish for them to grow up faster when they were younger."

"And now you wish they were children again?" she asked.

I hesitated. "Not often, but sometimes," I said.

She looked at her boys, and I could see her pride in them. She was right to feel it; they were good boys, which reflected well on her as a mother. Beneath Maria's reserve, I sensed a quiet strength, completely different from her husband's. I wondered how she and Greg Hope managed to get along.

Maria went over and spoke to the boys until they were settled on their beanbags, silently reading. She'd spoken in English, which made me wonder how much Spanish they knew. The books they were reading were old English classics, The Berenstain Bears, Arthur, and a Shel Silverstein poetry collection with that ghastly photo still on the back. Those weren't the books I'd purchased in anticipation of when Carla would be interested in reading with me.

After a few minutes, Maria came back to me. "My husband

says we should buy a bigger house so they have more space, but I love this home so much. Why do we need a bigger one when it's just more space to clean?"

But surely they would have the money for housecleaners, if she wanted? Hope's business seemed like it was doing gangbusters. "Would you be moving far away?" I asked.

"No, just another home in the area. Celestial Security hasn't done as well beyond Utah, and we wouldn't want to leave the ward."

She must have enjoyed being the bishop's wife of this particular ward. Maybe that was part of her husband's continuing appeal?

Maria told the boys to go get pajamas on and get ready for bed. Then she came back and told me a few stories about trouble her boys had gotten into. I trumped those with the story about when Adam had driven Kurt's truck into the river when we were on a family camping trip. He'd just put it in the wrong gear and then got out. No one thought to look back until they heard the sound of the truck hitting the water.

At this point Kurt and Greg finished their conversation and rose from the couch, and Maria took that as a cue to bring out a blueberry, cream cheese, and whipped cream combination with a nutty crust. She called it, appropriately enough, "Luscious Dessert."

"My mother-in-law gave me the recipe," Maria explained. "It was Greg's favorite growing up."

Of course it was.

As we ate, I considered what would happen if Maria let her sons have this. Blueberry was particularly bad at staining. Almost as bad as beets, which I'd given up for many years when my boys were young. But she never called the children to have any.

By then, it was clear that Maria needed to get back to her sons' bedtime routine and Kurt seemed ready to go, so we said our goodbyes.

Back in the truck, I asked Kurt why he'd given Hope his business card. Kurt informed me that Hope had asked if he would be interested in doing accounting work for Celestial Security.

"What did you say?" I asked. Had this been the real reason for the dinner, the one he hadn't wanted to tell me about?

"I told him I'd think about it," Kurt said.

I wished he wouldn't. "Aren't you worried about getting entangled with that kind of business?" I asked. Kurt usually steered clear of multi-level marketing schemes and anything he deemed remotely questionable. I certainly thought Celestial Security qualified. Not to mention all the questions I still had about Gabriela's murder, which I didn't bring up.

Kurt looked away. "I don't see why I should be, as long as it's legitimately run. I still have space in my client list."

He'd lost a big client last year when an insurance company had pulled out of Utah. Was he embarrassed that we'd lost income? We hadn't had to cut back on expenses, just our investing.

"You shouldn't take someone on out of desperation if you don't like their business model," I said. Especially not this someone.

"I won't, Linda. Don't worry," Kurt said. "I'm not going to do anything stupid."

And whenever I made those kinds of promises, did that make him feel better? I thought not.

CHAPTER 34

The next day, something in the back of my mind gnawed at me as I worked on pies. I got on my laptop and went to the Celestial Security website again. If Kurt was thinking about getting into business with Greg Hope, I really should do some digging to lay my fears to rest about his company. Or the opposite.

This time, I figured that instead of getting official, sanitized information, it might be better to ask actual customers what they thought. I could have asked Gwen to come with me, but I was worried she was letting this case get to her, so I decided to do this alone.

There were hundreds of photos of houses on the site. Every time I had a break, I came back and looked through a few more of them, until I finally found one that looked familiar. I stared at the view of the mountains behind the house, trying to place where I knew it from. It didn't work. I wished Samuel were here. He'd have found some trick online to pinpoint the location of the house.

Then finally, remembering Samuel's lessons, I managed to use Google street view to look through a section of Sandy that I thought was the right place, going south a few times, and then east, until the mountain line in the photo matched exactly. I found the right house (or what I thought was the right house) and then checked my watch. It was lunchtime, but I'd snuck so many bites of pie that I wasn't hungry.

I wasn't exactly sure how I'd get people to talk to me, but hoped my natural housewifely demeanor might just make their defenses fall. I drove down to the street I'd found on Google street view, amazed at how big the houses here were in person. Every single one on the block looked like it must be 20,000 square feet inside. Not much property, though. The gardens were tiny, but immaculate, reminding me of what Anna's husband Tobias had done with their yard when he'd been alive.

I went to the house number I thought was right, and was pleased when I saw the Celestial Security sticker on the bottom corner of the front window nearest to the door. I rang the bell, half expecting a servant to answer.

Instead, it was a fit woman with perky breasts wearing expensive-looking sweatpants, her hair damp from exercise. "Oh," she said, visibly disappointed. She glanced around me. "You weren't the delivery person I was expecting."

"My name is Linda Wallheim," I said. "I was driving by when I recognized your house from the Celestial Security website. You use their company, right?"

She was taken aback. "Why, yes, we do."

"Do you mind if I ask about the service? My husband and I are considering signing up, but we want to know if it's worth it," I lied. "The monthly fees are very expensive, aren't they?" I tried to look conflicted. "But is that what's necessary in this neighborhood, do you think?"

She smiled and patted at her hair, then invited me inside. The house was exactly the kind of picture-perfect inside that it looked outside. I thought some of the decorations were over-the-top in size—that giant Coke bottle savings bank, for instance—but who was I to tell someone else how to live? She introduced herself as Sylvia Loveland, and led me past the living room and into the kitchen.

"We've loved this house and this area. Celestial Security came along just as we were closing, and I must say that it's been worth every penny, just to have the sense of security they offer. When you own a home like this, you worry about it. But in the ten years we've lived here, we've never had a break-in, and we've become evangelists of a sort for their system. If our neighbors are well secured, too, it makes us all safer. Our children especially," she said with an air of someone who enjoyed being in the know.

I wished I could ask if she got a bonus for referring people. Not that she seemed to need the money. "Thank you. I really appreciate your honest opinion," I said.

"Are you thinking of moving here?" she asked.

"We're looking at a house up the way," I said, gesturing vaguely. But I wished I hadn't lied, because she stared at me like she was evaluating me for a position in her ward Christmas program. I should have put on something nicer, though I didn't think I owned anything that would impress her.

"Well, this is the best neighborhood in the Salt Lake Valley. We looked everywhere, I assure you. And everyone here sings the praises of the neighborhood and our security systems."

"Oh, I believe you," I said, making a note to myself not to ever sell our current house. If I thought I had problems in our ward, they could always be worse.

She stood up and walked me to the door. Yes, I was clearly of no interest to her anymore.

"Anything else I should know about Celestial Security?" I asked, because this woman seemed the type not to notice me prying for too much information.

She leaned in and said to me in a confiding and superior tone, "I know the owner, Greg Hope, and his wife, Maria. They are just wonderful examples of upstanding citizens. You can trust people like that."

I thought again about the Hyde I'd seen the last time I was at Celestial Security, and the Jekyll at dinner last night. She must have only ever met the latter.

"What about the monthly service?" I asked.

She waved a hand. "Oh, that. It's worth every penny. The maintenance people come every year to do updates and make sure everything is working well. There are never any problems, and I just appreciate knowing that people with my values are earning money doing something that's so important."

So she saw the protection of her massive home and valuables as of paramount importance. I refrained from responding. This woman was the kind of person I'd expected Greg Hope's wife to be, though I knew it was unfair to make that kind of snap judgment about a stranger. I had a prejudice against women who cared so much about their appearance, though I knew that for many women, it was what they were expected to do, especially in Mormonism.

"Just one more question," I said, "Is your husband by any chance a bishop?"

"He is," she said, tilting her hand in surprise. "How did you know?"

It had just been a guess on my part. I didn't think it really mattered, but it made sense that the other people in her ward might want to follow her lead in particular as the bishop's wife. I'd never considered that I might have a similar ability to set trends in my own ward. I'd always complained about not having power, but clearly, I did. It just wasn't a power I cared about. If I started wearing my hair one way, would other women in the ward start doing the same thing? Heaven forbid.

I walked around the rest of the neighborhood, knocking on doors and using the name "Sylvia Loveland" as my key. At the mere mention of her, a couple of women not only offered to talk to me, but invited me inside and gave me milk and cookies. I wasn't one to refuse cookies, even if they weren't my own well-tested recipes.

One thing was certain—there was a lot of tithing being paid by the people who owned these homes. They were all wealthy, and all good members of the Mormon church.

At the last house on the block, a tall, slender woman with hazel eyes and caramel-colored hair, Candice Stevens, invited me in after I used Sylvia's name. She looked a bit embarrassed, and I didn't understand why until she said, "We went off the monthly plan for just a few weeks, but then there was a break-in and we had a whole bunch of things stolen."

"I'm so sorry," I said. "That must have been terrifying." Certainly an interesting coincidence.

"It was very scary. I wasn't sure we could stay here after it happened. For the first night, we went to a hotel so the police could look through the house and take fingerprints. But after that, I wanted to come home. Only I discovered this didn't feel like home anymore." She shuddered and I thought it a little odd that she was telling me so much until I realized that she felt so vulnerable about the break-in that all her normal boundaries must have been ripped from her.

She went on, wrapping an arm around herself, "It felt like someone had turned the house I loved into a place I didn't recognize. I couldn't sleep for more than a few hours at a time, and I had to set up monitors so I could hear the children in the next room."

"How awful," I murmured.

Her eyes were haunted and her voice was thready as she said, "We prayed about it and eventually realized that the solution was simple. We'd taken our safety for granted, just like the Nephites in the Book of Mormon before Captain Moroni came along and taught them to build up their fortifications."

I felt a cold tingling sensation down my back as she mentioned that story from the scriptures. I suspected she hadn't come up with it on her own, but she might not remember that it had been fed to her.

Captain Moroni had led the Nephites to victory against the Lamanites under the "title of liberty" flag, on which he had written:

In memory of our God, our religion, and freedom, and our peace, our wives, and our children.

It had been a purely defensive war against an aggressor, and was thus considered "righteous." And of course, as Gwen had reminded me, the light-skinned Nephites were almost always the good guys in the Book of Mormon, while the dark-skinned Lamanites were the aggressors in all the wars.

"Did they ever catch the criminals?" I asked, coming back to the present.

Candice tightened her lips. "They eventually recovered some

of our items at a local pawn shop, but I didn't want them back at that point. We ended up selling them on KSL." The local classifieds, owned by the Mormon church.

"Did you have insurance, at least?" I asked. I wanted to somehow feel better about all of this. She was a rich woman. Surely this didn't matter to her, did it?

"Oh, of course. But that didn't make me feel safe. I'm glad that the children, at least, never had nightmares. We tried to keep as much information from them as possible so they wouldn't worry." It could have sounded privileged, but instead it just struck me as sad.

"Thank you for talking to me about this," I said, and stood up. I felt I had no right to intrude further on her privacy.

"You absolutely must get Celestial Security," she urged. "I promise you it's worth every penny and more. It's like paying tithing, but the blessings you get are right now, in this world."

Again, her echo of church language bothered me, but was certainly in line with my other dealings with people connected to Celestial Security. All in all, it had been a very productive outing, and I felt only a little guilty at the pride I had for undertaking it on my own. Walking back to my car, I debated whether to share anything with Gwen. I didn't want her to go off halfcocked on some scheme to get at Greg Hope, but maybe I wanted her to give me a little praise, too, so I drove straight to her house and sketched out what had happened.

She started bouncing even before I'd finished telling her about the "title of liberty," which I wasn't sure was a good thing.

"Wow, Linda! This is fantastic! It's just the break we needed. There has to be some connection between those thieves and Celestial Security."

"But how? Why would Hope want to rob his own customers?" I asked, thinking that here she was, making a big leap again without much logic behind it other than her hatred of Greg Hope.

"Former customers. And that woman went right back to the company, didn't she?" Gwen asked.

"Yes, but just because she was scared." It hadn't been a rational decision. Surely a business couldn't rely on that kind of strategy.

"He can't have people backing out once they realize the monthly fees aren't worth it. It's a bad look. Like people leaving a cult—others follow suit. You have to stop the first ones to go." Gwen's lips were pursed, and I couldn't help but think that she was talking about Mormonism as she said this.

I'd heard lots of people refer to Mormonism as a cult, but that seemed unfair to me. We lived in the real world and while there was encouragement to pay tithing, there were no fees to join and no real threats beyond heavenly ones if you left. The way the leadership worked also didn't seem like a cult-like reverence for a single man.

"Even if it is someone in the company, it doesn't have to be Hope," I said, attempting to dissuade her.

"You don't know him like I do," Gwen said. She was almost glowing with energy now.

"I don't think we should confront him again." I was afraid of him, I realized.

"Oh, I'm just going to see what I can find out online first," she promised.

I was nervous about what she might do next, but she did have me wondering if Celestial Security might have something to do with the robberies, after all.

CHAPTER 35

The day before Thanksgiving, Gwen called me to tell me she had found a definitive Celestial Security connection to Candice Stevens's robbery.

"I looked up the news articles about it. The man arrested was Jesus Gonzalez." She sounded excited.

"And? I asked.

"He's a member of the Spanish ward. I know him. I didn't hear about him being arrested or serving time or anything. I guess everyone kept that quiet for him. But I've met him. And I know he works at Celestial Security."

"Wow," I said. Did Detective Gore know about any of this? I couldn't see how it had to do with the murder, but it signaled that there was something deeply wrong at Celestial Security, as we'd suspected.

"It gets worse, Linda. A lot worse," Gwen went on, still sounding excited as a kid on Christmas Day.

"What do you mean?"

"Well, I started looking up any mentions of ward members in newspapers online. It took hours. I was up all last night." She yawned. "I didn't want Brad to know what I was doing, so I pretended I was asleep and got up after he was snoring, then snuck back into bed when I was finished, but even then, I couldn't sleep."

This was the Gwen who would one day make a good police officer, then detective. "What did you find out?"

"Like I said, I had to sift through a lot of unrelated information. But there was another ward member who was arrested for a series of robberies last year. Bertran Lopez."

"A series of robberies?" Could this lead back to Greg Hope?

"Fifteen," Gwen said.

"And he's still working at Celestial Security?" I asked in amazement.

There was a hesitation. "No, not anymore," Gwen said. "He was fired when he was arrested, but Hope paid for his lawyer and he's still in the ward, so that has to mean something."

Hope was paying for Carlos's lawyer, too. Had everyone interpreted this as sheer goodwill?

"I've tracked down Jesus and Bertan's addresses. I want to talk to them. Would you be willing to come with me?"

I couldn't say no. It was too exciting; it felt like we were so close to wrapping things up. How could I let go of this case now? "Can you give me a half hour?" I asked, thinking about the family's visit tomorrow.

"Sure. I guess I should shower and put on some clean clothes. Linda, do you know what this means?"

"I have an idea," I said, but clearly Gwen wanted to put it out there in words. Maybe she was still working through the consequences herself.

"I haven't been able to track all of the fifteen homes that Bertran Lopez robbed, but of the three I can find direct mention of, all were former Celestial Security clients, and all three are back on the website with photos. It could be all fifteen. And there could be homes that didn't ever call the police to report break-ins, or homes that did call but no one's been caught yet. This could be huge."

Yes, it could. Or it could be nothing more than the coincidence I'd first assumed.

I mixed up the brine for the turkey and decided everything else could wait until tonight or tomorrow. We were on a late dinner schedule so that the married couples—Joseph and Willow, Adam and Marie, and Kenneth and Naomi—could see both of their families on the same day. Zachary was bringing a young woman with him, and although he hadn't told me her name yet, I was very excited to meet her.

Gwen picked me up and drove back to Gabriela's building, which seemed to be where most of the Spanish ward lived. We walked briefly by her apartment, and the door was wide open; overall-clad workers moved in and out, performing loud renova-tions.

"Gwen, let's just make sure we don't throw any wild accusa-tions out there, all right?" I attempted.

"But we've practically got them!" she said with the fervor that worried me.

"You have to remember that these men are victims, too. They've been used, and they're probably frightened about what might happen to them and their families. Let's tread lightly, all right?" I didn't want anyone punching the wall—or Gwen.

"I know that, Linda," Gwen said, but from her expression, I didn't think she did.

We went up a floor and she pointed at the door at the end of the hallway, number 56. "Jesus Gonzalez," she said cautiously.

"He lives with his mother." She knocked on the door and a woman opened it.

"Hermana Ferris," she said, without much warmth.

"Hermana Gonzalez," Gwen said soothingly. "May we speak to Jesus, *por favor*?"

Sister Gonzalez looked at us suspiciously. "What is this about? He is very busy and has to get to work soon. I don't want him to be late."

Considering that he was technically a convicted felon, I could see why she was nervous about that.

Despite my reservations, Gwen was indeed gentler this time around. "We just have a few questions."

"Questions about what?" asked Sister Gonzalez.

"Well," Gwen glanced at me. "I've been asking people about Gabriela Suarez. Her children are all alone now, maybe not even in the same household. We're trying to get justice for their mother. They deserve that much, don't you think?" I might not have put it so directly, but at least she hadn't mentioned anything about robberies or jail.

Still, Sister Gonzalez stiffened. "You're not one of us. Pretending to be—" She launched into Spanish then. It didn't sound nice.

But Jesus himself came out from behind her. "Mama, what's . . . Oh, Hermana Ferris?" he said.

His mother said something about Hermana Gabriela and waved in our direction.

Was that an expression of guilt I saw chase across his face?

He was over six feet and walked with a humble hunch, as if he thought being tall was some kind of sin. His hair was thick and curly, just beginning to grow wings around his ears.

"Please, Jesus, for Gabriela. And the children," Gwen said.

Jesus sighed, then nodded and stepped forward.

His mother licked her fingers and tucked his hair back behind his ears, then said something in Spanish that I suspected was remarkably similar to what I'd have said to one of my sons: Time to get a haircut, or you'll start to look like a shaggy dog.

He nudged his mother out of the living room, insisting loudly in Spanish that the three of us needed privacy. "What about Gabriela?" he asked. "She's gone now."

"We wanted to ask you about Celestial Security and why she was so afraid of Bishop Hope in the days before she died," Gwen said.

Jesus's face fell, and he seemed to collapse on the worn lime-green sofa. He held his head in his hands. "I warned her. She wouldn't listen to me," he muttered.

"Jesus, what do you know about Gabriela's death?"

His eye twitched, and I thought of what Kurt had said—that people had tells when they didn't lie often. Finally, Jesus seemed to make a decision. He shook his head and stared Gwen in the eyes. "Nothing. Carlos killed her. They were having an affair. Everyone knows that. The police have made an official state-ment. He confessed. There can be no question about it."

But obviously, there was a question. Or an answer. He knew something here, if we could just get him to say it.

"Jesus, you work at Celestial Security. What was your job there before the arrest?" Gwen asked. Her tone was getting harder, though I wasn't complaining. I agreed that it was time to apply a little more pressure where kindness hadn't worked.

He hesitated, then answered, "I helped with installations. Equipment and electronics."

"But you robbed one of the homes a few months ago," Gwen said.

He bowed his head. "I did." This was all on the public record, no reason for him to deny it.

"Why did you do it?"

He glanced up for a moment, incredulity on his face. "For money. Of course. Why else would I do it?"

Gwen looked at me, and I nodded for her to continue. "I think there was another reason, Jesus. Were you asked to rob them? Since they'd gone off the monthly monitoring system?"

He just stared at Gwen without answering. I couldn't tell if it was in anger or resignation.

"Did someone in the company ask you to do it? Greg Hope, for instance?"

"No," he said emphatically. "No, of course not. I did it on my own."

Did he protest too much?

"But when you got out of jail, Greg Hope rehired you at Celestial Security. Why was that? Why trust you after what you'd done? You'd used company information to hurt their customers. Wouldn't you be the last person they'd want to take back?" I asked, unable to stop myself from stepping in now.

"I told him I was sorry. I promised him I would never do it again." There was something behind Jesus's eyes that resembled satisfaction, or even pleasure. Maybe he'd had some kind of leverage against Hope?

"I'm not sure I believe that, Jesus. Are you sure you don't want to tell the truth?" I said in my best motherly tone.

A faint smile now. "What would I get out of that?" he asked.

"Knowing that the truth about Gabriela comes out," Gwen said.

That shut Jesus down immediately. "Gabriela had nothing to do with any of this," he insisted, standing up. The whole tone of the conversation had just changed, and I knew we'd lost him.

"Wait," Gwen said. "What about your case? Did you have a court-appointed lawyer?"

"No," said Jesus.

"Bishop Hope paid for your lawyer, didn't he?" she pressed.

"He is a good man. He cares for the people in the ward," Jesus said, and moved to the door.

"Did he have you plead guilty?" Gwen insisted. "Did you ever think about whether that was in your best interest or Hope's?"

"It was a good deal," he said, more slowly now. His hand was on the doorknob, but he hadn't turned it. "They said it was a good deal."

"Can't you see that he used you? Just like he used Bertran. And Gabriela. And Carlos. It's all for his own sake. He's letting you take the fall for his crimes. All of you."

This was all guesswork, but I didn't try to cut her off. Maybe it would make Jesus think twice about his position, even if I doubted he'd call us back later.

"Please leave now," said Jesus, and opened the door.

"Jesus, tell us what was going on. How was Gabriela involved?" Gwen asked too loudly as we walked through.

Jesus's only answer was to shut the door firmly in our faces.

"This is it, I can feel it," Gwen said, her fists tightening at her sides. "That told me everything I needed to know. Hope's going down for this."

For what? She'd gone too far, and even if I wanted to believe her theory, I wasn't sure I could.

"Gabriela must have found out what was going on and threatened to expose him," Gwen went on.

"We can't assume that," I said.

Gwen nodded to Jesus's door. "He said that Gabriela was involved."

"No, he didn't. He refused to say that she was involved." But in a way that made me pretty sure Gwen was right.

"She had to have been." She counted off on her fingers. "Carlos, Bertran, Jesus, Gabriela. They had to have been involved in the robberies."

"Proof," I said again. "We have to have proof."

"All right, let's go talk to Bertran," Gwen said, checking her phone for the right apartment number.

"Remember, let's try to be nice again, at least in the beginning to get him to talk," I said, but I wasn't sure she was even paying attention to me.

We went down two flights to apartment 34 and knocked again. The door didn't open fully, and we got only a glimpse of a young Hispanic woman's face. Bertran's sister? Girlfriend? Wife? She didn't seem to recognize Gwen, or if she did, it didn't make her open the door.

"Is Bertran home? We need to talk to him about Bishop Hope."

She was handling this too roughly, so I stepped in, "Yes, about a ward matter. We need his help," I said calmly.

The woman looked at Gwen. "Hermana Ferris?" she said.

"Yes. I was friends with Gabriela Suarez. You knew her? The one who was murdered—"

That was as far as she got before the door closed. So much for our good not-cop/bad not-cop strategy.

"Now what?" Gwen asked.

"You're not even listening," I said. Why was she bothering to ask me anything?

"There has to be proof of all of this somewhere. Maybe if I go back and look through the newspapers again, I'll find another name. Or maybe one of the members of the ward will decide to come to me." She shook her head, clearly frustrated.

"Maybe we can come back after Thanksgiving?" I asked. People might be more relaxed then. I was certainly having a hard time focusing on anything but my plans for tomorrow.

Gwen let out a long breath. "Yeah, sure."

Together, we walked out of the apartment complex. I thought we were headed home, but Gwen pointed suddenly ahead of me and then started running. I did my best to keep up with her as she ran to the back entrance of the apartment building just in time to collide with a young Hispanic man who was small, but muscular. His face was riddled with acne, and he looked like he couldn't have been older than Samuel.

"Bertran?" Gwen asked, her face flushed with triumph.

His head jerked to the side. "What's it to you?" he asked. He didn't seem to recognize her from the ward. I wondered if that could be to our advantage?

"We were wondering if we could talk to you for a minute," I said.

"About what?" he asked.

"Your mother seems worried about you," I said, nodding back to the apartment.

"That's not my mother," he said. "That's my aunt."

Damn. Well, I'd blown that one.

Gwen took over. "We want to ask some questions about Greg Hope and Celestial Security," she said.

Bertran's response was as clear as it was disgusting: he spat a gob on the ground, then glared up at us. "I'm not saying nothing without a lawyer," he said.

"We're not accusing you of anything," Gwen said quickly. "We just want to know the truth. Don't you think people deserve to know who Bishop Greg Hope really is, and how he's making so much money?"

Bertran stared for a long moment. "Why should I trust you?"

"We wouldn't be here unless we already suspected something was wrong," Gwen said. "We just want to hear your side of the story." Finally, she was following my less confrontational lead. But too late, it seemed.

Bertran spat again and looked up, then pushed past Gwen, nearly knocked me over, and ran headlong past us in the door.

"Damn it!" Gwen said.

"We can't force him to talk," I said. "Look, let's take some time to process this. We can regroup on Friday."

But Gwen was fixated. Her whole body was tense. "He's afraid, just like Jesus was. This is what Hope is to them, do you see that? Not a bishop, a monster."

Softly, I said, "They seem more scared of you right now than Bishop Hope."

Her face fell. "That's not fair, Linda. They're afraid of me because of him. They're afraid of what he'll do to them if the truth comes out. I'm trying to help them. They just can't see that because he has so much power over them. If it ever comes down to his word against theirs, they must feel like they can't win. He's a bishop and a successful, well-known businessman with endless resources. He might even be dangerous."

I didn't argue. I was just as disenchanted with Hope and his business as she was. "We can't just make it seem like we're using them, just like he has," I said.

Head bowed, Gwen walked back with me to the car. Once we got there, I wanted to relax, but I couldn't quite yet.

"He's making money off both ends," Gwen said bitterly. "Sign up and pay every month, or you get robbed to make you sign back up."

A sour taste filled my mouth. Even if by some miracle Hope wasn't involved in this string of robberies, I didn't like the idea of Kurt working with him.

Gwen dropped me off at home.

Frustrated with the whole situation, I got out one of the pumpkin pies in the outside fridge, eating half of it as I tried to think. Then I started making two new ones, because that was how I dealt with stress.

CHAPTER 36

I woke up at 5 A.M. on Thanksgiving Day to put the turkey in the brine. We were using one of the old root beer coolers that Kurt had taken to scout camp on many occasions. It still smelled faintly of that, but I didn't think it would affect the turkey's flavor.

I tried to go back to sleep after that, but couldn't, and when Kurt woke up, we occupied ourselves more pleasantly for a while.

"I've got to go get the bread drying," I said eventually.

"You know, you could just make stuffing with pre-dried bread from the store," Kurt said.

I goggled at the suggestion. Who would want to eat stuffing that was made from stale, store-bought bread? That wasn't going to happen at my house, not while I was still breathing. Though he'd hit on one of the reasons I hadn't allowed any of my daughters-in-law to volunteer for certain dishes. I didn't want to eat stuffing made from a boxed mix. Or rolls from a store, either.

I didn't particularly care when it came to sweet potatoes or anything green. Marie was bringing a salad, Willow a green bean casserole, and Naomi a dessert that wasn't pie. I wasn't going to complain about more dessert, though I suspected it might be near midnight before our stomachs were empty enough to give them all the attention they deserved.

I put the turkey in the oven at around noon without Kurt's help, though he offered. It wasn't that big, and if there came a time when I couldn't lift a turkey into the oven, maybe I would start going to the gym. Until then, I got enough of a workout kneading my roll dough by hand, as it should be. If more people took their aggressions out on dough, the world would be a better place, in my opinion.

Kenneth and Naomi arrived first, along with Talitha. She had brought a turkey-building craft activity with Rolos (the head), Reese's Peanut Butter Cups (the body), and candy corn (the feathers). More sugar, thank goodness!

Naomi asked me if there was anything she could do to help. "I feel so guilty, just showing up here and eating. That's not the way it was at home."

She came from a huge polygamous ex-Mormon family, and as the eldest daughter, she'd acted more like mother to her younger siblings in many ways. But I wouldn't let her do that here. "I've got it handled. You just go sit down and enjoy yourself," I said, and nudged her out of my kitchen.

Adam and Marie arrived next. Marie had indeed brought a green salad—a green Jell-O salad. After all, what would any Mormon gathering be without Jell-O? I guessed Marie had missed the memo on how much I disliked Jell-O, especially in salad form. This one had shredded carrots and cucumber in it, along with chunks of mandarin orange and apple.

"Mom, I want your roll recipe someday," said Marie as Adam snuck a piece of the dough.

I slapped his hand, but he'd already put it in his mouth.

"That'll grow in your stomach and make you explode, you know," I teased. This was one of our oldest jokes.

Zachary was next. After being so excited for us to meet his new girlfriend—or whatever he was going to call her—he came alone.

"What happened?" I asked.

He only shook his head, tight-lipped, and refused to give any details. I gave him a hug and told him I loved him. Then I sent him to play with Talitha—he'd always gotten along well with kids.

Finally, Joseph and Willow and baby Carla arrived. She had plumped up nicely and was just about the chubbiest little thing I'd ever seen.

As promised, Willow had brought a green bean casserole, complete with a layer of cornflakes toasted on the top. I liked the Mormon classic more than I cared to admit.

"It looks delicious," I told her.

She smiled. "Thank you. I know you don't give compliments about cooking easily."

Was it true? Was I stingy in that way?

After that, I shooed her out of the kitchen. It was time for me to start mashing the potatoes that had been boiling for twenty minutes, and then simmering the gravy. And the rolls had to come out of the oven fresh and golden. And the turkey had to rest before Kurt carved it.

Once I'd disgorged the turkey's insides, I put the stuffing back in the oven for a moment to make sure that it was warm and crunchy on the sides, just how I liked it. I wished for the umpteenth time that I had a second oven. But only twice a year. A disappearing second oven.

People talked about how quickly the food you spent all day cooking got eaten, but it took us well over an hour to get through it. Then Carla started to cry, and Willow said the baby needed a nap. She already knew she could go upstairs and lay the baby down in Samuel's room in the portable crib we kept there.

When she came back, we made the candy turkeys Talitha had brought, and Kurt had us go around and say what we were thankful for this year.

No one mentioned my stuffing or rolls, but I was pretty sure that was implied, judging by how much had been eaten.

Joseph said he was grateful that Carla would start walking soon, so he wouldn't have to carry her around everywhere.

Adam said he was grateful school was almost finished.

Kenneth said he was grateful for Naomi and Talitha.

Zachary said morosely that he was grateful for text-message breakups, which the rest of us tried carefully not to react to.

I said I was thankful that my family was growing each year without me having to have more children myself.

Kurt said he was thankful that I was still in one piece, which made all the boys laugh. They'd heard about what had happened to land me in the hospital last summer.

"How's Samuel doing?" Kenneth asked after a lull.

"It sounds like he's having a great time," Kurt said effusively. "I think we're going to have to get him a warmer coat this year, though."

Kenneth looked at me with intent. "I heard he was transferred three times in two weeks. That seems unusual."

"He called me about that," I said.

"What?" said Kenneth.

"I thought that wasn't allowed," said Naomi, whose brothers

hadn't gone on missions, though perhaps her father had, before he'd decided to practice polygamy and been excommunicated from the church.

"It's not, usually," said Kenneth. "He must've gotten special permission."

Kurt was trying to communicate something to me with a meaningful stare. Probably that I should go along with his cheerier take on Samuel's mission life since it was Thanksgiving.

"He called from the mission home with special permission from President Cooper," I said.

"Really? Why?" asked Adam, who was now curious as well.

"Because your mother was worried about him, that's all," Kurt said.

I considered leaving it at that. But these were Samuel's older brothers. They deserved a more accurate version of events. Especially Kenneth, after what had happened to the gay companion on his mission, a young man who had been sent home and ended up committing suicide. "I called the mission president and chewed him out the week before."

Kenneth laughed. "Go Mom!" he said.

Based on Kurt's dark expression, he was not thinking the same thing. He didn't want to spend Thanksgiving talking about problems like this. But I wasn't sure I understood what the point of family was if you couldn't talk about what was really going on.

"I think Samuel deserves to be treated well, and if the other missionaries are mistreating him, they should be the ones punished, not him," I said.

"That's not always the way it works," said Adam, subtly siding with his father.

"One of the many times I'm glad I didn't go on a mission," said

Joseph, who had gone to school and gotten married instead. That wasn't always accepted as a legitimate choice in Mormonism, but the older Joseph got, the less people questioned it. There was other proof now of his devotion to God and the church.

"One of the transfers wasn't about Samuel at all. He was helping clean up a messy relationship between other companions who'd become physically violent with each other," I added.

"Better him than me," muttered Joseph.

"Sounds like the kind of thing the mission president's pets get asked to do," said Adam.

"But Samuel isn't even an AP," said Kenneth.

"What about the other two transfers?" asked Naomi.

I relayed the stories Samuel had told me about the homophobic companion, and the one who'd come out of the closet and gone home.

"You know, if the Mormon church didn't teach people that being gay was wrong and had to be fixed in the next life, it wouldn't be such a big deal," Kenneth said, fists clenched and face flushed.

"Our church is about love and inclusion," Kurt insisted. He'd turned his back on the conversation, but he couldn't let it go without saying something like that.

I sighed, unsure what to do to make Kurt feel better.

"Let's play Pictionary, okay?" said Willow.

"That's boring," said Talitha. She suggested Scribblish, which was like Pictionary combined with telephone. You drew a picture, then someone guessed what it was, wrote that down, folded the paper down to cover the picture but left the words showing, then passed it along for someone else to draw for the person after that to guess, and so on until you ran out of paper.

We played for an hour. I ended up with several Book of Mormon-themed pictures that were easy to guess, including the one with Ammon cutting off dozens of arms and Captain Moroni with the "title of liberty." I also got one that looked too risqué for a game in mixed company, so I guessed that it was a banana, ignoring the genitalia-esque hairs, and found that I was actually right. Kenneth had intervened along the way to make it funny, since he'd known it was coming to me next and that Talitha wouldn't see.

Finally, it was time for dessert. It seemed that the bad feelings of the day had dissipated, and I didn't have to make an official apology. Kurt and the boys started cleaning up and I relaxed on the couch with my daughters-in-law. When they were all gone, it was just me and Kurt.

"That was a good day," Kurt said, pulling me close for a hug.

So he wasn't mad? "If every day was like today," I started. "We'd—"

"We'd all end up as wide as we are tall," Kurt finished for me.

I pushed him gently. "No, we'd all forget about going to heaven, because we'd be perfectly happy right here and now," I said.

CHAPTER 37

The next morning I was watching television on the couch in a post-Thanksgiving-indulgence coma when the phone rang.

"Hello?" I answered unhappily, not ready to leave my comfortable spot.

It was Gwen, of course. "Linda, we have to go back and see Carlos again. I want to ask him about the robberies and if he and Gabriela were involved. That has to be what he was holding back on the last time we were there."

I decided it would be rude of me to ask how her Thanksgiving had gone. "I thought we were going to try with Jesus and Bertran again," I said.

"No, I've been thinking about this for the past two days. We have to talk to Carlos now, before word gets back to Bishop Hope," she said, her words rushed. "I keep thinking about the phone message she left. She was terrified. She must have known she'd pushed Hope too far. She'd become too big of a threat, and he had to make sure she was out of the picture."

She was right; I wasn't ready to let this go either. "If you're sure," I said.

"I've already arranged it. We have to go, Linda. It's the only way to figure out the last piece of the puzzle," she said.

I sighed. "All right. I'll come."

"I'll be there in a few minutes," Gwen said.

I thought about Kurt, still asleep upstairs. Today might be the only day he took off all year. We didn't go shopping on Black Friday as a rule and he had no bishop commitments. He'd been talking yesterday about watching my favorite old movies all day while eating leftovers, and now I was skipping out on him.

He wouldn't be happy with me when he woke up—did I care? Of course I did. But I also didn't want Kurt thinking he was in charge of me. This was an issue of conscience, and I couldn't let it go for the sake of convenience within my marriage.

"I'll wait for you outside," I said, though I knew I was behaving like a teenager, sneaking off so she didn't have to talk to her parents.

I met Gwen outside and got into her car. I'd left no note at home. Nothing. I'd even turned off my phone so I wouldn't be bothered with questions while I was out.

"What are we going to say to him?" I asked.

"He must have known something about the robberies. We can bring it up with him."

"But that won't necessarily get him to talk," I pointed out. "He's probably afraid, just like Jesus and Bertran were."

"Then we have to remind him that Hope can't be trusted," Gwen said. "Why should Carlos do anything for a man that evil? Especially something as huge as prison time. We can get him out, and we're the ones trying to get justice for Gabriela, whom he loved. He has to trust us—we're on his side in every way, and we already know what's going on."

This seemed reasonable to me, so I nodded. Gwen had made some bad mistakes here, but so had I when I'd first gotten drawn into a murder case. She was on a steeper learning curve, and I was proud to be helping her, though I was sure Gore and Kurt might have something to say about that "help."

At the prison, we went through the routine security checks and eventually got to Carlos.

He'd had a haircut since our last visit, but it was awful. It looked like he'd done it himself—maybe put a belt around his head and shaved everything under it, then snipped the rest haphazardly with scissors.

"How are you?" Gwen asked anxiously. His eyes were red, and he looked jumpy.

"I don't know if I can survive in here," he said softly. "It's so much worse than I thought." He glanced around, then crossed his arms.

I felt a wave of pity for him, but selfishly wondered if his despair might make him more forthcoming.

"We want to understand what happened to Gabriela, Carlos. Now more than ever. We talked to some of your friends at Celestial Security," Gwen said, subtly introducing the subject of the robberies.

He held still for a very long moment. "What do you mean?" he asked warily.

"Jesus and Bertran told us what was going on."

Carlos tried not to react, but his eyes widened.

"We know you only did them because Bishop Hope forced you to," I said.

"He didn't force us," Carlos said after a long moment.

What did he mean?

Gwen said, "But he still paid you to do them. He told you which houses to rob, and when. He gave you all the information you needed. And then when the police got involved, he threw Jesus and Bertran to the wolves."

What? This was another guess, but it did make some sense. I looked to Carlos for a reaction.

He began fidgeting, his fingers tapping incessantly on the table. This seemed like another one of those tells Kurt would have pointed out. He was coming up with a lie, I suspected.

"Did he pay them for their time in prison? Or was him hiring their lawyers enough?" Gwen asked.

I remembered that Bertran hadn't been given his job back, but Jesus had. Why the discrepancy there? Was it just because Bertran had been connected with more of the robberies?

"And then Gabriela was murdered, and Bishop Hope got you to confess to it because he said your life would be harder otherwise. Isn't that right?" Gwen was trying to make eye contact with Carlos, but he looked away deliberately.

She was forgetting the leverage Hope held over him. I wondered if more people than Carlos were under threat of losing something here. I waited and asked, "At the Pro-Stop, you were arguing with Gabriela about the robberies, too, weren't you?"

"I was arguing with her about how stupid she was being," Carlos admitted.

I glanced up at the camera in the corner. There was probably a videotape of us talking to Carlos right now, but would that audio be enough to use against Hope? I didn't know, but I was sure Hope could easily get out of it with only this testimony against him.

Carlos jerked up and tried to look away again, but when I caught his eye, I could see his tortured pain. I resisted the urge to pat his hand or shoulder, to comfort him somehow. I knew we weren't allowed to touch the prisoners. The rule had been drilled into us when we signed in.

"I told her that she needed to stop pressing him," he said softly. "She wouldn't listen to me. She called him twice while we were there, insisting he come talk to her."

Wait a minute. All my thoughts about getting Carlos to talk about what Hope held over his head vanished. How could Hope have been at the gas station? He'd claimed to have a rock-solid alibi. Could that have somehow been faked? I glanced at Gwen and realized she was as surprised as I was by Carlos's statement.

"Hope says he wasn't there," I pointed out. "That he was at a business dinner."

Carlos went still. "Ah, yes, he was. I forgot." He shifted uncomfortably.

"Carlos, why are you so afraid? What's he threatening you with?" I asked.

"You can tell us," Gwen said. "We can help you."

But as I stared at Carlos, it struck me. It wasn't about a threat. It was about a promise. "What did he say he'd do for you if you took the fall for him? Did he promise to take care of your family? Your mother? Your sisters?" I asked, guessing blindly.

Carlos flushed.

"Once the trial is over and you're in prison, do you really think he'll follow through on that? Think about what you know about him. He only does what's in his own best interest. If you can't give him any more, he'll think of you as a bad investment," I said.

Carlos didn't say anything, but I thought we had him.

"Carlos, think of Gabriela," Gwen said, going in for the final blow. "Think about what she would want. If Hope killed her, she wouldn't want you taking the blame for it and getting him off the hook. She'd want you to help her. You say you loved her."

And that did it.

"I did love her. So much," Carlos said emphatically. "I wanted to marry her, but she kept putting me off. We were—it was wonderful when we were together."

"And Hope ruined all that. You could have gotten back together with her, had a life with her. She wouldn't have gone back to Luis, not after everything he'd done," I said. And although it was too late, I hoped that was true.

"He took all of that from you. You have to tell the police what he did. Everything," Gwen finished.

Carlos put his hands on the table in front of him. "Nothing I say or do will bring her back."

"But you didn't kill her, did you?" Gwen said breathlessly. "You were there to try to protect her from Hope because you knew he was dangerous, weren't you? Hope was the one who wanted Gabriela dead, not you." She was practically pulsating with excitement.

Carlos folded his arms across his chest and frowned.

I was loathe to say anything. Gwen was doing so well. She was so close.

"Carlos," she said urgently. "Help us stop him from getting away with this. Think of her children. Don't Lucia and Manuel and Amanda deserve to live in a world where they know what really happened to their mother?"

At the mention of Gabriela's children, Carlos started to weep.

"It was Hope's idea, wasn't it?" she asked. "He wanted to meet at the Pro-Stop. He told you to talk her into it." I remembered

Gabriela's panicked phone call on Halloween, her repeated mentions of Hope.

Carlos wiped at his eyes and gave a short nod. "It was close enough to the meeting he was at," he said.

I felt a strange sense of relief, a cold sensation spreading through me. Of course! He'd planned it all out carefully. A man like him certainly would. Gabriela had pressed him by getting President Frost involved in the bogus embezzling charge, and for revenge, he'd arranged for her death.

"So he came there. After you were caught arguing on the gas station camera?" Gwen asked. Her voice had smoothed out now, more in control. She sounded like Detective Gore again.

"Yes," Carlos said with resignation.

"And he killed Gabriela?" Gwen pressed.

There was another long silence.

Finally Carlos said, "He acted like he always does. Smiling, pleasant, nodding along. Like he was going to do exactly what she asked, give her the money. He even took out his wallet. Then he reached for her, and it happened so quickly I didn't know how to stop him."

"What happened so quickly?' Gwen asked.

I was horrified at all of this, but I couldn't turn away.

Carlos spoke dully, as if he were trying to distance himself from the events he'd seen so clearly. "He put his hands on her and held her throat so she couldn't breathe. She tried to kick at him, but he was too big, too tall for her. He pushed her back against the wall and then to the ground."

I didn't want to hear any of this. I didn't want to imagine it happening, but I couldn't help it. I'd been at the Pro-Stop. I'd seen the wall he was likely talking about, away from the lights of the convenience store, away from the camera. God, had Hope planned things down to that detail? Had he driven to the Pro-Stop and scoped out the right place for a murder hours, even days before?

I thought of the man who'd met us at Celestial Security and had walked us through the building, emphasizing every detail he wanted us to see, pretending to answer our every question. I thought of the man who'd invited Kurt and me to dinner, and his little boys all in a row. This was a man whose life was perfectly manicured, a man who was always wearing a mask. I'd had that one glimpse behind his façade and convinced myself I'd imagined it. But I hadn't. What I'd seen had been the truth.

"Are you willing to testify to this in court?" Gwen asked quietly, exhausted now, her fidgeting gone.

Carlos looked around the room, as if afraid that Hope would find out about this conversation. "Who would believe my word against his?" he asked. "And what about my mother and my sisters? Who will take care of them while I'm in prison?"

It seemed to always boil down to that—about reputation, and about race. Hope was a bishop. He was a white Mormon in a land of white Mormons. I wouldn't have believed how much that mattered before seeing it this starkly.

"You have to tell the truth, Carlos. You have to get justice for Gabriela. And for her children. If you go free on the robberies because of this information, you can be the one who's there for your mother," I said.

Carlos gathered himself enough to say, "What about all the people who depend on Bishop Hope? If he goes to prison, how will they pay their rent and buy food for their families?"

Had he thought of this himself? I doubted it. More likely it was another pressure point Hope had used to get him to confess.

"There will be a new bishop, Carlos," Gwen said. "And people will find other jobs, maybe even better ones. Gabriela depended on you to protect her, but instead, you stood there while Greg Hope strangled her to death. You watched her die. Are you going to walk away from justice for her now?"

She was harsher than I could have been, but this was probably what had to be said.

"I can't," Carlos said.

"So you're going to stay in this horrible place because you're afraid of the criminal who killed the woman you love? I thought you were a different man," Gwen said.

Our words were awful, but they were a last resort. We didn't have much time left.

But it didn't work.

"I'm sorry," Carlos said. He stood up and knocked on the door to ask the guards to go back to his cell.

I was speechless, shaking as we walked out of the jail and to the car. Gwen sat at the steering wheel with tears pouring down her cheeks.

"We have to get him," Gwen said when she had regained some measure of control.

We did, though I didn't know how. Greg Hope could not continue to act as a Mormon bishop, or a Mormon of any kind. He couldn't be part of my religion. I had to do everything in my power to push him out, to make people see him as he really was.

CHAPTER 38

"I'll text Detective Gore, and maybe she'll agree to meet about what Carlos told us," I said to Gwen as she drove back toward our neighborhood. I had no idea how likely this was, or how helpful it would be in building any kind of case against Hope as a murderer.

"Make sure she understands it's important," she said.

I worked on composing a text that might pique Gore's interest:

I visited Carlos Santos in jail today. He has information I don't think you know about Greg Hope, Celestial Security, and Gabriela Suarez's murder. There was a lot more going on the night he and Gabriela were at the Pro-Stop than an argument about their relationship. He may even recant his confession. I just thought I should give you a heads-up.

Good enough. I sent it off. I hoped she was even getting these.

"Brad working the night shift again?" I asked as Gwen pulled up in front of her dark, empty-looking house.

She nodded. "Want to come in?" she asked.

"Sure," I said, since I wasn't particularly eager to go home and explain myself to Kurt.

We got out of the car and she locked it, leading me inside.

I came around here occasionally, and it looked the same as always. The green curtains matched the textured green-flecked carpet, and there were some nice prints on the walls, including some of Brian Kershisnik's angel paintings and Kirk Richards's black Eve portrait, as well as a photo of Gwen and Brad at the Jordan River temple, where they must have been married.

To my surprise, Gore responded almost immediately, saying she wanted to talk to us about both the visit with Carlos and the phone message from Gabriela, which she hadn't seemed to think was important before.

"Have her come here?" Gwen said after I'd called her and explained.

I texted Gore Gwen's address. She didn't complain about coming to us, and said she'd be there in fifteen minutes. Did she finally think we had useful information for her?

"Do you want some cookies?" Gwen asked.

"That would be lovely," I said before realizing what she meant. She brought out a package of Keebler Fudge Stripes. I dutifully took one and worked on it for the next few minutes, but I couldn't help comparing them ruefully to Anna's homemade cookies—or my own.

Detective Gore was true to her word and arrived just a few minutes later. She was wearing far more casual clothes than I'd expected, just jeans and a sweatshirt, but then again, I'd called her on a holiday weekend about a case she'd thought was closed.

"Linda, nice to see you again," she said as she came in, looking at me and not Gwen.

It seemed like she meant it. Mostly. Her expression was kind, but wary.

"Do you want to know what Carlos told us about Gabriela and Celestial Security?" I asked.

"Do I?" she asked.

"Carlos admitted that he and Gabriela were at the Pro-Stop to meet with Greg Hope. The three of them argued about a robbery scheme she had encouraged him to go along with at Celestial Security, and about her blackmailing Hope with the threat to expose his involvement in it." It could have been ruinous for Hope if that had come out, even if he'd been able to prevent legal consequences.

But Detective Gore was clearly unimpressed. "That's it?" Gore said. "I already know about the history behind Celestial Security and Bertran Lopez and Jesus Gonzalez."

I hadn't even had to name them. She really had done her research thoroughly; I should never have doubted her.

Gore went on, "It's unpleasant, but unless I have more than suspicions about Hope's involvement, someone who has an email or a phone message directly from him ordering a robbery or offering a reward for it, I don't see how I can prosecute him. We've looked through all Gabriela's emails and everything on her phone, but we couldn't find anything incriminating. Hope holds his cards close to his chest." She shook her head and stood up, ready to leave.

"Wait! Carlos said that Hope killed Gabriela. And he was there!" I didn't know if he'd be willing to repeat this in court, but I had little doubt after hearing him that it was true.

Gore stared at me, waiting.

I hurried to explain the rest. "Hope was the one who set up the meeting place at the Pro-Stop. He must have planned it somehow so that Carlos and Gabriela would be seen together there. He knew where the security camera was and made sure he was never caught on it." I was desperate to make her pay attention. I didn't know these things for certain, but they seemed logical assumptions to make, given what Carlos had said.

"More importantly, Carlos saw Hope murder Gabriela. He can testify against him in court," Gwen added.

Gore looked sadly at us and shook her head. "The only witness to this is a man who confessed to the murder himself? I can't see how that would hold up in court. If he'd said it in the first place, it might have been worth something."

I felt empty at her words. So a murderer was simply going to walk free, his position in the church and his company intact? I'd always trusted Gore, believed that if we got her the truth, she'd be able to exact justice. But it seemed I'd been wrong.

"Hope is a powerful man. Carlos was afraid of him," Gwen said, unwilling to give up. "Wouldn't that explain his not having spoken up sooner?"

Gore held her breath for a long moment, then let it out and shook her head again. "There are a dozen witnesses who place Hope at a business meeting at the time of the murder. They're all going to be much more reliable witnesses than Carlos Santos, who already confessed to the crime himself. The video footage and the existing relationship between Carlos and Gabriela are too damning." She clearly wasn't happy about it, but she seemed to shrug, as if to ask, what could she do?

"Are you absolutely sure about the alibi?" I asked, trying one last gambit. "If these witnesses for Hope have a financial interest in his company, they might have a reason to lie for him. Do you have security footage of him at this meeting? Any real proof he was there at the exact time of the murder?"

Gore made a face. "Most white-collar businesses don't keep security cameras inside their boardrooms," she said.

"And how close was this meeting to the Pro-Stop? Have you considered that they wouldn't have noticed him being gone for fifteen or twenty minutes, and that's all it might have taken for him to kill Gabriela?" I asked.

I was sure I saw a flicker of light in Gore's eyes. Maybe all wasn't lost, after all.

"You're saying he went there with the intent to kill Gabriela," Gore said slowly. "And the business meeting was a cover, planned for days beforehand."

"Yes!" Gwen said, punching a hand into her fist. "He's the kind of man who plans everything. He doesn't do anything he thinks won't pay off for him."

Gore hesitated. Then she sighed. "Thank you for bringing this to me, Linda. But I need you to trust me at this point to take it from here. You, too, Mrs. Ferris." A quelling look at Gwen. "I appreciate that you're trying to help, but I'm the detective here."

Her tone was less patronizing than pitying. I wasn't sure which was worse.

"Are you going to do anything?" Gwen asked, despair warring with anger in her voice.

"I told you, I will handle this. I'll be watching Greg Hope carefully and checking into everything I can." Her tone was curt now, dismissive. "Now, about that phone message?"

Gwen looked defeated. She simply held her phone out and pressed the button for Gore to hear Gabriela's terrified voice.

I had to reach for a wall to remain standing.

"I see. Thank you. We may need that. I'll send it to myself."

She pressed another button on the phone, then typed in her own number. After a moment, she picked up her own phone to make sure it was there, then played it again, to ensure it had come through perfectly clear.

It was devastating, especially after Gore had said it still wasn't enough to prosecute Hope.

"He's a murderer, and no one knows," Gwen muttered.

Gore moved past her. With her hand on the door, she turned back and said, her tone cold, "I'm going to warn both of you one last time that this investigation is finished, and that you're interfering in the judicial phase by trying to coax a criminal into retracting a sworn confession. In addition, if you continue to place yourself in dangerous situations when it is completely unnecessary, we may have to charge you with something ourselves, if only to keep you out of harm's way."

I had the impression she'd prepared this speech for us because she'd known last time that we weren't about to give up. She stared hard at Gwen, then me. I thought I saw a hint of compassion, but maybe just because that was what I'd been hoping to see.

She added, "I just need you to wait a week or so, Linda."

What an odd thing to say. What did she mean?

She put up a hand to stop me from asking anything else. "That's all I need. For you two to stay out of trouble for a week. Goodbye." She closed the door behind her, and Gwen and I stood there, shocked, as she drove away.

Gwen thumped the door with a fist and then turned back to me. "How can she just ignore the truth like this?"

I didn't know what to think or feel. Was this Gore's fault? The system's? Or even Mormonism's?

CHAPTER 39

S till depressed about the abrupt, disappointing end to Gabriela's murder case, I was out running errands for Christmas
the next week. It was hard to focus on such everyday things, but
I was trying. I was sending a package to Samuel, and I wanted
Kurt to sign a card for him, so I stopped by his office, which was
conveniently located downtown by the shopping centers.

The receptionist seemed to have stepped out, and I realized
when I stood outside the door to Kurt's office, which was ajar,
that he was with a client. In fact, it was Greg Hope. I saw him as
he leaned forward, his outline clear from the doorway, instantly
recognizable by his wavy blond hair and strong shoulders. I
hadn't told Kurt everything that had happened with Carlos and
Gwen and Gore, but I'd told him enough that I couldn't believe
that he was still thinking of taking on Hope's business. The man
was a conman and a murderer! Had Kurt decided that my opin-
ions were really so worthless? I felt sick that he'd ignored my
reservations so thoroughly.

I considered walking out then and there, but decided that
would let Kurt off the hook too easily. So I decided to listen in.
Neither of them deserved privacy at this point. I glanced in
quickly to get a sense of where they were, both standing over

the desk, looking over a set of papers together. Then I crouched down just outside the door and shamelessly eavesdropped.

"I don't know what you're seeing in those books, but there's nothing missing," said Hope. His voice was smooth and confident, but it raised my hackles, sounding completely canned to me. Did he practice these excuses standing in front of a mirror? Knowing what I knew of him now, probably. But it was Kurt's attitude that really concerned me. He seemed conciliatory and eager to please.

"I can't help you with this if you don't tell me the full story about your finances," he said to Hope.

Where was the moral core of the man I'd loved my whole life? Kurt was usually so unforgiving when it came to schemers like Hope, and I knew he hated multi-level marketing. Had the money offered been enough that even he'd been swayed?

Kurt continued, "What you've given me so far is clearly missing some important pieces. I've got a degree specializing in corporate accounting, and I've been in the business for forty years. I know when there's something fishy, and I can tell you that the IRS does, too. If they haven't audited you yet, they will soon. They're not idiots."

Okay, well that sounded better. Maybe he wasn't just going to let Hope push him into whatever his dubious new business plans were. I was still crouched with my back pressed hard against the wall near the door, trying to hold myself very still and breathe as quietly as possible.

"It sounds like you're saying that I've done something illegal," said Hope.

I wished Kurt hadn't brought Hope into the office. If he hadn't wanted to work with him, surely he could have just handled this by phone with a brief and firm "No, thank you."

"Have you done something illegal?" Kurt asked.

"Of course not," replied Hope immediately.

If Kurt said Hope was lying about his financial situation, it wasn't debatable. Kurt had been at his job so long that he could sniff out shady dealings like a bloodhound. I silently cheered him on.

"Then why are so many of these expenses unspecified? There are dozens of employees on the payroll who haven't clocked any hours. And you were so close to bankruptcy just two years ago, how is it that you now seem to be swimming in cash?" Kurt asked.

There was a bit of a silence, and then Hope's chair creaked.

My heart shot into my throat as I worried that he was going to try to harm Kurt.

But Hope sighed and the chair squeaked again—which meant he was still in it. "I'm just trying to help out my employees. You know they're not here legally, Kurt. They don't have many other options, and if I paid them the going wage, they and their families would end up going hungry. There's no ill intent on my side."

So Greg Hope was trying to play the bishop card with Kurt, get him to go along with his sketchy accounting practices because he was a "good guy." If Kurt were anyone but the man I knew, it probably would have worked.

"You're going to owe some fines when it comes to the illegal workers," Kurt said. "If it were just that, I'd be on board. I agree that it's important to help people who are trying to better their lives, whatever their citizenship status."

"Well, then—" Hope started.

But Kurt cut him off. "What I'm concerned about is your role in Gabriela Suarez's murder."

What? I had to put my hand over my mouth to cover a gasp. Why was Kurt confronting him directly like this? My mind whirled, and I could only think that somehow, Kurt was doing some kind of sting here. But why would he do that without any backup? Unless . . .

Detective Gore had said in a week, I'd understand what she was doing. Had this been her plan? Maybe the only way to get evidence against him was to go inside with someone like Kurt.

Hope said in that smooth, placating tone of his, "You know they already have Gabriela's murderer in custody. I'm not proud of the way that I let her relationship with Carlos Santos go on under my nose, even though she was married to another man. That inaction led to her murder, I suspect, but I can't be held legally accountable for it. I've already talked to President Frost about my lack of proper judgment and asked him to release me if his confidence was lost. But he said that every bishop makes mistakes, and that he feels God still wants me in this calling."

Yuck. Hope was so swarmy. I hated him even more now.

"If that's so, then why were you at the Pro-Stop when she was killed?" Kurt asked.

I froze. This was dangerous now. Was Kurt recording this? If Gore was behind all of this, where was she now? Close enough to protect Kurt if something went wrong? I hadn't seen anyone outside the office when I came in.

"I don't know what you're talking about," said Hope. "I was at a meeting for Celestial Security that night. Ask anyone there."

"You were there, but why did you choose that location? You rented a meeting room two miles from the Pro-Stop when you could easily have had the meeting at your own offices instead. That would have made much more sense, in fact. But they weren't close enough for you to step out and convince your clients that you'd just gone to the bathroom to deal with some stomach distress when you headed over to the Pro-Stop to meet with Gabriela and Carlos."

This had to have been fed to Kurt from Gore. I was both hopeful and terrified, holding my breath for Hope's reaction.

Hope paused, his chair creaking yet again, and finally spoke. "Fine. I went there to talk to her very briefly at the Pro-Stop the night she was killed, but I had nothing to do with her murder. She was trying to blackmail me, Kurt. She had this idea that I owed her more than I'd already paid for her years of work at the business. She'd already tried to ruin me by talking to your wife about the money I'd given her from the ward. President Frost called me, and then I had to deal with the threat of a stake audit."

"So you're saying you never threatened to accuse her of embezzlement?" Kurt said.

Hope made a sound of disgusted derision. "Of course not. She was the one who benefited from that salvo. And when I met her at the Pro-Stop, she made more threats against me. She was going to tell the police I'd been involved in some kind of robberies. And that I was blackmailing our customers on a grand scale. It was all lies, I swear to you."

Here was all the truth about Gabriela I wanted. I'd have felt a sense of relief and triumph if it wasn't all so sad. And if Kurt wasn't still in danger from the suspect in question.

"Why didn't you call the police on her, then?" Kurt asked.

"Because I wasn't afraid of her, Kurt. I walked away and went back to my meeting. I swear to you, Kurt. I never touched her. Carlos Santos killed her because she was going back to her husband and he was jealous."

Hope was starting to sound a little panicked. I wished I could see his face. Or maybe I didn't. That glimpse into his real self wasn't something I particularly wanted to repeat.

"Why would you leave your dinner for a conversation you could have had during daylight hours at the Celestial Security officers?" Kurt said. "Unless it was about something untoward. Something you didn't want anyone else to know about. Something you knew was going to end in a crime."

"I—I—" Hope stuttered. It was the first time I'd heard him really rattled, but it didn't last. "Kurt, you can't think I'm a murderer. I would never harm anyone. I might have been frightened and reacted badly to the threat to my family's safety, but I would never do something so far from the light of Christ within me. I know God's laws."

"Do you? If you did, you'd confess to killing her. You'd remember that if you don't admit to your sins, you have to pay for them all by yourself, and Christ's Atonement has no application to you," Kurt said harshly.

I could hear the tension in my husband's voice. He wasn't used to this kind of interrogation. He was probably sweating buckets. And at some point, Hope was going to realize this was a sting operation. If Gore had given this information to Kurt, hoping he would confront Hope like this, did that mean she was nearby somewhere, listening in to see if Kurt had gotten all the admissions she needed? I really hoped so, but I wasn't sure I could count on it.

"But I didn't kill her, Kurt!" Hope insisted. "She was unhinged. She just wanted money. Gabriela Suarez was a greedy woman. That's all these illegal immigrants want when they come to America. They're trying to take what's ours."

Wow. I couldn't believe he'd said that aloud, after the earlier show of his supposed sympathy for his ward members and employees.

There was a long silence. I tried to breathe shallowly, evenly—and quietly.

"I can see why you couldn't allow her to ruin everything you and your family have worked so hard for, just because she wanted to line her own pockets," Kurt said.

I guessed this was a concerted effort to sound like a potential co-conspirator. If I hadn't been so afraid for him, I would have laughed. Good old Kurt, still the man I'd always known he was.

But Hope sounded a little more self-assured after this. "She was a woman with only one thing in mind. She pretended to be a member of the church, but that was just a blind. She was using her membership to get to me, to ruin me."

I rolled my eyes and for one moment, was less worried about Kurt. Maybe Hope was too self-obsessed and venal to realize what was going on.

"And I can see how you'd feel like it wasn't just your reputation on the line," Kurt offered. "It was the church you were protecting, too. If you allowed her to smear your good name, it would make the whole church look bad."

"Exactly. Not to mention the fact that my company would go under, and all the people I'm working with in the Spanish ward would lose their livelihoods. Their families would suffer enormously. I had to stop her for their sakes, not just mine."

I was pretty sure that I couldn't have gone along with Greg Hope like this, pretending I agreed with him. Which must have been why Gore had gone to Kurt instead of me. And of course, the fact that Kurt was another bishop, a fellow priesthood holder in the church, whom Hope would think he could trust—and manipulate.

"Listen. I might be able to help you with this if you explain the details behind the robberies you mentioned Gabriela being involved with," Kurt said softly. "We can find a workaround on this if I have the full picture. The IRS doesn't have to know the details. We just have to make sure that the proper taxes are paid. Was there any compensation for the robberies that needs to be masked as contract labor? Did any of the stolen goods come back to the company?"

My whole body strained in anticipation of the answer. Would Hope react poorly to Kurt trying to get him to incriminate himself? He wasn't a stupid man.

But he was still comfortable enough talking to a fellow bishop, it seemed. He said, "We paid five thousand dollars per home as a lump sum. The stolen goods never came back to us, though. I told them they could manage that on their own. Whatever they took was theirs."

"Five thousand?" Kurt said, whistling. "That's a lot."

"But you said you could call it contract labor, right? There's always a vague category you can list things under that the IRS can't question, isn't there?"

I wondered what kind of accountants he'd worked with before. "Vague" wasn't in Kurt's professional vocabulary.

"Of course," Kurt said easily. "Though there'd be less of a tax burden for the company if it was listed as a performance bonus. Then the tax burden is on your employees to pay."

"Ah. That makes sense. I can see why you're so good at your job," Hope said warmly. As if Kurt needed his approval.

Kurt said clinically, "All right, so if I've done my research properly, it looks like there were twenty-five or twenty-six homes involved."

Hope hesitated, then said, "I believe there were twenty-six. It was really a small number, considering the effect it had. Word spread like wildfire from those who'd ended their contracts, and in addition to them returning, new clients signed up in the dozens over the next few weeks." He seemed to warm up as he told the story, congratulating himself by the end, looking for Kurt's approval, as well.

"How efficient," Kurt said drily.

Surely this was enough for Kurt to stop and for the police to rush in?

But there was nothing but silence outside the building and the thunderous beat of my own heart.

There was another long pause, and I realized that there was no real reason for me to assume the police were outside, waiting to come in. Kurt might have done this all on his own. Waiting for the cavalry was stupid—and could possibly be fatal.

"You can't really write off those bonuses, can you?" said Hope after a too-long moment of consideration. "Not for illegal activity."

"No, I can't," whispered Kurt.

Why would he say that? Why say anything at all? Because Kurt was an honest man who was as bad at lying as I was. Hope must've spotted his tell somehow.

The chair's squeaking ended abruptly, and I realized Hope had stood up. "What's going on here?" he asked.

"The police have been listening in to all of this," Kurt said.

I sagged in relief.

Unless—was Kurt lying?

"You bastard," Hope cursed.

I couldn't bear it anymore. I wasn't waiting to hear Hope strangle my husband, as well. I rushed inside the room, flung myself at Kurt to protect him, and kicked at Greg Hope's legs on the way. I might not be an athlete like he was, but I knew enough to make him drop to his knees.

"Linda, what the—?" Kurt started to say.

He was cut off by the sound of uniformed officers streaming in through the front doors, past reception, and into Kurt's office wide open. They pulled Hope's arms behind his back and cuffed him, then read him his rights. And finally, Detective Gore came striding in.

She saw me and said, "Linda, I should have known you would somehow figure this whole thing out and make sure you were here for the climactic moment."

I didn't know what to say. I'd been here purely by accident. I wished I believed that God had led me here, but I didn't. I hadn't felt any sense of divine protection. "Thank God you're here," I said, still a little winded from my run.

Gore shook her head and extended her hand toward Kurt. He met the gesture with a firm shake. "Thank you so much for your help," Gore said. "This will all be very helpful at the trial. I assume that you'll be willing to testify there, as well?"

"I will," Kurt said. He reached for my hand and pulled me close. I could feel his heart beating so quickly, it was a wonder he hadn't had a heart attack. He should really leave these kinds of things to me, the expert at this kind of craziness.

"We already had the books, but you got him to confess on tape to his presence at the murder scene, as well as his collusion in the robberies. That, along with Carlos Santos's testimony against him, should be enough to get a conviction at trial. We can thank your wife for her help in this, too," Gore said, nodding to me.

It felt good to get some credit, though I felt like the lion's share of it really should have gone to Gwen, who had been so dogged about investigating Bishop Hope and proving Carlos Santos's innocence.

As the police officers dragged Hope out of the office threatening everyone with church discipline and eternal consequences, I kissed Kurt's cheek, almost as I would have done with one of the boys.

"Let's go home," I said to him.

"Good idea." He steered me through the office and into the parking lot, where the police car was just heading off with Bishop Hope in its backseat. I could see him glaring menacingly at us through the rear window.

"His poor wife and sons," I said. I felt for Maria, who had seemed genuinely like a good mother. What would happen to her and her boys?

"Are you really saying that, after you and Gwen did everything you could to make sure he went to prison for his crimes?" Kurt said.

Yes, I was. "Of course. I can still worry about them," I said. "They're innocent in all this." Wasn't that what Mormonism was about? Taking care of the people in your community? Making sure families had the best chance they could?

He sighed. "Yes, I guess you're right. We'll make sure they're okay, Linda. You know the church takes care of its own."

And what about Gabriela's children? Did the church take care of them, too? Or didn't they matter? I vowed to myself that I would do something for them somehow.

At home, I called Gwen to tell her about our crazy morning.

"I was right all along, then." I could hear the happy gloating in her voice.

Well, I wasn't sure if she'd been right every step of the way, but we'd gotten to the truth first. "You're going to be one hell of a detective," I said.

"I hope so," she said. "Thank you, Linda."

"Anytime," I said. "I'm always here for you. And not just for murders." I was trying to re-establish our friendship outside of this case, but it didn't quite come out that way.

"We'll see," Gwen said, and hung up.

After that, Kurt and I slouched on the couch together, not even bothering to turn on the television. We were too wrung out.

"Seeing Hope led off in handcuffs has given me a new appreciation for you," I said, snuggling closer to him.

"Well, that's good," he said. "Maybe we'll have to do more murder investigations together." He looked at me and winked.

Was that what we had done?

The next day, I called DCFS and asked about Gabriela's children, but they absolutely refused to tell me a thing. They wouldn't even let me send money to them, which made me cry and bang my phone against the table. But I told myself that I would try again through other channels, and that this didn't mean I couldn't help anyone. I remembered that most members of the Spanish ward would likely be out of a job soon. And the attention of Hope's trial could scare them enough to simply leave the ward in order to avoid attention from ICE.

I went back online to MWEG. I posted about the Spanish ward and asked for advice. The post was flooded with suggestions of things I could do, but more than that, people were volunteering.

There were contacts for lawyers to help, volunteers to do a rally to raise money for those who were losing their jobs, and the idea of starting a job fair to help connect those who needed jobs with employers who wanted someone with their skills. Gwen was joining the Police Academy, and I knew I couldn't join her, but I could do this. I could take part in making a better future.

AFTERWORD

Mormon Women for Ethical Government (MWEG) was formed in November 2016 by Sharlee Glenn, Linda Hoffman Kimball, Melissa Dalton-Bradford (old, dear friends of mine) and Michelle Lehnhardt, Jacquie White, and Diana Bate Hardy (new, dear friends of mine) and now has nearly 6,000 members. These non-partisan women have joined together to protest unethical government in a variety of contexts, from immigration issues to health care reform and even connections between Trump and Russia. They've worked hard on letter-writing campaigns to help reconsider repeal of the ACA, to stop the new tax bill with its deficits and tax breaks for mega-corporations, and have also worked hard to send a statue of Martha Cannon, the first Mormon woman to serve as a senator (and first woman in any state to do so—after she won the election against her own husband!) to the Capitol. You can find out more about them at www.mweg.org.

ACKNOWLEDGMENTS

Thanks are owed to many people on this book. First, Juliet Grames, who encouraged me to actually outline a book for the first time, and then guided me through the tricky process of first tying it to a current year's timeline, and then separating it from it. Thanks also to Amara Hoshijo, who walked me through several content and line edits. And to Jennifer Lyford, who went above and beyond a copy editor's job. Thanks also to Kerina Espinoza for answering a series of questions about Spanish wards. As always, the mistakes are all my own. Thanks to everyone at Soho, the best publishing company on the planet. And to the friends I keep finding within Mormonism and without, who understand the work I'm doing, who are kind about the mistakes I make, and who allow me to cameo them when I have the chance.

Other Titles in the Soho Crime Series

Stephanie Barron
(Jane Austen's England)
Jane and the Twelve Days
of Christmas
Jane and the Waterloo Map

F.H. Batacan
(Philippines)
Smaller and Smaller Circles

James R. Benn
(World War II Europe)
Billy Boyle
The First Wave
Blood Alone
Evil for Evil
Rag & Bone
A Mortal Terror
Death's Door
A Blind Goddess
The Rest Is Silence
The White Ghost
Blue Madonna
The Devouring
Solemn Graves
When Hell Struck Twelve

Cara Black
(Paris, France)
Murder in the Marais
Murder in Belleville
Murder in the Sentier
Murder in the Bastille
Murder in Clichy
Murder in Montmartre
Murder on the
Ile Saint-Louis
Murder in the
Rue de Paradis
Murder in the Latin Quarter
Murder in the Palais Royal
Murder in Passy
Murder at the
Lanterne Rouge
Murder Below
Montparnasse
Murder in Pigalle

Cara Black cont.
Murder on the
Champ de Mars
Murder on the Quai
Murder in Saint-Germain
Murder on the Left Bank
Murder in Bel-Air

Lisa Brackmann
(China)
Rock Paper Tiger
Hour of the Rat
Dragon Day

Getaway
Go-Between

Henry Chang
(Chinatown)
Chinatown Beat
Year of the Dog
Red Jade
Death Money
Lucky

Barbara Cleverly
(England)
The Last Kashmiri Rose
Strange Images of Death
The Blood Royal
Not My Blood
A Spider in the Cup
Enter Pale Death
Diana's Altar

Fall of Angels
Invitation to Die

Colin Cotterill
(Laos)
The Coroner's Lunch
Thirty-Three Teeth
Disco for the Departed
Anarchy and Old Dogs
Curse of the Pogo Stick
The Merry Misogynist
Love Songs from
a Shallow Grave
Slash and Burn

Colin Cotterill cont.
The Woman Who
Wouldn't Die
Six and a
Half Deadly Sins
I Shot the Buddha
The Rat Catchers' Olympics
Don't Eat Me
The Second Biggest Nothing

Garry Disher
(Australia)
The Dragon Man
Kittyhawk Down
Snapshot
Chain of Evidence
Blood Moon
Whispering Death
Signal Loss

Wyatt
Port Vila Blues
Fallout

Bitter Wash Road
Under the Cold Bright Lights

David Downing
(World War II Germany)
Zoo Station
Silesian Station
Stettin Station
Potsdam Station
Lehrter Station
Masaryk Station

(World War I)
Jack of Spies
One Man's Flag
Lenin's Roller Coaster
The Dark Clouds Shining
Diary of a Dead Man
on Leave

Agnete Friis
(Denmark)
What My Body Remembers
The Summer of Ellen

Seichō Matsumoto
(Japan)
*Inspector Imanishi
Investigates*

Magdalen Nabb
(Italy)
*Death of an Englishman
Death of a Dutchman
Death in Springtime
Death in Autumn
The Marshal and
the Murderer
The Marshal and
the Madwoman
The Marshal's Own Case
The Marshal Makes
His Report
The Marshal
at the Villa Torrini
Property of Blood
Some Bitter Taste
The Innocent
Vita Nuova
The Monster of Florence*

Fuminori Nakamura
(Japan)
*The Thief
Evil and the Mask
Last Winter, We Parted
The Kingdom
The Boy in the Earth
Cult X*

Stuart Neville
(Northern Ireland)
*The Ghosts of Belfast
Collusion
Stolen Souls
The Final Silence
Those We Left Behind
So Say the Fallen*

(Dublin)
Ratlines

Rebecca Pawel
(1930s Spain)
*Death of a Nationalist
Law of Return
The Watcher in the Pine
The Summer Snow*

Kwei Quartey
(Ghana)
*Murder at Cape
Three Points
Gold of Our Fathers
Death by His Grace*

Qiu Xiaolong
(China)
*Death of a Red Heroine
A Loyal Character Dancer
When Red Is Black*

James Sallis
(New Orleans)
*The Long-Legged Fly
Moth
Black Hornet
Eye of the Cricket
Bluebottle
Ghost of a Flea*

Sarah Jane

John Straley
(Sitka, Alaska)
*The Woman Who
Married a Bear
The Curious Eat Themselves
The Music of What Happens
Death and the Language
of Happiness
The Angels Will Not Care
Cold Water Burning
Baby's First Felony*

(Cold Storage, Alaska)
The Big Both Ways

Akimitsu Takagi
(Japan)
*The Tattoo Murder Case
Honeymoon to Nowhere
The Informer*

Helene Tursten
(Sweden)
*Detective Inspector Huss
The Torso
The Glass Devil
Night Rounds
The Golden Calf
The Fire Dance
The Beige Man
The Treacherous Net
Who Watcheth
Protected by the Shadows*

*Hunting Game
Winter Grave*

*An Elderly Lady Is Up to
No Good*

**Janwillem van de
Wetering**
(Holland)
*Outsider in Amsterdam
Tumbleweed
The Corpse on the Dike
Death of a Hawker
The Japanese Corpse
The Blond Baboon
The Maine Massacre
The Mind-Murders
The Streetbird
The Rattle-Rat
Hard Rain
Just a Corpse at Twilight
Hollow-Eyed Angel
The Perfidious Parrot
The Sergeant's Cat:
Collected Stories*

31901067064966

e Winspear
England)
*Maisie Dobbs
Birds of a Feather*